THE ANATALIAN
SOLDIER

REBECCA
MIKKELSON

AUTHORS 4 AUTHORS PUBLISHING
Marysville, WA, USA

Published by Authors 4 Authors Publishing
1214 6th St
Marysville, WA 98270
www.authors4authorspublishing.com

Library of Congress Control Number: 2021946804

E-book ISBN: 978-1-64477-103-7
Hardcover ISBN: 978-1-64477-131-0
Paperback ISBN: 978-1-64477-104-4
Audiobook ISBN: 978-1-64477-105-1

Edited by Renee Frey
Copyedited by Brandi Spencer

Cover design ©2021 Brandi Spencer. All rights reserved.
Interior design and map of Aratia by Brandi Spencer.

Authors 4 Authors Publishing branding is set in Bavire. Titles and headings are set in Beguns and Goudy Twenty. All other text is set in Garamond.

THE ANATALIAN SOLDIER

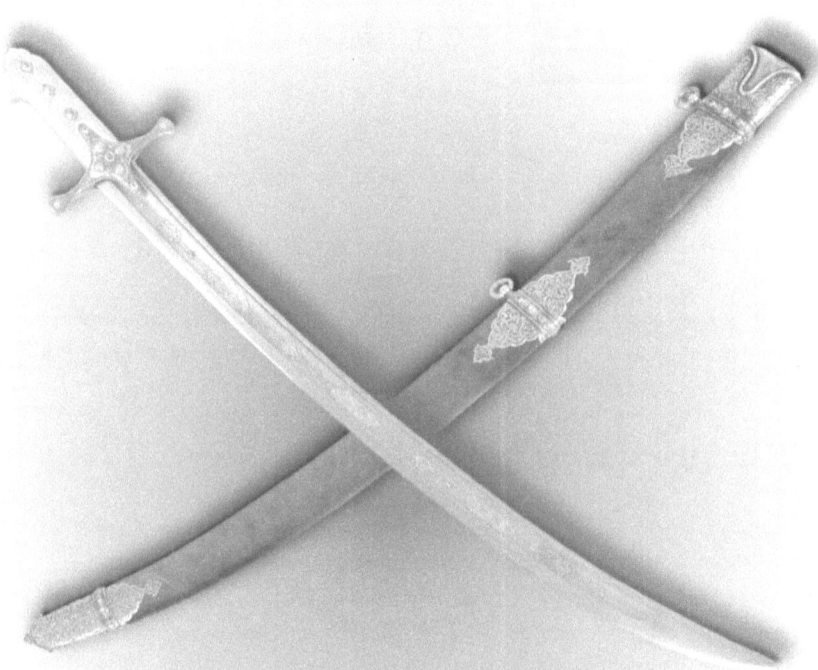

REBECCA MIKKELSON

Authors 4 Authors Content Rating

This title has been rated 17+, appropriate for older teens and adults, and contains:

- graphic violence
- strong language
- moderate sex
- mild tobacco and illicit drug use
- moderate alcohol use

Please, keep the following in mind when using our rating system:

1. A content rating is not a measure of quality.

Great stories can be found for every audience. One book with many content warnings and another with none at all may be of equal depth and sophistication. Our ratings can work both ways: to avoid content or to find it.

2. Ratings are merely a tool.

For our young adult (YA) and children's titles, age ratings are generalized suggestions. For parents, our descriptive ratings can help you make informed decisions, but at the end of the day, only you know what kinds of content are appropriate for your individual child. This is why we provide details in addition to the general age rating.

For more information on our rating system, please, visit our Content Guide at: www.authors4authorspublishing.com/books/ratings

DEDICATION

For my mother, who always said I would write a novel one day.

I finally did it.

WORKS BY REBECCA MIKKELSON

"*The Measure of a Princess*"

The Anatalian Series:
The Anatalian Soldier
The Anatalian Countess
The Anatalian Throne
The Anatalian King
The Anatalian Queen
The Anatalian Heir

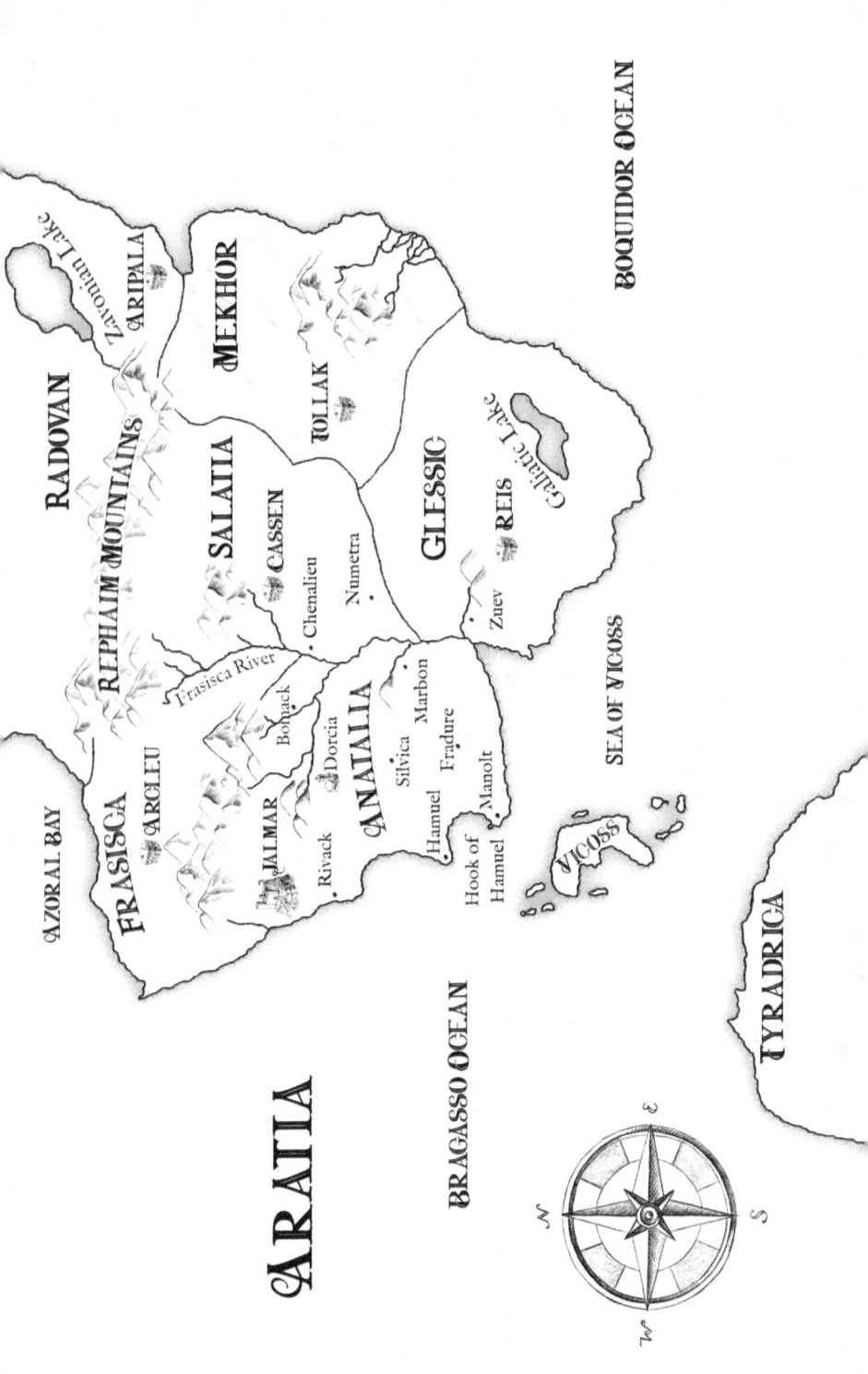

TABLE OF CONTENTS

 **1**

ooking around the dull room, a single pallet bed jammed in the corner and not much else, Liam Fulton longed for something more. This wasn't the life for him—he wanted more than being a tenant farmer's son, working on the country's most prosperous vineyard. The monotony of his days wore at him as a pumice; surely, if he stayed any longer, he would disappear into nothingness. He wanted a chance to go adventuring—to travel Aratia and find out what the continent could offer—and freedom from the cage of fear his mother had trapped him in.

With his haversack packed, Liam made his way into the kitchen, where his mother was. He had already spoken to his father at length about his decision, and they both thought it would be best to not tell his mother until the time came for him to leave. She had her back to him, stirring the contents of the cast-iron pot hanging over the flames. She fanned herself with a rag, pushing damp hair away from her face. He set his bag in the doorway, taking the time to memorize the moment. It was one he had seen so often, but today would not end the same as it always had.

"Mother?"

She turned, spoon in hand, a smile lighting her pale face. "Liam, darling, what are you doing home so early?"

Liam went to her side, his own smile wavering. "Mother—"

She stepped back from him, holding a hand up to pause his speech. "What's wrong?"

"What makes you say that?"

"Because there's something wrong." Her eyes started to widen. "What's happening?"

His jaw clenched, muscles quivering. He could do this. He had to tell her. He couldn't just disappear without a word. She would never recover if he did. "Mother, I'm leaving."

Her eyes narrowed, the wrinkles deepening in the corners. "*Leaving?* Why are you leaving? Where are you going?"

Shifting on his feet, Liam looked away from her. He had to stay firm. If he looked at her, he didn't know if he could bring himself to leave. "To Jalmar."

"Jalmar?" Her claw-like hands gripped his arm. Her voice quavered as she asked, "What business do you have in the capital?"

"It's where I'll be trained."

"Trained?" Her brows furrowed. "What's going on, Liam?"

"Yes, trained—to join the Anatalian military. I'm going to be a soldier, Mother." Clearing his throat, Liam extracted his arm from her grip and stepped back. He hated the broken look on her face. He had to stay strong. "I've already spoken to Father—"

His mother touched her cheek, her eyes wide, as though Liam had slapped her. Her voice small, she asked, "He agreed to this?"

Looking at the ground, Liam regretted not leaving her a letter and disappearing in the night. He hadn't thought she'd take it this badly. "Yes…he thought it was a good idea for me. He said he was proud."

Why was this so difficult for her? It should have been as simple as talking to his father, telling him he was going, and basking in the pride of wanting to serve his country.

Finally shaking free of her stupor, his mother cried, "I forbid it!"

"Mother, you can't stop me. I'm a grown man."

She let out a wail, grabbing his arm again. "It isn't safe for you to leave! You can't go, Liam. I don't allow it!"

"You don't have a choice." He couldn't let his resolve slip, no matter how upset she got—no matter how much it hurt to upset her. No matter how much she ignored how he already had his father's permission. He was leaving, and that was final. Liam couldn't live in her bubble of fear until one of them died. "I'm leaving today, and I wanted to say goodbye."

His mother stumbled back, eyes shining with unshed tears. "You can't go, Liam. It's not safe."

Liam straightened his shoulders, steeling himself. He couldn't allow her to rob him of his life. "I can't stay in this house forever, Mother. I'm not your little boy anymore."

"You *are* my little boy—you'll *always* be my little boy!" She wiped the tears from her reddened eyes. "You're only eighteen. Aren't you too young?"

"Most join when they're fifteen, Mother," Liam informed her. "I'll be the oldest recruit there."

"Then don't go! Stay here, follow in your father's footsteps. Stay here with us where it's safe."

Liam fought his rising disappointment. So much for a fond farewell. Nowhere was ever safe for her—would ever be safe for her. Liam gently took her shoulders and held her at arm's length. "I'm going to leave now, Mother. I'll say goodbye to Father on my way out."

Another sob escaped her lips. She put her hands on his arms, gripping them tightly. "Please, Liam. *Please*."

His mouth turned downward, heaviness settling behind his eyes. He had to leave now, or he wouldn't leave ever. Liam pulled her in close once more and kissed her on her hairline before letting go of her. "Goodbye, Mother. I'll send word once I get there."

"No!" She launched herself at him, grabbing onto anything that she could.

His shirt stretched in her hands as he walked away. Liam stole it from her fists, hesitating when she collapsed in a heap. Steeling himself, he took his bag from the floor. "I love you," he called over her sobs.

His father waited for him at the end of the property, hand stuffed in his pockets. "I could hear her all the way from here."

"She didn't take it well, as you can tell." Guilt rattled in his chest. He'd never seen his mother that upset before, much less been the one to cause it. "She wouldn't even listen when I said you'd already approved."

"No, I didn't think that she would." His father sighed. "So you're leaving now?"

Liam nodded, bottom lip trembling for only a moment. "Yes...I don't know when I'll be back."

His father pulled a small pouch from his pocket, handing it to Liam. "This is for your travels."

The coins weighed heavily in his hand. "You didn't need—"

"I did. I want you to be able to stay somewhere when you get to the capital."

Liam rolled his bottom lip between his teeth, unsure of what to say next. He stuffed the pouch in his own pocket. "So this is goodbye."

"I suspect it is."

He squared his shoulders, shaking his hands out. He inhaled deeply to keep his burning eyes dry. "I'll miss you and Mother."

Clapping Liam on the shoulder, his father said, "We'll miss you as well, but you'll do great things for Anatalia. I know you will."

Liam mustered a smile. "Thank you."

"Go on now," his father urged, waving toward the road. "You don't want to waste the day."

Nodding, Liam adjusted his pack. "Goodbye, Father."

"Goodbye, Son."

THE ANATALIAN SOLDIER

The day had finally come—Liam had finished his training and would swear his oath to the king and queen before he could formally join the Anatalian army. He ran his hand through his hair to straighten the fresh cut. A quick glance in the mirror confirmed it was just the way he liked. He and all of his fellow recruits had been pampered by servants to make sure they were presentable for royalty. It was the first time he'd ever been dressed by anyone who wasn't family.

He couldn't say he hated it.

When the servant returned with Liam's ceremonial gloves, Liam lifted one of the unearned decorations, raising his brow at it. "This shouldn't be here."

"It's for show, sir." The servant took it from his hand and laid it flat, smoothing out the ribbon holding it in place. "They will not be included in your uniform upon departure."

At last, Liam was the only soldier in the room. He would finally be presented to the king to swear his fealty. Liam loosed a yawn, covering his mouth with his fist. If he was tired, Liam imagined that the king must also be. He would keep his oath short. They were not given a script to follow but told to swear their oaths from the heart. Some of the men's hearts must have been full, as Liam had been waiting three hours.

The herald returned for him, only nodding in his direction. There was no need for names—he was the only one left. There would be no mistakes as to whom he meant. Liam stood, smoothing out his wrinkled clothing. At this point, he doubted the king would even care he was wearing clothes. He, like Liam, probably just wanted to be done with the whole thing.

Liam followed the herald down a gilded hallway to the throne room. The floor looked to be solid marble; he could find no seams as he traveled. Chairs lined the corridor for nobles to rest in while they waited for petitions, their plush cushions overstuffed with cotton. The corner of Liam's mouth pulled up. Why could they not have waited there instead?

The door at the end of the corridor opened when they approached, two guards pulling at the heavy oaken sections. Light poured through the open space, revealing a glittering throne room. There was more gold in the chandeliers alone than Liam had ever seen in his life. If he had been told to pick a single word to describe the throne room, it would have been gold. It extended from the chandeliers to the walls to the floors. It filled almost every corner, light bouncing off it, giving the room a slight glow.

Liam saw that both the king and Queen of Anatalia sat upon their thrones, simple circlets resting on their brows. The king's brown hair hung to his shoulders, beard shot with white, framing his hard blue eyes. Liam had expected to see them in their full regalia and was almost underwhelmed by their plain dress.

He waited until he stood before them to bow deeply at the waist, remaining there until he was told to rise. Liam stood straight, shoulders back. "Your Majesties, I am humbled to be in your presence."

"You may pledge your oath to me, soldier." The king waved his hand, sounding bored.

Pulling his sword from its sheath, Liam knelt on one knee. "To His Majesty, I pledge my loyalty and fealty, endeavoring to only serve you and the realm as you deem fit." Liam looked between the king and queen before continuing, "And to Her Majesty, I pledge my sword in protection if ever it need be used." Upon finishing his oaths, Liam kissed the blade of his sword to seal his commitment.

King Sorren rose. He motioned for Liam to stand, and after doing so, raised the blade to his own mouth. "We accept your humble oaths and wish to see only your success. You may leave with our blessing."

A thrill raced through Liam, his stomach tightening as he bowed his way out of the room. Once the doors were closed, he realized he had not even put away his sword. He let out a short laugh, returning it to its place.

With nowhere else to go, Liam returned to the training barracks. His things had already been packed for him and rested on top of his made bed. A note was pinned to the front of his satchel.

> Report to your new barracks on the east side of campus.
> Sergeant Edwin will assign you a posting to serve.

Liam smiled, pulling his satchel on to his shoulder.

 **2**

ord General Tobias Crompton, Duke of Rivack, arrived in the capital of Salatia on the first morning of Mamonat. He wiped his brow. It was unseasonably hot for this time of year; one would think the summer had already started. At his side was Lieutenant Alton Bryant, Crompton's aide-de-camp for many years now—he seemed to be suffering just as much. Alton's brown curls clung to his forehead, even as he tried to wipe his brow clean.

They rode up to the palace on black stallions, slowing once they reached the white gates to the palace grounds. It was smaller than the palace in Jalmar, though Crompton suspected it was due to the Salatians being more humble than his ancestors, who had wanted the largest palace in Aratia. Crompton turned on his horse, then opened his saddlebag and pulled out their diplomatic papers for the guards.

Interior guards escorted Tobias and Alton through the palace, stopping at the guest rooms to freshen up before the Duke of Rivack's audience with King Peralta of Salatia. Compared to the Anatalian palace, Salatia's was lackluster; Crompton had only seen three paintings in as many hallways.

"Get some rest." Crompton turned away from Alton, loosening the cravat at his neck. He grimaced at how wet it was. "When you wake, I want you to ferret out secrets about the king and queen from the servants."

"As you command, Your Grace." Alton bowed before retreating to his rooms farther down the hall.

Crompton's rooms lacked the luster he should have been afforded as a duke, but he didn't mind. As a military man, he preferred austerity to opulence. Crompton poured water into the basin. He had not brought any servants on this trip, opting only for his aide, whose duties went no further than secretarial—on paper, at least. Crompton didn't want anyone in Anatalia to know what he was planning. Once he had finished washing the dust off of him, he lay down on the bed to rest.

A servant summoned Crompton not long after the duke closed his eyes. It seemed being the king's cousin and closest advisor afforded him an audience with some urgency. He was brought to one of the king's private offices. The room was messy, with books strewn about and papers nearly sliding off the desk by the window. Crompton frowned at the lack of care—anyone could rifle through this room, and none would be the wiser. Perhaps this was a test to see if he would try gleaning information from the ill-hidden documents.

"His Majesty will be with you in a moment."

Nodding, Crompton settled in to wait—he could wait for hours before Sorren showed up. His king enjoyed showing his power this way. Crompton expected much the same from the Salatian king but was pleasantly surprised when Peralta arrived mere moments later.

Crompton hastily stood. "Your Majesty, thank you for seeing me."

"What is it that you want, Your Grace?" The Salatian king looked Crompton over with a frown. He poured himself a drink, neglecting to offer Crompton one. "This is highly unprecedented."

Ignoring the slight, Crompton waited for the Salatian monarch to sit before he did. This was too important to let pettiness ruin it. "My apologies, Your Majesty, but it's a matter of great importance that could not wait for approvals."

"Yes?"

"It's been known for quite some time your distaste for the Anatalian king." Crompton watched the king closely as he spoke, but there was no change on the monarch's pallid face. "There are many who also detest him within my country and without."

"I don't have all day, Your Grace," Peralta snapped. "Get to your point already."

Crompton tried not to let his irritation flare. He needed the king more than the king needed him for this scheme to work. He took a deep breath before he continued, "I would like to dethrone him with the help of Salatia."

King Peralta let out a boisterous laugh. "You cannot be serious, man. You come to me with this? Why not hire your own men?"

Crompton closed his eyes for a moment and counted to three. He mustn't let the foreign king's amusement set him off. It was dangerous enough for him to come ask for help from the Salatians, but it would be even worse to provoke the anger of their king. "Because you have more resources than I do."

"And how exactly do you plan to do this?" Peralta leaned back in his chair, swirling his drink. Amusement lit his face, bringing color to his cheeks.

Crompton wished he could punch the smirk off the king's face. Instead, he said flatly, "With a war."

The king let out another laugh, this time, one of incredulity. "You expect me to start a war just to replace your king? Do you know how expensive wars are?"

"I'll ensure you win—I'll hand over troop locations, movements, and the makeup of each unit. I don't want the throne; I want someone else to have it, as long as it isn't a Platiri. No good can come from our line." Crompton leaned forward in his seat, staring intently at the monarch. "I'll even let you select the next ruler. You can put someone who will be sympathetic to Salatia, as long as they're Anatalian. The people won't tolerate a foreign ruler."

"You don't want this for yourself?" King Peralta's brow furrowed, and his eyes narrowed as he examined the Duke of Rivack.

"I do not. Anatalia will find no one who loves her more, but I am not the correct ruler for her."

"And why is it you think I should dethrone him?"

Wasn't it obvious? The kings had met before—anyone could see Sorren was not meant to lead. "He is unfit to rule. He's a letch and does not care for his people."

"Many of us are unfit to rule, but that does not stop the monarchies from allowing us to." Peralta crossed his arms over his chest. "I'm sorry, Your Grace, but without good reason, I cannot help you. Disliking him is not enough to start a war over. I'm afraid I am going to have to ask you to leave immediately." The king rang a bell on his desk, and the door to the study opened.

"As you wish, Your Majesty." Crompton stood, bowed, and backed toward the door. "By your leave," he muttered before backing into the hallway. Crompton waited for the doors to close before he stood, his mouth in a tight frown.

That had failed spectacularly.

Crompton assumed the hate the King of Salatia held for his cousin and the promise of picking a puppet ruler for Anatalia would be enough incentive. He would find Alton, and they would depart quickly. Hopefully, his aide had been more successful than he and learned some information they could use.

Upon his return to his temporary chambers, Crompton found Alton sitting in the window. He had one foot braced within the frame and the other on the floor. He was chomping on an apple and swallowed quickly when he saw Crompton. "Your Grace." Alton stood, tossing the apple onto the table. "What news?"

"We will not have our war." Crompton grabbed the bag he hadn't had the chance to unpack. "And we must leave now. We'll find an inn to rest the horses overnight and leave in the morning."

"But, Your Grace—"

"Grab your things, and meet me in the stables. We can talk about what you've found on the way home."

Alton bowed his head before leaving the room.

Crompton went immediately to the stables, ordering the stable boys to saddle their steeds. They rode out as soon as Alton arrived and tied his bags to the saddle.

Crompton waited until they were outside of the city proper to speak. "What did you find?"

"The queen has taken several secret lovers, despite the fact the last three were executed and King Peralta threatened to make her next."

A slow smile spread across Crompton's face. "I can manage with that. Sorren finds nothing more enticing than a woman he's expressly forbidden from bedding."

3

Liam found the eastern barracks easily enough—it was a three-story building lined with small windows. Its utilitarian exterior, and multitude of small windows, signaled it could be nothing other than accommodations for soldiers. He ventured in, looking for the office of Sergeant Edwin, and found it at the end of the first floor. Liam lightly knocked on the open door, waiting to be invited in.

Sergeant Edwin glanced up from the papers on his desk, barely taking the time to motion him in before going back to his work.

"Private Liam Fulton reporting for duty, sir!" Liam made a face. He'd said it with more enthusiasm than intended.

The sergeant squinted at him. It was clear Liam was a greenie and overly eager—just what he didn't want.

"Fulton, you said?"

"Yes, sir."

Edwin riffled through the papers littering his desk before pulling one out with Liam's name on the top. The sergeant read it over before handing it to Liam. "Your first assignment will be to the city guard. You'll report to Sergeant Major Cooper in the morning to be assigned a unit. Take the rest of the day off, Private, and welcome to the Anatalian army."

Liam grinned, one cheek dimpling. "Thank you, sir."

Handing him the remainder of the paperwork, Sergeant Edwin waved him out of the room. "That's all, Private."

Excitement bounced around Liam's stomach—he was ready for his first assignment and didn't know if he would sleep that night. Liam looked over the paperwork as he walked down the hallway. His name should be on a plaque with his room number over a slot with which to receive their correspondence. He scanned the names until he lighted on his, tapping it with his finger. "Room two-eighteen."

He climbed the stairs to the left of the mailboxes and searched for his new room. Liam found it halfway down the hall and to the right. Four beds occupied the space, and nothing adorned the walls. The beds were unoccupied, but it was obvious which ones were in use. They had all been made, rather than topped with neatly folded sheets for Liam to make the bed himself.

Setting his things down, Liam made quick work of putting the bed together. At its end sat a chest for storage. Opening it, Liam found it was full. Confused, he looked around for another one. On the opposite end was another chest, which he discovered was empty. Liam put his things away, changing into civilian clothes. He might as well enjoy the rest of his day wandering the city he was to protect and serve. They were so rarely allowed outside of the barracks while they trained; this would be a nice luxury for him.

Dressed in his basic uniform of jockey boots, tan trousers, and a white shirt and vest under a dark blue woolen coat, Liam went in search of Sergeant Major Cooper. He had never seen the city guardsmen in any ceremonial garb while they made their patrols. The fanciest thing about his uniform was the cape, and that was only to be worn when it rained. He found the sergeant major in the courtyard, already surrounded by other newly-inducted soldiers. Liam waited his turn, fidgeting with his tricorn hat under his arm and cursing himself for not getting there earlier.

When finally he reached the front of the line, Liam stated his name and stayed at attention while he received his placement. He would be with the Third Guard Brigade, which would patrol the inner city. Pride welled in Liam's chest. There were only four Guard Brigades, the first at the gates of the city, and the fourth and most prestigious settling in around the palace itself, with the second and third stationed within the city. The Fourth Guard Brigade were the elite of the Guard Brigades, usually reserved for the nobility who joined, and as a nobody, Liam was placed right below them.

"Report to the guard house on Fasch Street, and you will be brought to your unit," Sergeant Major Cooper commanded.

"Thank you, sir." Liam turned and sprinted from the courtyard. When the light hit him, he placed his tricorn on his head.

Liam slowed once he reached the palace gates. He wanted to show decorum as a soldier—to show that he was not green and could comport himself as well as any of the more experienced men. Ants crawled through his stomach, the muscles tightening the closer he got to Fasch Street. By the time he did reach the guard house, Liam felt ready to piss himself if another soldier spoke to him.

He scolded himself. There was nothing to worry over. He would be among the experienced, and there would be nothing strenuous for him to do his first day. They would simply patrol the streets and ensure no one was committing a crime. It would be simple.

Liam knocked on the door to the guard house, jumping back when it opened quickly. "Private Fulton reporting for duty," he squeaked. Liam resisted the urge to slink off and never come back. What a first impression.

The man who had opened the door let out a raucous laugh. "Sent us another greenie, did they?"

Liam shifted uncomfortably, unsure how to answer.

"You can wait here, Fulton. The Third will be making their way back around in a short while." With that, the man shut the door.

Pursing his lips, Liam settled himself against the wall of the guard house. He hadn't gotten the man's name, but he figured the man residing in the building would not appreciate being disturbed again.

True to the man's word, Liam heard footsteps approaching. Once he pushed himself away from the wall, he saw the unit he would be working with. He didn't know what he'd expected, but Liam was disappointed that the unit was not full of legendary-looking warriors ready to snap the heads off any threat that came near. They were all ordinary-looking men. None of them were even particularly tall. Liam stood half a head above all of them, though he mentally conceded that he was unusually tall.

"Ho to the house!" the leader called.

The man Liam had met earlier exited, standing at attention. "Report, sir."

The leader of the unit told him all they had seen on their circle of the city, concluding they had found nothing out of the ordinary. Once he had finished reporting, his eyes landed on Liam. "And who is this?"

Snapping to attention, Liam proudly—and with no squeaking—told them, "Private Liam Fulton reporting for duty, sir."

"Welcome to the Third, Fulton. I'm Borodin; these are Nadelman, Cropsey, Peale, and Bierstadt." Borodin pointed to each man in turn, the names quickly said. "Each team—there are five—is composed of six members. You'll be our sixth."

Liam nodded to each man, trying to remember each name with the face so he would not make any mistakes later. He began walking with them as they started their next round of their section of the city. "What should I be looking for?"

"Anything out of the ordinary. A vendor looking to sell illegal wares, someone stealing—anything you think shouldn't be happening." Borodin's eyes roved the streets as he spoke. "You'll only be observing for the first few days, so watch what we do, and you'll be fine."

Simple enough, Liam supposed. "How often do you find those sorts of things?"

"Not very, which means either the First or Second Guard Brigade has done their job, or people are minding us as they should."

"So they bear the brunt of it?"

Borodin nodded. "Makes our job much easier."

Eyes scanning the street, Liam puckered his lips. He wondered if the prestige actually lay with the Third and Fourth Brigades, or with the First. It seemed to him he would be doing much more important work in the first wave of the city.

"I see that look on your face, Fulton." Peale stopped Liam where he stood. "You should feel honored to be part of the Third. We are one of the last defenses for the king in the city, and he trusts us enough to be that barrier. We're less disposable to him, and if you think you'd like to be fodder, we're more than happy to ask for your transfer."

Liam cleared his throat before speaking. "I'd like to stay here."

"Good. Show some pride, then." Peale turned away from Liam and led the group on their next round.

Collapsing on his bed, Liam let out a heavy sigh. Exhaustion pulled at him as he tried to kick off his boots. He hoped he would soon adjust to the amount of walking he was doing each day. His feet were covered in blisters, and his lower back ached after a week of walking the city in an endless circle. He had yet to see any of his roommates since moving into his barracks room. They were, he assumed, away on an assignment as their clothes still occupied the chests at the heads and feet of the beds.

He lay on his bed, not even bothering to take off his coat, and threw his arm over his eyes. He just wanted to get some sleep and stop walking.

When a throat cleared next to him, Liam bolted upright, nearly hitting his head on the bunk above him. Another man occupied the room, placing things on his bed.

He stood. "I'm your new roommate, Private Liam Fulton."

The man on the other side of the room held out his hand. "Private First Class Jorren Vojvo."

"Liam Fulton," he responded automatically, shaking Jorren's hand. Jorren's laugh brought color to Liam's cheeks. He'd already given his name and showed just how nervous he was to meet new people. Liam wanted to retreat to anywhere else.

"You settling in well?" Jorren ignored Liam's embarrassment.

"Well enough."

Jorren quirked his head slightly and crossed his arms over his chest. "Have you made any friends yet, Liam?"

The color on Liam's cheeks deepened. "No," he confided, "but not from lack of trying."

Giving him a small grin, Jorren clapped Liam on the shoulder. "There are always trials at first, and if you give up in the beginning, you'll never accomplish anything."

Liam cast his gaze in the direction of Jorren's hand. "Thanks," he said quietly.

Jorren waved a hand, walking out of their room. "Come on."

"Where are we going?" Liam hesitantly followed.

"You'll see!"

Jorren introduced Liam to every man on their floor and invited them to join himself and Liam at the Whistling Squire. They went to the favorite local watering hole to have a celebratory drink for Liam's first assignment in the Anatalian army.

"A round of ale!" Jorren called to whichever serving wench was listening as they sat at a large table.

Only four of the men Liam had met agreed to come to drinks with them. It was not many, but it was more than Liam had expected. Liam took a long drink of his tankard when it was set in front of him.

"To our new friend." Jorren held up his own cup, foam sliding down the side.

"To Liam," the other men repeated, taking drags of their ale.

Jorren clapped Liam on the shoulder. "I think we are going to be very good friends, Liam."

4

Margaret flew down the hallway as she finished tightening the last bindings on her kirtle. "I'm leaving, Papa!" she called once she reached the foyer. Just a few more steps, and she could leave without a lecture…again.

"Hold!" her father boomed from his library.

Reluctantly stopping before her hand hit the door handle, Margaret turned to the direction he'd be coming from. "Yes, Papa?" she asked innocently.

"Where are you going?"

"Annalise and the others have asked me to walk the market with them," Margaret told him, voice pregnant with excitement.

Her father raised his brows, folding his arms over his chest. "Aren't they the ones who call you a parvenue?"

Deflating slightly, she nodded. "Yes, Papa."

"Then why are you spending time with them?"

"Because they're my friends, Papa, and Mama likes them."

Her father sucked something off an eye tooth, looking his daughter over critically. "Don't let your Mama choose whom you spend time with, Margaret—especially if they make you unhappy. Your position at court is secure, no matter who you're friends with, despite what your Mama thinks."

Margaret looked down. She wasn't so sure he was right. She had seen the way the women behaved at court and how those women swayed their husbands one way or the other based on petty rivalries. "Yes, Papa. May I go now?"

Sighing, her father pulled out a coin purse and handed it to her. "Please be careful, Margaret, and don't be afraid to leave early if you aren't enjoying yourself."

Margaret turned her nose at the coin purse. "I don't need money. We have receipts sent to the house to be paid."

"The Doremises always carry money," her father scolded, putting the purse in her hand.

She clutched tightly to the leather pouch. "I don't have any pockets."

"I happen to know very well, all the seamstresses we use are told to put pockets in your dresses, Margaret. Put it in your pocket."

Margaret's knuckles went white holding the coin purse. "I can't. I sewed them shut."

Her father inhaled deeply before responding. "Why would you do that, Margaret?"

"I don't want to give them another reason to call us parvenus, Papa!" Margaret looked at him desperately. "They still think us farmers who were lucky enough to catch the eye of the king."

Sighing, her father held out his hand for the coin purse. "Very well. Have your bills sent here."

"Thank you, Papa!" She flashed a bright grin and dropped the money in his hand before darting from the house.

Margaret made her way to the market without an escort. At fourteen, with her rank, she should have one, but her father had never found one for her. It was just another way that showed she had not grown up in the social hierarchy her friends had, that she was what they called her. And they were right: she was new money. She had only been a count's daughter for eight years, having been raised on a tobacco farm before that.

Her father had built his green empire from the ground up, amassing a fortune to rival any of the noblemen who'd held titles for more than four hundred years. The king had thought to make her father an ally to the crown and sought also to receive a portion of his wealth in taxes. The king granted Margaret's father the title of count, making her mother a countess, giving them an estate in the capital city of Jalmar. All the lands he owned would be known as Dorcia, and he would need to produce an heir to inherit them or name one, according to the Laws of Inheritance. Margaret was only six at the time and had been immensely happy at the prospect of a younger brother. As a count, her father would owe the king ten percent of his profit to add to the royal coffers.

It would be no great loss to their own wealth, hardly even enough to notice; tobacco was in such a high demand with nobles and commoners alike that Margaret and her mother wore only the finest silks colored with the highest quality dyes money could buy. At times, they even dressed better than the queen. Margaret's mother only let her associate within the highest circles. Her family had been invited on a regular basis to attend the king's private dinners with only the wealthiest and most prestigious of families.

Margaret smoothed her skirts as she reached Fasch Street, preparing for the onslaught of vendors waving their goods in her face. She was to meet her friends in the fabrics. They only ever seemed to shop for fabrics, or flowers, with her. It seemed to Margaret they only thought themselves capable of arranging a fine bouquet or finding fabric for their newest dress. Margaret doubted they would ever be able to survive without the aid of a father or husband. There was no pragmatism in their lives, though Margaret knew they never thought they needed it. In their world, money bought everything, and they had a lot of it—or, at least, their fathers did—with no care of how much was spent. Her father had taught her the basics of managing money and how to stick to a household budget to ensure she never lived outside her means.

Eventually, the fine fabrics came into view. It was odd to Margaret that fabrics, especially ones of high quality, would be sold in the public market instead of in an indoor shop so there was no chance to be damaged, but it was fully covered with tents and always full of ladies wanting to buy. She shrugged; less work for the vendors, she supposed.

"Lady Margaret!" Lady Clairissa Beauchamp called out to her, waving a delicate hand nearly invisible under the lace of her sleeve.

Waving back, Margaret smiled.

"Take care behind you!" a deep voice yelled.

Margaret turned in time to be shoved aside, her arm smashing into the wooden frame of a vendor's tent. A man raced past her, followed by one of the city guardsmen.

"Stop, thief!" the uniformed man yelled. "In the king's name, I command you to stop!"

Margaret pushed herself off the frame of the tent, letting out a small cry as her arm smarted. She cradled it against her chest, examining her injury. Her forearm was red where it had been hit; no doubt it would turn dark by the morning. Margaret made a face at it—she'd surely hear about this from her mother until it went away.

The sound of several pounding feet echoed off the buildings, and she turned to see more city guardsmen slow to a halt. One came to her side. "My lady, have you been injured?"

"Not terribly so, sir."

He motioned toward the arm she still cradled. "Do you know who has done this?"

Margaret shook her head. "I heard a man yell to take care, and when I turned around, I was shoved aside before I could see what was happening."

Lady Ingrid came to Margaret's side. She nodded to the guard speaking to Margaret—any time there was a man around, Ingrid needed to be there. "My dear Lady Margaret, what has happened to your arm?"

"It's only a bruise," she commented, raising a brow at Ingrid. She had never used that tone with Margaret before, and she was sure it was due to the guardsman being decently handsome. "I'll join you in a moment, Lady Ingrid."

Ingrid moved closer, putting a hand to her breasts and widening her eyes. "Do you think that terrible man will come back?"

Color dusted the guardsman's cheeks, his eyes drawn to her hands. "No, my lady. Our Liam will outrun him, and we will add bringing harm unto persons of the peerage to his list of crimes."

The other three ladies joined them. Ingrid barely acknowledged them, while Margaret lifted her hand in a silent hello.

"Even so," Ingrid mused, moving closer still, "it has given us all quite a fright, hasn't it, Margaret?"

Margaret resisted the urge to roll her eyes at Ingrid's blatant flirting. She shouldn't even be flirting—at fourteen, they were far too young for these men. "Quite a fright, indeed," she monotoned.

Smile still plastered on her face, Ingrid's eyes turned gelid while looking at Margaret. "Perhaps then, sir, you might escort us all to the safety of our homes?"

"It would be our pleasure, my lady." He bowed before offering his arm. "Third, we will be escorting these ladies home after the fright the thief and Private Fulton have given them."

The men of the Third came forward and offered arms to Elise, Clairissa, and Annalise. Margaret sighed. She always came last when her friends were around, even with those who did not know the Doremises had the newest title in the entire country.

Finally, the last of the Third, a sour-looking gentleman with gray blooming at his temples, offered his arm to Margaret. "Where shall I escort you, my lady?"

"To Cerule House, sir."

5

iam pumped his arms as he ran after a thief who had stolen a handful of jewels from a table. Despite it being Amonat, it felt as hot as summer, making his chase even more unpleasant. He followed him through each section, never slowing as they approached the fabric market. Liam saw the thief fast approaching a young woman who had her back to them.

"Take care behind you!" Liam yelled, hoping he'd be in time for her to move away.

He was not. She turned in just enough time to be shoved aside, her arm hitting the wooden frame of a vendor's tent. The thief continued without even pausing. Though he wished to, Liam also did not stop. He could not let the man get away.

"Stop, thief!" Liam yelled. "In the king's name, I command you to stop!"

As expected, the thief did not stop. Liam doubted he would stop unless someone forced him or he dropped dead of exhaustion. Opportunity presented itself when a carriage pulled into the street, slowing the thief down. Liam threw himself on the criminal, tackling him to the ground. Wind rushed out of both guardsman and criminal as they hit the hard cobblestone. Liam was lucky the thief took the brunt of the fall; only Liam's shoulder smarted from where it touched the ground.

"With the authority of the King of Anatalia, you are under arrest for thievery and disrupting the peace and will be brought to the royal magistrate to receive your punishment," Liam recited the official line they were to tell criminals they caught. After three years working in the Third, he could recite almost any edict in his sleep.

"I didna do it!" The thief scrambled under Liam, clawing at the cobblestones to try to get away.

"No one ever does." He pushed himself up against the thief, receiving a groan in return, and pulled the criminal up by his arm. Liam dug in his pockets, pulling out the stolen ring, raising a brow at the criminal. "This way, if you will."

The thief spat on the ground in response, only moving when Liam pulled roughly at him. He returned the way they had come, hoping to find the young woman still in the market to apologize for her being shoved, but she was nowhere to be seen when they reached the fabric market. Annoyed, Liam tightened his grip on the thief's arm and marched him toward the magistrate's office within the palace grounds.

The magistrate was located at the courtyard entrance to the dungeons, the only door to the left of the entrance. The doors to the right led to the dungeon guards' barracks and dining area. They had previously petitioned to be allowed residence with the other guardsmen of the city, but the king and his councilmen deemed it necessary they stay close to the dungeons in case there was an escape. They would be the best and first defense against some of the more dangerous criminals residing underneath the palace.

Liam pounded on the door, shaking the flimsy wooden structure. He feared he would break it, but the magistrate was hard of hearing, and only a ruckus would alert him to his duties. The door flew open, revealing the scowling magistrate. His squat form ambled away from the entrance, sitting behind his desk.

"I don't know why you guards won't just open the door instead of making all that racket." He turned another scowl Liam's way.

Liam shoved the thief into the room. "Because, Mr. Slanic, the last time someone did, you were enjoying your time with a woman of questionable morals."

Laughter erupted from Mr. Slanic, his rotund belly jiggling with each bark. "I suppose you'd not want to see that either."

"No, sir."

Mr. Slanic spoke once he calmed his humor. "Who do we have here?"

"State your name for the magistrate." Liam pushed the thief into the chair sitting in front of the magistrate's desk. He kept his hand firmly on the criminal's shoulder so he wouldn't be able to bolt. Liam had learned that lesson the hard way the first time he'd caught a thief.

The thief refused to speak.

"As you wish, then. What crime has he committed, Private Fulton?"

Liam placed the stolen ring on Mr. Slanic's desk. "Thievery, disrupting the peace, and possibly causing harm to a young lady of noble birth. I could not question her, as she was gone by the time I was able to apprehend the criminal."

Nodding, Mr. Slanic wrote the crimes out on a piece of parchment, the tip of his quill scratching pleasantly against the paper. "Is that all?"

"Yes, sir."

"Very good, then." The quill continued to move for a few moments more. Mr. Slavic pinched sand between three fingers and dusted it over the drying ink. He waited a moment before dumping it off into a bowl filled with darkened sand. "He'll have a hand removed and two fingers knocked."

"I canna lose my hand!" The thief tried to rise, but Liam firmly pushed him back into place.

"Where will he be receiving this punishment?"

Mr. Slanic shrugged. "Take him to the surgery so he has a fighting chance of staving off infection, or the butcher—it matters not. He will lose the hand either way."

Liam's face twisted. This was the first time he would take someone to a fate other than imprisonment. "Where is the surgery?"

"You'll find one on the other side of the dungeons, past the interior entrance. Be off with you, then."

"A good day to you." Liam pulled the thief, white in color and devoid of complaint, from his seat. It must have been shock, as he had not been an easy man to handle to begin with. Liam led him through the upper level of the dungeon toward the surgery, his stomach souring the closer they got.

Halfway there, the thief finally spoke. "Please, sir, ye canna let them take my hand! I promise I'll return to my home and be a law abidin' citizen for the rest of me days if ye just let me go."

"I can't do that. I'm sorry. You've committed a crime, and now you have to deal with the consequences of that."

The thief began to struggle once more. "No, please! Let me go!"

"You have been given your punishment. You'll have to accept your fate." Liam swallowed the sick feeling in his throat. He didn't want to be part of this punishment any more than the thief wanted to receive it. But he had a sworn duty to uphold the law, and uphold the law he would.

Upon entering the surgery, Liam shut the door behind him and blocked it. The thief looked for any other exit, drooping in on himself when he could not. Surgical instruments lined the walls, saws in one section and blades in another. For a healer, it was rather well organized.

"Can I help you?" the only healer in the room asked.

"Yes, Healer…"

"Woolsey."

"We've just come from the magistrate's, Healer Woolsey." Liam lifted the sentencing paper in his hand. "He's to have a hand removed and two fingers knocked."

Nodding, the physician started to remove the tools he'd need from the wall. "It's a shame you missed Healer Orion. He's truly the more skilled at removal."

Liam shifted, unsure of how to respond.

"Did Mr. Slanic say which hand?"

"N— His non-dominant hand is to be removed."

A smirk lifted the corner of Woolsey's mouth while he let out a soft snort. "Mr. Slanic must have been feeling generous today."

Liam, not wanting to let him think otherwise, quickly agreed. "Indeed he was."

The last item taken off the wall was a long iron bar that was in the shape of a spade, though more pointed at the end. There were several sizes from the width of Liam's finger to the width of his thigh. He thought it unlikely any patient would survive the need of one so large.

Healer Woolsey shoved the instrument into the fire to heat. "Sit him down over here, and pour him a drink from the pitcher."

Liam pulled over the criminal, putting him in the seat before lifting the pitcher. Taking a whiff, it reeked of cheap alcohol. He poured it into the only cup, sliding it in front of the thief. "I would strongly suggest drinking it."

The thief put it to his lips without argument, letting out a choking cough when the alcohol hit his tongue. He took another drink, pouring the rest of the cup's contents down the back of his throat. After two cups full of alcohol had passed the criminal's lips, he leaned back in the chair and let out a belch.

"Which is your dominant hand?" Healer Woolsey asked.

The thief lazily threw up his right hand, leaning his head against the back of the chair.

"Very good, thank you." Healer Woolsey grabbed his left hand and started to examine it. He prodded certain areas and pulled at the hand while the thief watched.

"What was in that?" Liam had never seen someone affected so quickly by spirits.

Healer Woolsey shrugged. "A little Poppy's Milk mixed in. It will help keep him calm, and there will be less pain for him."

Liam supposed that made sense. "Shall I leave you, then?" He was already edging toward the door. Liam had no interest in staying for the removal.

"Oh, no. Without Healer Orion, you'll have to stay here to help me—don't give me that look—all you have to do is hold him down."

The healer glared at Liam when he unconsciously backed up. Liam's stomach sank with the thought of having to witness such a punishment. "Are you sure I can't go find Healer Orion for you?"

"No, now come over here." The glare persisted while Woolsey put a wooden rest stained with blood under the thief's hand. "I want you to hold his arm steady, no matter how much he moves. One wrong cut, and he could bleed out."

Liam gulped but firmly grasped the thief's arm without protest. He hooked a leg between the thief's spread ones, trying to do the work of two men at once. "Ready."

"You're going to lose your balance like that, Private." Woolsey scolded.

Liam shot him an annoyed look. "I'll be fine. Please proceed, Healer Woolsey."

With a shrug, Woolsey pulled on the thief's hand before he began cutting with a sharp blade. The thief screamed into Liam's ear, his whole body bucking against him with the onslaught of pain. Liam felt jarred and wished he'd have listened to the Healer about his position. Liam leaned heavily against the criminal to try to make him stay still, but it was no use. The only thing Liam could do was try to keep the arm still so the only person who lost anything was the thief. And not lose his stomach on the thief.

"Hold a moment more!"

Blood poured over the table as the saw moved. Liam dared not look, but he could feel the hot blood running down his fingers and down his arm, cooling by the time it soaked into the fabric at his elbow. The criminal was starting to weaken, his convulsions not nearly as strong as when the blade first licked his skin.

The healer grabbed the smaller of the two blades he'd put in the fire and put it to the flesh he'd cut to staunch the bleeding before he grabbed the saw. "You'll really have to hold him now, Private."

Liam switched positions to get a better hold on the arm, his back blessedly to the gory scene. It didn't help much when the healer began to saw the bone—Liam could feel the vibration up the thief's arm. He was glad the thief only groaned; maybe he would faint soon, and they could finish in peace.

"Private, I'm going to need your help," the healer said. "I'm going to need you to hold the flaps closed while I put a stitch in."

"Don't you just cauterize the wound?" Liam asked, feeling queasy. He did not want to touch the separated skin.

"The stitch will burn up with the heat, but I want as small a wound as possible."

Liam groaned. It just had to be him to spot the thief first. He turned around and gagged at the bloody stump. The healer was already putting the stitch together, making Liam shiver. Next time, he'd wait for Healer Orion to return.

"Just hold it together here—that's it—and I'll put in the stitch."

Stomach roiling, Liam closed his eyes while he held the stump. Luckily, the thief made no more noise while the healer worked.

"Bring his arm up," Healer Woolsey commanded as he retrieved the iron, now glowing with its own heat.

Liam did as he was told, making sure to keep his hands away from the iron. "Hurry!" He could feel the bile in his throat and wanted to let go of the thief as soon as humanly possible.

The healer laid the hot iron atop of the stump. The criminal loosed a scream Liam would never forget before slipping back into unconsciousness. His flesh sizzled as it cauterized, filling the room with the smell of burnt skin.

Liam released the arm, putting a wrist to his mouth to hold back the vomit crawling up his throat. "Will you require me any further?"

"No, you may return to your duties, Private. He won't wake up again after that." Healer Woolsey laid the criminal's hand flat on to the table. "Someone else will escort this gentleman to his cell for recuperation when he comes around."

Almost tripping on his feet in an effort to retreat from the room, Liam made it to the fresh air outside the entrance of the dungeon in record time. He was sure his face was as white as the criminal's had been once the iron was laid against him.

"Private Fulton, you're to report to Sergeant Edwin at oh nine hundred."

Liam pulled the pillow from his face. "What for? It's my day off."

"You don't ask questions, Fulton. Show up in uniform."

Sighing, Liam pulled himself out of bed. It was just like his higher-ups to give him only an hour's notice. He shaved and dressed as quickly as he could, making it to Sergeant Edwin's office ten minutes before his appointed time. "You wished to see me, sir?" Liam asked, standing at attention once he entered the office.

"Yes, Private Fulton, have a seat."

He sat stiffly in front of his superior and waited for him to speak.

"You're being promoted today, Fulton. From Private Class One to Private Class Two."

"Aren't those essentially the same rank, sir?"

"They are, but you have to reach all three classes before you can be promoted to Lance Corporal," Sergeant Edwin told him.

"Is there something I've done to be rewarded with this?" Liam asked.

"Your exemplary work capturing the thief in the market the other day. Borodin recommended you."

Surprise lit Liam's face, his eyebrows raising. He wasn't aware that Borodin liked him enough to recommend him for a promotion. "Thank you, sir."

Sergeant Edwin handed him a new pin for his uniform and a medal to put on his rack. "Put these on your uniform before you report for duty in the morning."

Liam put the new decorations in pocket. "Yes sir."

"That will be all, Fulton. You may go."

"Thank you, sir." He stood and saluted before returning to his barracks. Liam replaced his rank insignias before he put away his uniform and put the medal on his dress uniform. He climbed back into bed, intending on sleeping the morning away. Liam grinned. It would be a good day.

Liam walked his way through the streets with his unit. The days were once again monotonous as he patrolled the streets for wrongdoers. The people of the city were hardworking and liked to go about their business as usual. They saw the same people every day, doing the same thing day in and day out. It would stay boring until there was another thief or Liam was moved to another division.

Pulling his hood over his head as it began to rain, Liam trudged forward. He was ready for the day to be over already. He nearly ran into Borodin when his leader paused. "What's going on?"

"Aren't those the ladies from the other day, Peale?" Borodin asked.

Peale squinted, looking at the group of women pointed out. "I believe so, sir."

"What ladies?"

"We had to escort them home while you chased that thief." Borodin rolled his eyes. "The one I had was an absolute snake."

Liam let out a surprised laugh. "Oh?"

"All she wanted was to make her suitors jealous by making them think even a lowborn was preferred over them, the viper."

"What of the one who was hurt? Was she all right?"

Peale shrugged. "She was pleasant enough—very unlike Borodin's young noble. She kept apologizing for keeping me from my work and tried to send me away, saying she could escort herself home."

"Are they all like the viper here?" Liam asked, still watching the young women. They had pestered a soldier of the Third from another unit into carrying them over the muddy river that formed in front of them.

"Mostly." Borodin scoffed while he watched the man from Unit One struggle. "Poor Ragle. Should we help?"

Peale laughed. "If he was fool enough to offer, let him do it on his own."

"Which one is the viper?" asked Liam.

"The one being carried now."

Peale pointed to the one hiking her skirts to her shins. "That is the one who was hurt."

"Lady Margaret, you will scandalize us all!" the Viper yelled at Lady Margaret as she skipped over the rivulet. "You put your skirts down!"

Liam could feel the eye roll from Lady Margaret where he stood. Once she was over the offending water, she dropped her skirts and waved a limp hand in the Viper's direction.

"I pity the husband who tries to control her," Liam said. A lady who would raise her skirts in public was certainly not one who would care what a husband had to say.

"If she can ever find a husband; she seems far from demure," Peale countered.

Snapping his fingers, Borodin brought their attention back to him. "We have work to do. We need to stop standing around and gossiping like women."

Standing up straighter, Peale said, "Yes, sir."

"Yes, sir," Liam echoed.

"Come along, then." Borodin walked away.

Liam followed behind, glancing over his shoulder at the group of women. They were surrounding Lady Margaret, giving her some what for. He was tempted to turn around and help her, but she looked as though she could handle herself.

6

Margaret sat in the library with her mother, reading through the morning. She would not be allowed to go out again until her ungainly—in the words of her mother—bruise went away so that her appearance was once again pristine. That, and Ingrid had tattled on her for lifting her skirts in public. Her mother would never say her imposed reclusion was primarily driven by that, especially since her father wasn't upset. Appearance was the only thing that mattered to her mother, something she said should matter to Margaret as well, but Margaret disagreed. There were much better things than being pretty. Margaret knew her mother was only trying to make sure her daughter had the best. Margaret tried not to fault her for it—her mother still had a hard time being an outsider in the court after all these years.

The butler, Bruggen, entered the library with Charles Luther, her father's business partner, in tow. "My ladies, Mr. Luther to see his lordship."

Margaret's eyes roved over the tall, lean man, his strawberry blond hair gleaming in the afternoon light. Resisting the urge to gasp with excitement, she calmly laid down her book. "How nice to see you again, Mr. Luther. Was Papa expecting you?"

He bowed to the both of them as the butler left the room. "My lord was not, Lady Margaret."

"Please, sit while you wait, Mr. Luther," her mother gently commanded. "My husband will not be long before he sees you."

Heat pinkening her cheeks, Margaret asked, "Will you sit with me and tell me of your day, Mr. Luther?"

"It would be my pleasure." He took the open end of the chaise, turning in Margaret's direction. He smiled, but it dropped when his eyes landed on her arm. "Lady Margaret, have you been injured?"

Her mother spoke before she could even open her mouth. "Oh, it was horrible, Mr. Luther! Margaret came home not two days ago with an ugly black bruise on her arm, escorted by a city guardsman for her own protection. She had been assaulted by a common criminal as he rampaged through the city, stealing as he pleased."

Margaret resisted the urge to roll her eyes. "It wasn't as bad as Mama makes it seem. I was only pushed out of the way by the thief while he was running from the Third Guard Brigade, and one of them kindly escorted me home."

"I'm glad to hear that you're all right, Lady Margaret." Charles rested a hand over hers, his smile reaching his eyes.

A thrill ran through Margaret, settling in her stomach as it buzzed with excitement. His crow's feet deepened as he smiled, bringing attention to the white bursting at his temples.

"Enough of me. How have you been, Mr. Luther?"

"I'm afraid you'll find me rather boring, Lady Margaret. I do nothing but work with your father. Soon enough—hopefully tomorrow—I'll be leaving for Dorcia to speak with our workers on how to better improve their efficiency of delivery."

Margaret smiled. "On the contrary, Mr. Luther, that sounds quite exciting. How is it you wish to improve the deliveries?"

"I would like to hire more workers to not only package the product, but deliver it. With more than one person on the road per carriage, they can go faster. While one sleeps, the other drives." Charles's eyes lit as he spoke.

Margaret frowned, her brow furrowing. "Doesn't that seem…too taxing on the workers—and the horses?"

"Not at all, Lady Margaret. The faster the deliveries happen, the more time they can spend with their families, and we can have horses along our common routes to switch out in regular intervals so no one beast gets too worn."

"But with the increased delivery rate, won't that also raise product purchase and expectation, making them work even harder than they do now? They would be able to spend time at home even less than they do currently. Surely, Papa would not see this as a good thing."

Charles looked over at her mother. "She certainly has her father's gentle spirit, does she not?"

"She does. It makes my lord proud." Her mother almost looked annoyed as she agreed.

Margaret blushed, pulling her eyes away from him to land on her lap. "My apologies, Mr. Luther. Surely, Papa would have a much better idea of what is happening than I."

"You know more than you think you do, Lady Margaret," Charles assured, squeezing her hand. "I'll be sure to tell your father he has a most respectable heir in you."

Margaret smiled tightly. "Thank you, Mr. Luther. All I can hope for is to make him proud."

Her father had not officially made Margaret his heir yet, but she did not want to correct Charles. His petition was still being looked over by the king, and it could take years before an official answer was given—even for the king's friends. The petition had only recently been drafted, so Margaret did not expect anything in the near future. And as far as she knew, it was the first of its kind. The other women of court who were sole children were married off and their husbands made heir to their father's estates.

"You do, my darling," her father said from the doorway, an affectionate smile adorning his face. "You make my heart burst with pride."

Margaret lowered her lashes in a display of humbleness. "Thank you, Papa."

"Come, Charles. Tell me more of this plan of yours."

Charles quickly stood and bowed to her father. "Good day, Lady Catherine, Lady Margaret." Charles nodded to both of them before following behind her father.

Margaret felt the distinct absence of his body heat when he left, drooping back into the corner of the chaise longue. She sighed heavily, looking at the hand he had touched. There was nothing particularly extraordinary about the touch, but Margaret felt something special had happened. He had gone out of his way to touch her this time. She wondered if he had finally stopped seeing her as the little girl he once knew and now saw the woman she was becoming.

Only time would tell, but time was too slow for Margaret's taste.

A scream erupted near the front door of Cerule House, startling Margaret.

"Margaret! Margaret, come here right now!" her mother yelled.

She picked up her skirts and hurried toward her mother, worry tightening her chest. "What is it?"

"We've been invited to dine privately with Their Majesties!"

"What?" Margaret snatched the parchment from her mother's hand, reading it quickly.

"We have to call the seamstress here immediately. We cannot wear anything they might have seen before." Her mother opened drawer after drawer until she found a blank piece of parchment. She wrote a short summons to their seamstress before calling out for their butler. "Bruggen!"

A few moments later, he appeared. "Yes, your ladyship?"

"Find someone to deliver this to Mistress Marrywick immediately."

"As you wish, my lady." Bruggen took the parchment and bowed.

"Mama, will we have time for new dresses? The dinner is in three days." Surely, they couldn't ask Mistress Marrywick to create two gowns in such a short time; the poor woman would have to work until her fingers bled.

She smiled, cupping her daughter's cheek gently. "Of course we will, my love. There's nothing we can't have when we want it."

Her lips turned upward unbidden. "What colors should we wear?"

"They have to send a message. Everything we do needs to tell them something."

"Our house colors, then?"

"I think perhaps the Platiri colors. We must show them we are loyal to Their Majesties."

Margaret followed behind her parents as a servant escorted them to the royal family's dining room. This was the first time they had ever been invited to dine privately with the King and Queen of Anatalia, and there was nothing that her mother wouldn't do to make sure that it went perfectly. They all wore new clothes in the colors of the Platiri family: red and black.

Her mother wore a black robe with her burgundy petticoat and stomacher embroidered in black. Margaret wore the opposite, though with more ornamentation on the bodice. Black silk thread was woven into a bouquet of flowers native to Dorcia at her shoulders. Her father was the only one of them who did not strictly follow the color scheme. He wore all black with a silver vest, the colors bringing out his pale skin—it seemed no matter how long he spent in the sun, he never tanned.

"Please wait here, my lord, my ladies," the servant said when they reached a closed door. He bowed to them before going through.

Margaret clenched her fists in her voluminous skirts to hide her shaking hands. Her father had dined privately with the king on many occasions, but this was the first time they had all been invited. She was sure she would stick her foot in her mouth at some point in the night. Margaret lacked the conversational skills needed at court, and it showed painfully in social situations such as these.

A few moments later, the servant returned. "If you will please enter, the table has been set."

"Thank you." Her father stood to the side to allow his wife and daughter to go through first.

Margaret pulled a chair out to sit but was stopped by her mother slapping her hand with her fan. "We do not sit until Their Majesties have been seated."

"Yes, Mama." Margaret blushed deeply, going to examine the artwork while she waited. How could she have not remembered something so simple?

Paintings by the most famous artists of their time lined the walls throughout the entire palace. The art ranged from before Anatalia was a country to the current year 2271. In the new year, the monarchs would host a showing for all the new artists to allow them to be seen and their art to be purchased by the nobles invited to attend. It was another way to find out where one was in the peerage hierarchy. Only the closest friends of the monarchs were invited, and it was something Margaret's mother was dying to attend.

The door opened beside Margaret, and she fell into a quick curtsey. "Your Majesties, Your Royal Highness."

The king nodded to them, a broad smile stretching his face. "Jerone, my good man! Thank you for coming—and bringing your lovely ladies with you."

"It is our honor to be here, Your Majesty," her father said once he straightened. "We were delighted to receive your invitation."

"It was high time we invited you. Please, sit, and we'll eat." King Sorren motioned to the table for them to take their places.

Servants peeled away from the walls and pulled out chairs for them, pushing them in as they sat.

Margaret looked around the table before settling her eyes on the plate in front of her. There were times she wished she could go back to only being a farmer's daughter. She would do as she was bid by her mother—let the adults talk and only speak when addressed. That was something she was very comfortable with. In any case, her mother was content to talk for her; her mother much preferred it, actually.

"Lady Catherine, Lady Margaret, you both look lovely this evening." Queen Lillian offered them a slight smile.

"You're very kind to say so, Your Majesty, but we certainly could never match your beauty." Her mother bowed her head humbly.

Queen Lillian waved a hand. "Surely, Lady Margaret will grow up to be the crown jewel of our court."

Her mother smiled at Margaret. "I would like to think she will."

Margaret shifted uncomfortably in her seat. She didn't enjoy being talked about like she wasn't in the room, even if it was complimentary. She looked to her left, where the crown prince sat, to find he was already deep in drink. It seemed he wouldn't be any help in keeping her from being the object of conversation.

"Jerone," King Sorren finally said, "tell me about what you're doing now."

Margaret's father sat straighter. "Not much has changed, but we're trying to find a way to make our deliveries more efficient while still letting our men see their families."

"Why not just hire more men?"

Her father smiled patiently. "If I hired more men, that means that I would have to pay my current workers less than what they make now, because there would not be as much work for them. That, in turn, would make it harder for them to survive on their salary. My people depend on me to ensure their families can live and prosper."

The king nodded as her father spoke. "And how do you propose to solve your problem?"

"Perhaps creating incentives for the men without a family to work longer hours." Her father shrugged, taking a sip of his wine. "Perhaps finding more investors to be able to pay more salaries."

"You'll find a way, I'm sure of it. You always do; otherwise, you wouldn't have risen so far." King Sorren raised a glass in her father's direction.

"Your Majesty's faith in my husband is beyond heartening." Margaret's mother lowered her lashes demurely. "It inspires us all to be better to deserve your confidence."

Margaret looked between her mother and the king. Something palpable radiated off her mother that she couldn't identify. She looked over at her father and saw his nose dipping into his glass of wine. Margaret jumped when the doors opened and the servants returned with steaming food. They served the king first, followed by the queen and the prince before they came to the Doremis family. It was a hearty spread of pheasant, roasted beef, and potatoes.

Looks continued to pass between the king and her mother throughout the dinner, the king personally helping her from her seat once dinner was finished. "My lady, we must be sure to do this more often. Perhaps after I've returned from my visit in Salatia?"

Margaret looked to her father and saw his eyes tighten as he looked at the king and her mother. She didn't understand what the issue was—her father and the king were the closest of friends.

Her mother smiled brightly. "It would be our pleasure."

 **7**

rompton stopped beside Sorren as they came to the capital city of Salatia. Even from here, he could see no fanfare prepared for the king. The retinue paused behind them. Crompton could hear murmuring from them, most likely noticing the same. "Do you wish to remain outside the city until you've had a chance to rest, Your Majesty, or do you wish to proceed?"

"We'll go now. I don't want to spend another night in a cot." Sorren ran a hand down his face, looking tired with the bags under his eyes.

"As you wish, Your Majesty." Crompton clucked his stallion forward, taking the lead for the king's safety.

Crompton rode up to the familiar gates of Cassen. It was still blocked by guardsmen, but that was of no matter. "Make way for King Sorren of Anatalia and his retinue."

The guards bowed before opening the gates.

Crompton rode through first, followed closely by Sorren. There were no people lining the streets cheering the foreign monarch, no fanfare, no excitement filling the streets as there had been on previous visits. Crompton couldn't help but grin. This could be good for him; if King Peralta saw that the people did not welcome the foreign king, he might not either.

The palace came into view, windows gleaming orange in the evening light. Only two members of King Peralta's council waited for them on the steps of the palace. It was a great insult, and Crompton knew it would not go unnoticed by Sorren. Crompton dismounted, clapping his horse on the shoulder. He bid the king to wait before following suit.

Crompton approached the two council members. "What is this?"

"I don't understand, Your Grace."

"Where is King Sorren's welcome?"

"That is what we are here for." He straightened himself.

Crompton raised his brow. "Where is the fanfare? The people in the streets?"

The second councilman cleared his throat. "Word has reached the capital of His Majesty's tax on imports from Salatia that has not been imposed on the other Aratian countries, and they are not happy for it. It has hurt some of their chances of selling their wares in Anatalia."

"I see." Crompton tried not to smirk. He had pushed another noble to suggest the tax to replenish Anatalian coffers. He knew it would ruffle feathers, but this was more than he could have hoped for. "Then escort us in, please, so we can refresh ourselves."

The councilman bowed. "We will be happy to, Your Grace."

Waving the red-faced Sorren down, Crompton gestured for the king to precede him before following after the king and the Salatian councilman. This boded well—very well, in fact, for him. No doubt, King Peralta was as irritated as his subjects over the new taxes implemented by Sorren, and Crompton would stoke the fire while they were here. Crompton could think of nothing better to do with his time.

"Let the games begin," he murmured to himself, letting out a pleased snort.

Crompton was making his way to the library to wait for his appointment with King Peralta when he heard raised voices.

"Pig! You are cumbersome and unwanted!"

Crompton waited in the corridor to see if the people would walk past him. The least that would happen was he would enjoy some gossip; the most would be he would have ammunition to use to get what he wanted.

"You could be sleeping with a king," a familiar voice countered.

"I already *am*, you buffoon!" a woman yelled, storming past Crompton.

Crompton raised his brows in surprise. That surely wasn't whom he was expecting. Sorren followed after her, but Crompton reached out to stop him. "Where do you think you're going?"

"After her. Now stand aside," Sorren commanded.

"You cannot try seducing the Queen of Salatia for your own fun," Crompton scolded. "Buy a whore like the rest of them."

Sorren rolled his eyes. "You should have seen the eyes she was giving me. She wants me to seduce her. She's just playing hard to get by saying no."

"You're going to ruin our time here before it even starts," Crompton raged at the king, but he secretly wished Sorren had been successful in his seduction. "Go back to your chambers; I'll have a courtesan sent to you."

Sorren rolled his eyes again. "Remember to whom you speak, cousin."

"You would do well to remember where we are, cousin," Crompton countered, standing firm. "Someone will be along shortly to serve your needs."

"There better be." With nothing more to say, Sorren walked away.

Sighing, Crompton leaned against the wall. Things would be much easier once he no longer needed to keep up this charade. He would wait until after his meeting with King Peralta to send anyone Sorren's way. Hopefully, that would make him angry enough to act a petulant child at dinner and further bring relations south.

Sorren wrapped an arm around her, pulling her close to him. Sweat slicked the sides of his neck, and his fingers slid easily against her damp back. He let out a small noise when she moved even closer, wedging herself under his shoulder with her head on his chest. Sorren smiled, tracing circles on her tanned skin. She kissed his chest, nuzzling closer while running a hand down his torso.

"Surely, you cannot be in need of more already?" He nipped at the skin of her arm, producing a giggle from her lips.

She raised a brow, her mouth quirking into a challenging smirk. "And what if I am?"

"Then I'll have to oblige you," he growled, pulling her onto his chest.

"Good." She grinned, planting her hands on his chest while she settled back on his hips.

Grabbing her by the back of the neck, he pulled her forward. "Come here." He attacked her mouth, planting his other hand against her hip with an audible smack.

She let out a short squeal against his mouth.

The door burst open behind them, shedding light onto their entwined bodies. She jerked, trying to pull away, but Sorren kept her in place.

"What is the meaning of this?" demanded King Peralta.

"I do believe I'm taking your wife at the moment."

Queen Alaxia squirmed, trying to pull away from King Sorren.

He grabbed on to her hips tightly, glaring at her. "We're not finished, Your Majesty. You can't go until we are."

"Take my lady wife to her chambers to clean herself," King Peralta commanded darkly, his voice nearly a growl. "And ensure King Sorren's bags are packed. It seems he's overstayed his welcome."

"Yes, Your Majesty." One of the guards stepped forward. He pulled off his mantle, covering the queen with it as he pulled her away from the foreign king.

"Husband, please!" Tears streamed down her face. "Please forgive me!"

Sorren rolled his eyes, pulling the bedding over himself. "Stop sniveling. You're a queen."

"You, stop talking," snapped the King of Salatia. "After this day, you are no longer welcome in my home, in my city, or in my country." With that, he left the room.

King Peralta stormed from the room, waiting until he was in another part of the palace before letting out a yell. He slammed his fist into the wall several times before shaking it out. He turned to look at one of his guards and barked, "Find me Lord General Crompton, and bring him to me in my chambers."

"Yes, Your Majesty." He bowed before scurrying off.

Running a hand over his face, he winced once he realized it was the one with bloodied knuckles. The King of Salatia returned to his rooms, thinking all the while how he would punish his wife. He did not want to be a barbarian and execute her as earlier kings had, but he also could not let her go unpunished. He had just sat in his chair when Crompton entered.

"Your Majesty, you sent for me?"

"I did." He extended his arm toward the seat in front of him. "I was wondering if you might counsel me, Your Grace."

Crompton looked at him expectantly.

"How would you punish an unfaithful wife?"

Crompton's face hardened. "Did he get to her, then?"

"He did."

"Do you love her?"

"I do." Peralta slumped back in his chair, covering his face for a moment before recovering himself.

"Has she given you any children, even unborn ones?"

King Peralta hesitated. "No."

"Then strip her of her lands and titles and send her to a nunnery." Crompton shrugged.

"And how will the people accept their beloved queen going to a nunnery?"

"Tell them she wished to devote herself to her faith," Crompton said slowly, thinking as he went. "Have her make the proclamation to the court. Put on a show. She has been visited in the night by an angel telling her she's barren and her true calling is a sister of the faith, spreading the good word to everyone."

King Peralta leaned back in his seat, examining Crompton. "A very good idea, thank you." He grabbed the decanter between them and poured himself a drink. Peralta looked to Crompton, holding until he got confirmation.

Crompton shook his head. "If that is all, Your Majesty, I assume I should be packing."

"Indeed you should be." Peralta waved a hand. "You may go."

Crompton stood and bowed to him while backing up toward the door.

"Your Grace?"

"Yes, Your Majesty?"

Peralta's face darkened, his knuckles white as he clenched his fists. "You'll have your war."

A grin slid slowly across Crompton's face. "Thank you, Your Majesty."

 **8**

Captain Marius Vojvo walked into the tavern, scanning the mass of people sitting at a myriad of tables, none of which were the same shape or size. The interior was smoky, the smell of tobacco invading his senses. He squinted, looking for his son, the dim light making it difficult to easily identify any one person. His son, Jorren, was supposed to meet him for lunch while he was still in town. He had been recalled to the capital to get his orders, rumors of war with their neighboring country, Salatia, running rampant in his circles.

Finally spotting Jorren, his back to him, Marius walked through a cloud of smoke that stung his eyes. Vojvo clapped Jorren on the shoulder before sitting at the table. They were at their favorite tavern, the Whistling Squire, which was always crowded with a plethora of patrons. This would be their last meeting before the Captain went to wherever he was ordered. Captain Vojvo was pleased Jorren had followed in his footsteps, joining the Anatalian military when he was old enough. His son had been assigned to Captain Baleran's regiment, while Marius was leading his own battalion wherever the lord generals saw fit to place him.

"It's good to see you, son," Marius almost shouted to be heard over the crowd, looking over his son slowly. He looked older than the last time he had seen him, but Jorren still had his boyish smile. "Lance Corporal looks good on you."

Jorren grinned at him, taking note of the close examination. "Would you like me to sit for a portrait, Father?"

The captain rolled his twinkling eyes. "And have to see your face every day?"

Jorren let out a barking laugh before his face lit with excitement. "Do you think there will be a war?"

Marius turned serious, the lightness of his mood evaporating. He leaned forward on the table, clasping his hands in front of him. "It is certainly a possibility."

"All of us in the barracks hope that we go to war," Jorren said excitedly.

"War is a very serious thing, Jorren," Vojvo sternly scolded. "There's no guarantee we would win."

Jorren furrowed his brow. He looked uncomfortably at his father. "We are the best army in all of Aratia!"

"Whether we are or not, it is all dependent on who allies with us and who allies with Salatia," Marius lectured. "If neither Frasisca nor Glessic come to our side, and Salatia convinces Radovan to join them, we have no chance of winning. Radovan has an almost endless supply of men to use for Salatian fodder."

"Both Frasisca and Glessic hate the Salatians," Jorren countered, his frown deepening. "Why wouldn't they come to our aid? Salatia will have no chance against us."

"Even if we win, there is no guarantee we make it back alive," Vojvo reminded him. He was pleased to see some of the delight taken out of his son's face. Vojvo had seen his fair share of bloodshed in his career and wished that his son would never have to see the horrors he had seen himself. It saddened Marius that Jorren was so excited at the prospect of fighting the Salatian soldiers.

"Where will you be if there is a war?" Jorren asked.

"I can't be sure, but I suspect that I'll be in the borderlands, monitoring the bridges on the Frasiscan River with Captain Limburgh and Captain Magnor, likely close to Marbon. They are an easy place to cross with how narrow the Frasisca River is there," Marius speculated. "It would not be a dangerous assignment."

"Good—you are not as young as you used to be," Jorren joked, the twinkle returning to his eyes. "You can't go around swinging your sword all day like us young folk."

Vojvo let out a laugh, glad he had this time with his son before they would part company for an undetermined amount of time. "How is Elaine?" He wanted to change the subject.

Jorren's face fell at the mention of the woman he had been trying to court. "She is still being evasive."

"There are always trials at first, but if you give up in the beginning, you will never accomplish anything," Marius told his son. It was something he always said to Jorren and what his own father had always said to him.

"I don't even know if there is a beginning," Jorren murmured sullenly, perking up when a serving wench arrived with the food. "I ordered before you arrived."

Marius muttered his thanks before digging into the steaming food. "Maybe if we go to war, Elaine will have changed her mind and want a man with a pension," he teased.

"I doubt it, Father," Jorren countered, gulping down his ale. "She will probably have a brood of children by the time we return."

"We shall see," Marius tried to placate his son. "Maybe she'll fall madly in love with you, and she'll be begging to be Mrs. Jorren Vojvo."

Jorren laughed at him. "What are we, women?"

Marius clasped his arm. "Not that, surely."

Jorren mopped up the juices on his bronze plate with a heel of bread, tearing into it. "We should return before we're missed."

His father nodded, finishing his pint of ale in a large gulp, some of it spilling into his beard. He pulled Jorren into a tight hug. "I don't know when I'll see you again," he started awkwardly. "I love you, Son."

Jorren gave his father a boyish grin. "I love you too." He chuckled. "I'll see you when I see you."

Marius watched his son walk off into the city, easily disappearing in the throng of people crowding the streets. He sighed, pushing his way through the crowd in the opposite direction, hoping that the rumors of war were not true.

9

argaret struggled with the door, her arm loaded with flowers from the market. "Mama?" she called once the door was open. "Where do you want the flowers?"

Her mother came to the door. "Margaret, why didn't you send for a servant to get them?"

Margaret shrugged, blooms falling from her arms as she did. "The day was hot, and I wanted to return home. I didn't want to wait for a servant just to carry some flowers."

"You have more important things to be doing than shuffling through the market like a servant, Margaret." Her mother snatched the fallen flowers from the floor, squinting at her daughter. "Bring them down to the kitchens so the servants can arrange them."

"Papa told me you used to make the most beautiful arrangements when you were first married."

"Things are different now." Her tone was still sharp, though her face softened. "That was before we could afford servants, and I collected the flowers myself from the fields."

Margaret pulled the blooms closer to her. "Will you teach me?"

"You will marry a great man one day, and you'll have no need to make your own arrangements. You'll have hordes of servants to do it for you, and you'll be the one to manage them." Her mother handed her the fallen bloom, wiping her hands as though they had been sullied.

She looked down. "Yes, Mama."

Her mother sighed as Margaret reached the doorway. "Margaret, stop. Bring them into the library. It will cheer your father up."

Margaret smiled brightly, changing her course. She set the flowers on the long oak table in the library and separated them by type of flower. She had roses of three colors—white, red, and pink—amaryllis, and white-green hydrangea. Once Margaret was content they'd been well separated, she pulled the rope to summon a servant to the library.

Her mother came up beside Margaret. "These colors will go together nicely."

"Thank you, Mama." Her cheeks heated from the praise.

When the footman arrived, her mother turned to him. "Bring us hand shears, a vase, and water."

"Yes, my lady." The servant bowed before leaving the library.

"First, we need to decide how we want the arrangement to look," her mother instructed. "Then we need to cut the ends of the stem so the flower will sit where we want it."

"How should it look?" Margaret asked, glancing at the flowers.

"However you'd like it. You get to decide."

While they waited for their servant to return, Margaret paired flowers together to see how they looked. She clustered the roses together with the amaryllis, looking at it with a tilted head. She liked it, but she wasn't sure it would look good with the hydrangea. "What do you think, Mama?"

"It doesn't matter what I think as long as you like it. Always remember, Margaret—other people's likes and dislikes cannot dictate what you do." Her mother looked at her with narrowed eyes. "You cannot allow people to influence your every move because of how you think they will like it."

"Yes, Mama." Margaret looked back at the flowers. She couldn't help but feel her mother's words were hypocritical—wasn't nearly everything she made Margaret do to please others for a better match?

The servant returned, laying the supplies out on the table for them. "Will there be anything else, Lady Catherine?"

"No. You may go."

He bowed before leaving.

"See how they look in the vase before deciding, Margaret."

She nodded, filling the vase with the hydrangea until there were three layers going upward. Margaret then stuck the clusters of roses and amaryllis between each of the fluffy white-green hydrangea. She stepped back to examine them.

"How do you find it?" her mother asked, looking with her.

"I like it."

"Then cut the stems so they fit perfectly."

Margaret did, grinning at her finished product. "What do we do with the scraps?"

"Let the servants clean it up. You don't want to do their job for them, do you?"

"I suppose not..." She looked back when the door opened, her eyes lighting up when she saw it was her father and Charles. She resisted the urge to call out to Mr. Luther, instead saying, "Papa!"

"Good evening, Margaret."

"Do you like the flowers?"

"They are lovely, my darling, made lovelier by the women surrounding them." Her father cupped her cheek, kissing her on her forehead.

"You were born with a silver tongue in your mouth, my lord," her mother praised. "You were made for this life."

"I don't know about all that." He took her in his arms, kissing her cheek. "I would be content to still be a farmer with you at my side."

Margaret watched her mother's brows twitch, but a smile stayed plastered on her face. "Be that as it may, we are no longer simple farmers."

"That we are not." He produced a letter from his vest. "We have another invitation to dine privately with Their Majesties."

Her mother let out a small gasp. "They honor us greatly!"

"The king seems to have a fondness for me," her father said modestly, his chest puffing slightly.

"You know it's far more than a fondness. Perhaps, when news of this spreads, Margaret will finally have suitors calling."

Margaret blushed deeply, looking down at her feet.

"Surely, she's too young for suitors to come calling? She's barely even fourteen!" Charles looked between Margaret and her mother with wide eyes.

"The nobility and the wealthy marry younger than the common people, Mr. Luther," her mother snapped. "I was married to Jerone by age fifteen. Do you think that was too young?"

Charles looked down. "My apologies, my lady. I did not mean to offend."

"You did not, Mr. Luther," her father assured, giving his wife a scolding look. "Will you be joining us for dinner tonight?"

He tipped his head slightly. "It would be a pleasure, my lord."

Margaret sat across from Charles at the dinner table. He'd changed into more appropriate clothes to suit her mother's standards. She was put in a high-necked gown, the stiff fabric resting on her collarbone. "Have you been well, Mr. Luther?"

"Very well, Lady Margaret, thank you." Charles smiled at her. "Have you recovered well from your encounter?"

She furrowed her brow. "My encounter?"

"With the thief, my lady. The last I saw you, you were bruised."

"Oh, yes. I'm very well recovered, Mr. Luther."

"A good thing at that; no one wants a bruised prize on their arm," her mother commented. "That's why I keep telling you to let the servants do their job. You'll be seen as the low born you're acting, and no one will want you."

"Hold your tongue, Catherine, or you will be excused for the evening." Her father glared at her mother, putting his fork down heavily against the table. "It seems you're not feeling well."

Her mother's jaw clenched, and her lips went flat. "Yes, my lord. My apologies."

Margaret gave Charles a shy smile. "Do you have any trips planned to Dorcia, Mr. Luther?"

"I'm sending him to negotiate with a new investor, Aiden Bennett," her father told her. "He's a very rich man with too much time on his hands. If all goes well, we'll solve our wage problem."

"I wish you the greatest success, then," Margaret told Charles with a hopeful look.

Charles raised a glass to her. "I'll bring you back a gift to celebrate my success, Lady Margaret."

Margaret grinned. "I would like that very much."

"My lord, my ladies, the royal carriage is here," Bruggen informed them upon entering the library.

Her father stood, holding a hand out to her mother. "Thank you, Bruggen. Inform the staff they have the evening to themselves."

"Very good, thank you, my lord." Bruggen bowed before he left the room.

Her father offered his arm to her mother. "Shall we go, my lady?"

She graced him with a smile. "We'd best not keep Their Majesties waiting. Come along, Margaret."

Upon exiting their home, the chauffeur, wearing the red and black royal livery of the Platiri house, pulled the carriage door open. Margaret's father helped her mother into the carriage before entering himself, sitting opposite his wife. The chauffeur offered a gloved hand to help Margaret up the steps, which she happily accepted. With her dress being smaller, she sat on the same side as her father to allow her mother comfort. She much preferred it, anyway. The nights were quickly growing warmer as they got deeper into Mamonat.

On this occasion, Margaret was not nearly as nervous as the first. Her nerves hummed low with excitement rather than anxiety. That, and she had not had to sit through a flurry of dress fittings before this outing. After the first invitation from the royal family, her mother had commissioned them both three dresses to wear only when dining with the king, each in the Platiri colors and embroidered with symbolism from each of their houses.

Stars appeared on the horizon as they wound through Jalmar toward the palace. Margaret rested her forehead against the door's window, sighing as she watched the faded stars. She longed for the days when she could see the whole sky unobstructed by the burning torches lining the city's streets. Before Margaret realized it, the carriage arrived at the palace. She jolted forward when the horses stopped.

Her father let out a chuckle, steadying her. "Were you off in your own world, my dear?"

Smiling, she nodded. "I was thinking of Dorcia and how clear the stars are there."

"You'll be back one day, I promise."

She had no chance to reply before the door opened and a hand thrust in to help her from her seat. Margaret gathered her skirts before taking it, clumsily descending the steps and teetering on her feet. The footman's hand tightened on hers to keep her upright.

"It seems we need to return to your lessons of grace, Margaret," her mother snapped from the carriage. "They seem not to have stuck."

Margaret snatched her hand from the footman's, cheeks hot. "Whatever you think best, Mother."

"Let's not keep the king waiting, shall we?" Her father led her mother to the doors of the palace.

Margaret followed behind, her eyes downcast.

Doors opened behind Margaret, and she quickly turned, falling into a curtsey when she saw the king.

"Rise, my friends." The king smiled to the room. "Be at ease. The queen has sent her apologies: she is feeling unwell this evening."

There was a small smirk on her mother's face when she said, "That is a shame. You will have to extend our well-wishes to her. We were delighted to receive your invitation once more, Your Majesty."

The king looked over her face slowly before extending a hand toward the table. "Please, let's not delay."

Margaret waited for a servant to pull out her seat before taking her place in the middle of the table across from Gareth, the Crown Prince of Anatalia. He looked bored, and she couldn't blame him. Margaret didn't particularly want to be there. She was no good at making idle chat, a skill needed for the world they lived in. She envied her mother her ability to talk about nothing as though it were the most interesting thing in the world.

Servants came behind them, pouring wine into their goblets. Margaret snatched hers and drank deeply before her mother could take it away from her. Her mother did not like for Margaret to drink, thinking it muddled her thoughts too much to make strategic decisions to advance their family. Margaret didn't particularly care; her mother did enough strategic talking for the both of them, and the wine helped calm her nerves enough to make tedious conversation.

She caught the eye of the prince over her glass. His mouth twitched as he tried not to laugh. He toasted his glass to her before taking his own long drink. Margaret blushed, putting her drink down, and stared at her plate. If her mother had her way, she and the prince would be courting by now, but Margaret did not like the older boy. He was rude, arrogant, and even at the age of seventeen, a womanizer. She did not think he had what it took to be a good king, and Margaret hoped that he would be spoken for soon so her mother would stop foisting her on the prince to make a marriage alliance. Clearly, neither party was interested in the other.

"I have unfortunately not asked you here for a purely social visit," King Sorren said once their attendants settled back against the wall. "Tomorrow morning, it will be announced that Salatia has declared war on us."

Margaret immediately looked to her father, her eyes wide. The color had drained from his face, and he leaned back against his chair. It was the only time she'd ever seen her father look afraid.

"How—why?" her father asked, mouth still moving but unable to form a full sentence.

"King Peralta has cited a grievance in our trade agreements, that we are causing a detriment to their economy." King Sorren looked around the room. "We have disagreed on this grievance, and he has withdrawn all trade to Anatalia and has blocked the routes from Mekhor and Radovan in retaliation."

Her father nearly stood before falling back against the seat once more. "They can't do that! Salatia is one of my biggest buyers. I'll be ruined if they refuse to buy from us."

"They have, and to add insult to injury, they are warring on us instead of the other way around." Sorren looked annoyed as he took a sip of his wine.

Margaret looked between the king and her father. How could the king not be more outraged? He looked more like a fly had flown at him, not like the lives of his people were at stake to fight a war. Was this the unflappability of a monarch, or did he just not care?

"I'll have to go to my people. I need to be there to support them." Her father looked close to walking out of the room right then and there. "Salatia is only a day's ride from my lands."

"I do not give you my permission to leave the capital," Sorren barked.

"But Your Maj—"

"There will be no negotiation, my lord. You do not have my leave."

"Perhaps some food will settle our nerves?" her mother suggested, resting a hand on her husband's arm.

He scooped up his wife's hand, kissing her knuckles. His hand shook in hers, and he closed his eyes tightly.

"Of course." The king raised his hand to signal the servants to serve their food. "I hope that you can forgive my bluntness for the evening; this was not a subject I could keep until the end of the meal."

"Papa?" Margaret asked quietly.

Finally, her father lifted his head and gave her a shaky smile. "I'm all right, Margaret."

"This must be weighing heavily on you," her mother said to the king, sympathy bleeding into her voice. "We are happy to share your burden for the evening."

King Sorren smiled at her. "You are too kind, my lady. Shall we move on to lighter subjects?"

"Whatever would please Your Majesty." Her mother looked at him directly.

Gareth coughed into his glass, setting it down quickly. He looked between his father and Margaret's mother with raised brows. "Lady Margaret, I heard you had a rough encounter in the city not too long ago?"

"Not recently, no," Margaret told him. "It was before our last dinner. A thief knocked me to the side while trying to escape, but one of your wonderful soldiers helped get me home safely. Will they all be leaving the city once the war starts, Your Majesty?"

"There will be fewer of them, but we will still have enough to keep us safe," the king assured her. "You won't have to fear for your safety, Lady Margaret."

The rest of the evening was filled with idle chatter. Margaret only participated when she was spoken to. Her mind—much like her father, based on his distant look—was on the war and what it would mean for Anatalia, and for Dorcia specifically. Would it even be safe for them to go back to Dorcia to lend support to their people, or would they be forced to stay in the capital with the rest of the peers there for the season?

She was happy when they left the palace. Margaret breathed easier once they were in the carriage, the king's private dining room now tainted with the news that thousands of Anatalians would likely die in the months to come.

Margaret broke the silence. "Papa, what will we do?"

"We will do anything asked of us, my darling." He squeezed her hand. "We will make sure our people are safe, and we will make sure we are safe. I will give His Majesty time to settle and petition him to allow me to go to Dorcia to gather our troops for the war effort."

Margaret's eyes went wide. "But Papa! What if something happens to you? What will happen to us?"

"I should not be exempt from danger simply because His Majesty thought I would make a good peer." Her father's brow furrowed. "Others already do not have the luxuries we do, and this should not be one to add insult to injury."

Sighing, Margaret dropped the subject. There was no talking to her father when he was like this.

10

L iam had been standing at attention for nearly an hour waiting for an announcement from Lord General Crompton. The newest soldiers had started to shift as they waited, impatience clear on their faces. They were not used to the endurance tests the Lord General Crompton would put them through. There were days where Liam missed being part of the Third Brigade, but he could not deny it was an honor to be selected for Crompton's regiment. They were revered for their skill and training. His appointment had come at the end of Amonat, and he suspected his friend Jorren had something to do with it.

Lord General Crompton passed by the rows of soldiers as he walked rigidly through the ranks to reach the front of the room. Lieutenant Alton Bryant followed, arms behind his back. Even though he stood straight, he had a lazy walk as though he had all the time in the world and the soldiers hadn't been waiting for them. Crompton looked them all over with a scowl. It was a known fact he detested the lesser ranks, never having a kind word for any of them.

"Soldiers," Crompton started, "His Majesty has just informed me that we are going to war with Salatia."

Liam felt a wave of shock run through the room as they comprehended the news. The room tensed, looks passing between friends. Liam could not tell whether they were looks of excitement or apprehension. He glanced back to the front of the room to the two officers. Lord General Crompton looked grim, while Lieutenant Bryant looked satisfied. Liam thought it an odd reaction to the news they gave—people would be dying.

"We leave in a week, men," the lord general said before leaving the room.

"Go home, see your families. It should take you no more than three days, and if it will, send letters," Lieutenant Bryant instructed.

Liam frowned. That was not a lot of time for anyone to go home, much less enjoy their visit. It was probably a good thing it would be so short, especially with his mother. She would look at him like she was in mourning the whole time. She still held some resentment for him leaving with only a few minute's notice when he joined the military. It tinged the letters she sent him.

"War, eh?" Jorren asked with a grin on his face. "These are interesting times we're living in."

Liam turned to the friend standing next to him, his own eyes brightening. "Mark my words, we'll be done in a month! We're the best in the world."

Despite his apprehension of actually participating in the bloodshed, Liam was excited to be in the army he knew would win the upcoming war. He would be able to travel—really travel—for the first time in his life, and Liam doubted he would see much of the fighting. Being on the lord general's personal detail would have its advantages. The highest ranking officers rarely saw any combat. Liam went to prepare his bags, both for the trip home and as much as he could for war.

Liam traveled the twenty miles to his home in the Duke of Rivack's provincial lands. The home looked just the same as when he left it, its exterior well-kept by his father.

Liam knocked on the door, disheveled after walking most of the day. He waited as he heard the numerous locks being undone. All his life, there had been multiple locks on every room of the house. His parents had been afraid some unknown threat would harm him. For the first time in months, Liam saw his mother's timid face peek out from behind the door, her blue eyes wide and the wrinkles in her forehead deepening in her confusion.

"Liam!" she gasped, and her drooping cheeks tightened with her smile, making her look younger. "What are you doing here?"

After opening the door, Liam gently grabbed his mother's face in his hands, kissing her forehead. She came almost to his shoulder, making him bend. "Mother, perhaps we can go inside before I tell you why I'm here?"

"Of course, of course!" his mother said excitedly, going into the main room. "Are you hungry?"

"Famished," he breathed out.

His mother went to the cupboard and got him day-old bread, cheese, and dried meats to tide him until she cooked supper for all of them. Sitting across from Liam, her face glowed in her excitement. "Eat, my darling!"

Liam voraciously ate what he was given. "Mother, I have some news you won't like hearing," he said, his mouth still full of food. He should wait for his father, but he didn't know how long it would take for him to return.

"What is it?"

"We are going to war"—he swallowed his food—"with Salatia."

The color drained from his mother's face. "War?"

Liam took his mother's shaking hands in his. "Mother, where's Father? We were sent home to say goodbye, in case we don't make it back."

"Don't make it back?" His mother shrieked. "No! No you can't go to war! You're too young for war—you're only twenty-one!"

Liam's father entered the room. He wiped his hands on the stained cloth over his shoulder, mouth flat. "What are you shrieking about now, Maria?"

Liam stood and extended his hand. "Father, it's good to see you again."

His father pulled him into a hug, a grin on his face. Liam noticed his father's hair was starting to gray at the temple, a new development that made him painfully aware of his father's age. "Liam, shouldn't you be in the capital?"

"He's going to war, Zachariah," his mother cried out in despair. "War!"

"Mother, I doubt that I will see much of the fighting," Liam comforted her. "I'm part of the detail assigned to Lord General Crompton, the king's cousin and most trusted advisor. The closest I'll come to combat is polishing his armor."

"You can't go to war!" she shouted at him. "Bully to the rest of them, you can't put yourself in danger!"

"Quiet, woman!" his father scolded her. "He will support *his* country."

"Zachariah, he can't! He's—"

"Be quiet!"

"Mother, I will be fine," Liam assured her with a gentle smile.

She glanced between her son and her husband, looking despondent. "He can't go," she said stubbornly.

Rolling his eyes, his father wrapped an arm around Liam's shoulder and turned him away from her. "Why don't you go out back and wash? You're covered in dirt, and I'm sure you'd like to be clean before supper is served."

Liam looked at his mother over his shoulder. "All right. How long do I have?"

"A few hours yet," his mother answered thickly. "The stew's only partially done."

His father clapped him on the shoulder. "Good. You can see the changes I've made on the land, then. Meet me out there when you're ready."

Liam found his father between the trellises in the back field, tying new vines back to train them. It was good to be home. He hadn't realized just how much he missed his family until coming back. Even his mother's paranoia did not bother him as much as it once had. He lifted his hand to grab his father's attention, smiling when he got it.

"I've only a few vines left, and then I can show you what I've done."

"Take your time," Liam told him. "I'm enjoying the fresh air."

His father looked amused, a smirk turning up the corner of his mouth. "Don't like the city air, eh?"

"The city has many things to boast of, but air quality is not one of them." Liam reached into the basket for some twine and pushed the cordons against the trellis to bind them. "Nothing will ever be better than the smell of the countryside."

"How long do you have left on your contract?"

"Seven years."

"Seven years!" his father nearly dropped the twine in his hands. "Why so long?"

Liam shrugged. "Ten years was the minimum contract they were offering."

"That's absurd! In my day, they only asked for two years."

"You joined?" Liam furrowed his brow. "Does Mother know?"

"She met me after my contract ended." His father grinned. "I doubt she would have courted me if she'd met me while I was soldiering, but it gave me enough money to support her before I became a vigneron."

"Good thing, probably. I don't have enough time to even look for a woman, much less properly court her."

"Ah, yes. They ran me ragged too." His father tied the last vine back before grabbing the basket from the ground. "Come on."

Liam followed his father back toward the cottage, taking note of a shed that hadn't been there before. "Did you do that?"

"The shed? I did. It was one of my first projects when you left."

Once they reached the structure, Liam found himself testing the rigidity of the shelves and bending forward to see if they were level. He had to laugh at himself; he'd seen his father do the same many, many times. "It looks good."

"I also built a pantry for your mother and replaced the stones for the fireplace with something she liked more."

Liam grinned. "I can imagine she was happy about the pantry. She's been asking for one for ages."

"She has." His father's eyes crinkled, obviously remembering her reaction. "We should get in. I'm sure your mother has supper almost ready."

His stomach full, Liam lazed by the fire. It might be spring, but the nights were still cool enough to need the warming flames. He yawned deeply, leaning back against the sofa. "Thank you for supper, Mother."

She smiled, leaning over to pat his knee. "It was good to have you here."

"I should go to bed; I have to leave early in the morning to return to Jalmar. We leave at the end of the month for Salatia."

Her face fell, the happiness vanishing in a moment. Her eyes welled with tears. "Just stay here."

"Mother, I'd be jailed, and you would be fined on my behalf if I deserted my contract." Liam leaned forward, his tiredness pushed back. "I have to go."

She started to say something else, but his father laid a hand over hers. "He's a man, Maria. He's made his choices, and he must honor them. You cannot keep him here for your own comfort."

"We all have to do our part," Liam said, "and my part is serving our country." His mother only sighed.

"I'll say goodbye before I leave in the morning, all right?"

"All right," she said. "Get some sleep. You'll have a long day tomorrow."

11

"I'll have to go to Dorcia to rally the troops." Margaret's father set down the bulletin that brought the news of war to the public. He ran a hand over his face before pulling it back through his hair. Dark bags hung under his eyes; he wasn't sleeping much. "I'll have to lead them to the front."

Margaret nearly dropped her scone. "Papa, you can't! You don't even know how to fight."

"I am their leader, Margaret."

"You know nothing of war, Papa. Mama, tell him!" Margaret protested, her voice raising as she whined. "Tell him he can't go!"

"He can make his own decisions without you putting your nose where it doesn't belong."

Margaret glared at her. "Don't you even care that he could die because he doesn't know what he's doing? That our people could suffer because he's never led troops into battle?"

"Your father knows what he's doing, Margaret," her mother sharply replied. "He certainly knows more than you do when it comes to these matters."

"Could you not go only as moral support as the troops gather? What would happen to Mother and me if you were no longer with us?" Her mouth went dry at the thought. They would have no one to protect them in the world, and without an heir named, the king could seize their lands and appoint whomever he'd like as the new Count of Dorcia.

"Margaret, that is enough," her father said.

"But—"

"I beg your pardon, young lady," her father snapped, "but I will not be the sole person making decisions. I will have advisors and tacticians who do have experience."

Her mother raised her hand when Margaret started to protest again. "That is enough, Margaret. If I hear any more from you, you will be sent from the table. Now apologize to your father."

"I'm sorry, Papa, but if it's you or them, I'd rather it be them."

"Margaret!" Her father looked shocked she would say such a thing.

"My dear, she's just worried." Her mother touched his arm. "I'm worried too, but we have to face adversity head on, or else it will get the best of us."

"Couldn't you at least appoint a lord general?" Margaret's blue eyes were stained with fear. "You could lead from behind or stay with our people to keep their spirits up?"

"I will only be allowed to do what His Majesty commands, but I will ask, if only to make you feel better." He sighed, leaning back in his seat. Margaret's nagging had worn on him.

"It will—oh, it will, Papa!" Margaret slid from her seat to kiss him on the cheek. "When will you ask the king?"

"I'm calling on the Duchess of Rivack tomorrow at the palace if you would like me to deliver a letter," her mother commented.

"Would you?"

She nodded. "It would be no trouble, I'll be there anyway."

"I'll have it for you by the evening, then."

Margaret grinned. "Thank you, Mama."

"So she said to him, 'If you cannot satisfy me, perhaps you can find me someone who can!'" Duchess Cecily chortled, resting her hand holding a handkerchief on her chest as she leaned forward.

Catherine laughed along with the rest of the ladies in the room. When the laughter died down, she stood. "If I may, Duchess, I have some business to attend before returning home?"

"Yes, yes." Duchess Cecily waved her hand. "You may go."

"Thank you, Your Grace." Catherine curtsied deeply before she left.

She wandered the corridors until she came to the king's private library. He spent most of his time there because it was a central location to all his advisors. Catherine slipped in through the cracked door, her wide skirts brushing against the dark wood.

The king sat with his back to her. He was at a table covered in maps, his advisors pointed to locations and murmured to each other, taking no notice of her intrusion.

Catherine cleared her throat delicately. "Your Majesty?"

King Sorren turned. "Lady Catherine?" He stood, straightening his clothes. "What can I do for you?"

Pulling a sealed letter from a hidden pocket in her skirts, Catherine offered it to him. "Lord Dorcia asked me to deliver this to you since I would be in the palace today."

He raised his brows. "What is it?"

"It has to do with the war, Your Majesty."

King Sorren waved his hand at the men behind him. "Leave us, please."

Catherine waited until the men had left before speaking again. "He is requesting you allow him to leave to lead his people in the war."

"I've already told him no, my lady."

"He knows." Catherine sighed. "Lady Margaret has suggested he go only as moral support to Dorcia and not leave for the war. I would implore you allow him to. Neither of us will hear the end of it if he is not allowed to leave."

Snorting, King Sorren finally took the letter from her hand and opened it, quickly skimming the contents. "I do not want to risk losing one of my closest friends to this pointless war."

"Please, Your Majesty. He will be miserable if he doesn't go, and he might even go without your permission."

The king sighed. "Jerone is headstrong."

"I think my daughter's solution will appease him and make him feel like he's doing something." Catherine stepped closer to him, resting a hand on his arm. "If you let him go, you will keep him closer to you by the end of it."

He still looked hesitant, his eyes starting to squint.

"I will do anything to make him happy, Your Majesty, even if it means him being gone for the entirety of the war."

Something lit behind his eyes. His voice was husky when he asked, "Anything?"

Catherine boldly kept her eyes on his while color came to her checks. "Anything," she repeated.

The king curled an arm around her waist and pulled her against him, bringing his face close to hers. "Kiss me," he commanded in a low voice.

Catherine's lips tingled when she pressed hers against his. A hand came behind her neck to lock her in place, and she let out a low moan. She reluctantly pulled away from him. "Does that please you, Your Majesty?"

"Greatly," he rasped, "but I am not sure it's enough for me to grant your husband leave."

"Perhaps I should try again?" Catherine bit her lip and did not waver in her gaze.

King Sorren grinned. "Perhaps you should."

Catherine stood on her toes to propel herself forward and met his mouth hungrily.

Catherine leaned against the king, sweat sliding down her neck. She sighed, closing her eyes, and moved closer to him. He kissed her forehead, stroking her hair back from her face. Excited chills ran through her stomach, and she looked at him with an adoring gaze.

"I'll give your husband my permission to go to Dorcia but nothing more. He must appoint a lord general to go to war in his place, or my offer will be rescinded."

"Thank you, Your Majesty." She smiled brightly at him. "Jerone will be so pleased."

"You and your daughter will stay here in the city for your own safety," King Sorren said. "Many of the other peers will be staying here as well; it's doubtful the Salatians will ever make it this far west, and I have requested additional troops from Frasisca to protect the capital."

Catherine's eyes went wide, and her brows raised. "Will they come?"

"Our lack of trade with the rest of Aratia will affect them as well. The less we can trade, the less they can get from us," he said. "They can't risk our economy failing and Salatia conquering us. They did not fare well the last time Salatia was too powerful."

"As Your Majesty wishes." Catherine pulled away from him, covering her chest with her chemise. "With your permission?"

"Yes, please." King Sorren stood, adjusting his own clothes. "I would like to see you again."

"Your Majesty?" Catherine looked at him with wide eyes.

"I'm giving up a great deal by letting Jerone leave. If he dies, who will inherit the lands? He has no heir, and someone who could be against me could marry Lady Margaret and use the profits of your empire for something that does not benefit my purposes. Did you think a single transaction will be enough to let him leave?"

"But you're a king! Surely, anyone who married Margaret would do as he's bid by his monarch."

"A king's subjects do not do as they're bid, my lady. As evidenced by your own husband fighting against my orders to stay in the capital."

Catherine remained silent as she laced her bodice slowly. She had thought many times about being with the king—he had a reputation among the women at court of being a very persuasive and skilled lover—but she had imagined it would be only once and she would forget about her indiscretion. She had enjoyed herself, quite a lot, actually, but the enjoyment was marred with his terms of their union.

"When you're ready, go to your husband. Tell him the news he wishes to hear, but remember that I would like to see you again, and soon."

"Yes, Your Majesty." Catherine finished dressing quickly and barely curtsied before she left.

Catherine barely remembered the walk from the library to the stables, where her groom waited to take her back home. "Ready the horses," she commanded, avoiding his gaze. She climbed into the carriage when it pulled up before her and rode silently home. She was not looking forward to seeing her husband. Surely, he would know. He would see it on her face that she had been unfaithful.

"Jerone?" Catherine called once she arrived home. Her voice sounded small to her, like it had lost its power to command.

He poked his head out from the library. "What is it, my dear?"

Tears welled in her eyes when she saw him. She put her hand to her mouth, unable to speak.

Jerone rushed to her side, pulling her into his arms. "Catherine, what's wrong?"

She shook her head, her throat tight. Catherine let out a sob and leaned against his chest.

"Tell me what I can do to help, my love." He held her tightly, rocking side to side ever so slightly to soothe her. "What's happened?"

"The king, he"—she broke into a sob before she continued—"he has given you leave to go to Dorcia to appoint a lord general and stay there for the duration of the war. Margaret and I are to remain here."

"My darling, you don't have to worry about me. I'll be fine, especially since I'll be staying in Anatalia." He smiled and wiped the tears from her cheeks. "And you and Margaret will be well taken care of here. I know His Majesty will look after the both of you."

That's what she was afraid of.

12

iam packed his bag on his barrack's wrack. He sighed heavily, unable to get his mother's weeping face out of his mind. He jumped when another pack bounced on his bed.

"You have to be more alert than that." Jorren flashed him a boyish grin. "Are you ready to go to war?"

"Almost." Liam stuffed his pack with another shirt.

Jorren's grin deepened to show his dimples. "I got myself switched to serve with you under the Lord General Crompton's command."

"How did you manage that?" Liam asked, surprised. It was rare to have a reassignment, and Liam suspected more so Jorren had something to do with his own reassignment.

"I called in several favors." Jorren sat on Liam's bed, examining the open pack. "Jackson is taking my place."

Once Liam finished packing, the two reported to their commander. They would start their march toward Salatia in only a few hours. "Were you able to see your family?" Liam asked Jorren as they waited.

"A few weeks ago, before the war was announced," Jorren told him.

Liam nodded and fell silent. He was glad he had been able to see his parents before they left, but he wondered if it was worth it, knowing he'd picture his mother's crying face before every march and battle.

The day's march was long and tiring. Liam wiped his glistening brow with the back of his hand as he walked. The scouts said they would reach their first destination in just a few hours. They only made it ten miles that day, and at this rate, it would take them two months to reach Salatia. It'd only been a week, but with their size, the army had to frequently resupply and could not travel more than two leagues a day with the soldiers carrying their packs and warring supplies.

"Partner up, men! This camp needs to be set up within the hour!" Lord General Crompton bellowed to the crowd. "We can't have an incident like last night where we almost didn't have shelter."

"Yes, sir!" Liam answered with the rest of the men. He jogged over to his commander, pack bouncing behind him. "Do you need any help setting up your tent, sir?"

"Do I need help?" Crompton looked amused. "I've been setting my own tents since before you were born, and I don't need you slowing me down. I saw the work you did yesterday."

"Er…yes, sir. Sorry, sir."

Crompton shook his head, laughing. "Do I need help?" he muttered as he walked away, laughing again.

His lips pursed, Liam went to find Jorren. "Let's get this over with. I'm ready to get off my feet."

"I'll grab a tent off the wagon." Jorren dropped his pack next to Liam before he joined the line of men for their supplies.

Liam gratefully threw his pack down and helped set up their tent when Jorren returned. He was thankful it was only two men to a tent and he could share it with someone he liked. Last night had proved if you didn't find the right person to share your tent with, there would be fighting—and there had been lots of fighting between the men. Liam climbed onto his bedroll and took his boots off, rubbing his blistered feet.

"Be kind, and put those boots back on!" Jorren boisterously jested.

Liam rolled his eyes and continued rubbing his sore appendages. All the soldiers had been given new boots and lacked the proper time to break them in before the march started. "Be quiet, and sit down."

Jorren complied, stretching out on his roll.

"Did you see Elaine at all before we left?" Liam inquired, realizing he'd never asked.

Jorren's dimpled grin said it all. "She likes the idea of a soldier going off to war."

Liam chuckled at him. "You've finally gotten what you wanted, then. Do you think she will be there when you return?"

"I guess we'll have to wait until we return, won't we?" Jorren asked.

"I suppose we will."

Liam groaned when someone shook him awake. He cracked his eyes open to glare at Jorren. "Leave me alone; it isn't even light out yet."

"That sound, my friend, is the rain." He shook Liam again. "We have to help roll up the tents before they get too heavy to carry."

"Shouldn't we just stay here until it stops raining?" Liam ran a hand over his face and grimaced at how sticky his skin was with the humidity.

"Lord General Crompton wants to travel as far as we can today. 'Every step counts,' when it comes to getting to Salatia."

Liam sighed, pulling on his boots before he got off his bedroll and packed it up. "How much of the camp is done?"

"Maybe a quarter of it. The other men are having a hard time dragging themselves out of bed with this weather." Jorren began pulling at the bindings keeping the burlap in place.

Liam helped him. "Why did no one have these waxed? It's spring for Heaven's sake. It rains!"

"Why don't you ask the lord general about that?" Jorren grinned. "I'm sure he'd be happy to answer all of your resentful questions."

"I'm sure he would be." Liam grimaced. He couldn't seem to get on the lord general's good side, despite his best efforts.

Once the canvas was off its frame, Liam and Jorren held it between them to wring it out. Water poured from the fabric, creating a puddle. They moved as quickly as they could to avoid the tent being soaked through again before they could put it in its bag. Liam grimaced. It would mildew by the time they had to take it out again. Whoever had neglected waxing the tents would make them all suffer. The bag, at least, had been waxed to keep the water out. Maybe, after this, the lord general would order them to take a day to properly prepare their tents for this type of weather. It would do none of them any good if half the army grew sick from sleeping wet.

The frame was torn down next and added to the same bag as the canvas.

"I'll take it to the wagon," Liam offered, holding the muddy bag away from himself.

"You sure?"

He nodded, scowling when the ground squelched as he walked. They would be lucky if they only had three broken ankles on their march today. Liam shook his head when he saw another soldier slip in the mud on his way to the supply wagon. "This is pure idiocy," he muttered to himself.

"What was that Private?"

Liam jumped, sliding in the mud. He went down hard, landing on his back. He groaned, trying to sit up.

Hands came under his arms and lifted him from the ground with ease. It was the lord general, and his mouth formed a hard line while he glared at Liam.

"Sir?"

"Do you have something to say to me, Private?"

"No, sir." Liam stood straight, keeping his hands tightly to his sides.

The lord general stepped closer to him. He was a shorter man than Liam, but it made no difference. He had the presence of a giant when he was angry. "Are you sure you don't want to tell me how idiotic this move is?"

Liam hesitated.

"Well?"

"Sir, I'm worried for the men. This mud will only make it harder to move, and we could lose several men to broken bones."

"Do you think all of Anatalia is made of mud, Private?"

"Well, no, sir, but—"

"Do you think I would risk good fighting men because I want to get to Salatia sooner?"

"No, sir, but—"

"I don't need to explain my orders to you, Private, but just a league past that grove over there are several grassy fields that can be easily walked on and won't sink when we move the camp there," Crompton said. "Don't question me again."

"Yes, sir!" Liam said as Crompton walked away. He slouched and let out a sigh when the lord general was out of sight. "Good going, Liam. He really likes you now." He tossed the tent into the wagon and returned to Jorren and his pack.

"What happened to you?" Jorren asked, laughing. "You're covered in mud!"

"The lord general surprised me when I was telling myself how stupid this was."

Jorren laughed again, bending at his middle. "Oh, I'm sure he loved that."

"He did—so much so, I got a talking to." Liam wiped some mud from his neck before digging his shaving mirror from his pack.

"You're going to have to change into your spare," Jorren said as Liam examined himself. "You look godawful, and if the lord general sees you like that again, you'll get another talking to."

"Why is it I just can't seem to get on his good side?"

"You're trying too hard. You want to be on his good side instead of just doing your job and excelling with your actions."

Liam sighed. "You're probably right."

"I'll see you in formation, yeah?"

Liam nodded, unbuttoning his uniform jacket. "Be careful of what you say."

"Never." Jorren laughed, snatching up his pack and slinging it over his shoulder before he walked away.

Liam sat on a stump to rest his feet while their group gathered to hear their orders.

"Do you think you're more special than the rest of us, Private Fulton?"

He jumped to his feet and turned around. Lieutenant Bryant stood in front of him, his brow furrowed. He was another leader whom Liam could not seem to get along with. Likely because Lieutenant Bryant and Lord General Crompton were thick as thieves. Liam had managed to avoid Bryant their first month of marching by some miracle. He had a worse time with him than he did Crompton.

"No, sir, I don't."

"You don't get a break just because you happened to find a stump. Everyone else is standing for their lord general," Lieutenant Bryant scolded. "Have some respect."

"Yes, sir."

Lieutenant Bryant gave him one last scathing look before going to the front of the crowd with Lord General Crompton.

"We'll be staying a few days next to Camaveia to recruit some new soldiers," Lord General Crompton told them. "You do not have permission to enter the town for any other purpose. You will have no relations with anyone in the city; you will not sleep in the city because it's more comfortable; you will only recruit men who want to join. No one will be forced into service like they do in Salatia."

There were a few groans from the men, but no one protested outright. They knew not to disobey Crompton. He was not afraid to exact punishment swiftly and thoroughly.

"We'll camp for the evening and get some rest before going into the city. I want all your uniforms cleaned and professional looking, and you will be inspected before you can leave. If you fail your inspection more than once, you will not be allowed to leave camp. Understood?"

"Yes, sir!" the group called.

"Back in formation!

The men fell in line as they marched away to make their campsite closer to the city. They were still too far away to see the city, and if they wanted to have enough rest to explore Camaveia, they would need to make it there in record time.

Liam brushed his hard leather boots with his boar-bristle brush to get the caked mud off them. He scrubbed until they began to shine, squinting at them in the light.

"Don't you think you're going a little overboard?"

"Hm?" Liam looked up, surprised anyone was in the tent with him. "I thought you left."

"I did. I've already been approved to go into the city. You've been scrubbing those boots for half an hour, Liam."

"I have?" He examined the boots again. "I don't want to be rejected. I'm already not liked. I don't want to fail my inspection."

"You won't. The lord general and Lieutenant Bryant are already in the city." Jorren took the boot from Liam's hand to inspect it himself. "This is cleaner than mine, and even I have approval. Get dressed, and go see Sergeant Flammel so we can go. He'll pass you for sure. I'm sick of seeing just the men here."

Liam laughed. "Have you already forgotten about Elaine?"

"Never," Jorren declared. "She's my heart and joy, but I want to see new people. And if they happen to be a pretty woman, all the better for my spirits. Now get up and go!"

"All right, all right!" Liam took his boot back and slipped it on. "Don't get yourself all in a huff. I'm going."

Liam grinned as they neared the city. Jorren was right, it was good to see new people. It'd been a month since he'd seen anyone besides his fellow soldiers, and it lifted his spirits to see the bright colors of everyday clothes.

A woman in a lavender day dress and yellow shawl passed by, smiling at them both in turn. "Good day."

Jorren took off his hat and bowed with a flourish. "Good day to you, miss."

She giggled and continued on, her cheeks rosier than they had been moments before.

Jorren grinned at Liam, returning his hat to its place. "It's good to be here."

"Do you smell that?" Liam's stomach growled as he sniffed the air. "It smells like bacon."

Jorren lightly tapped Liam's chest with the back of his hand. "Let's go get some breakfast. See if we can get any extras for defending our country."

Liam grinned at him, following his nose to an eatery named The Blue Vine. "Maybe we can actually find a recruit there. At least, that's what we'll tell people."

The Blue Vine had few patrons within, and only a few men sat at the bar, shoveling food in their mouths.

"Let's sit at the bar." Liam nodded toward the men sitting there. "I think we might have some luck recruiting after all."

The pair split apart and sat on either side of two of the men already at the bar.

The serving girl put ceramic cups of water in front of them within moments of being seated. "We've got eggs 'n' bacon, an' porridge."

"Bacon and eggs," they said together and laughed.

"It's been a while since we've had bacon," Liam commented, winking at the serving girl. "Could we have some extra?"

She smiled. "I'll see what I can do."

Jorren grinned at her. "Bless you."

The man between Liam and Jorren snorted, shoveling another fork full of food into his mouth.

"Something wrong, friend?" Jorren asked as the serving girl walked away.

"You'll be lucky if she even comes back," he said. "She doesn't like anyone in this town."

Liam shrugged. "We aren't from this town."

"That's obvious, isn't it?" The man looked between the two soldiers. "Showing up here in uniform. Should I be guardin' my cup in case you try to conscript me?"

"Ah, no." Jorren took a long drink from his cup. "I'm afraid the only people who drink at His Majesty's expense are the people who volunteer to."

"Can't say I'll be doin' that." The man sloppily drank from his cup, water dripping down his chin. He let out a gruff, satisfied sigh. "I like my freedom, thank you," he said with a smirk.

The serving girl came from the kitchen with three plates, two heaping with eggs and one solely dedicated to steaming bacon. "No extra charge," she said when she set them down. "Got to keep our soldiers strong."

The smirk fell from the man's face, and he let out a grunt of protest. "You told me you didn't have any extra to give when I asked!"

"Shut up, Ed!" the serving girl snapped. "These soldiers are hungry."

"But—"

"I said shut it!" she yelled before she turned to Jorren and smiled sweetly. "Let me know if I can get you anything else."

"I will."

The serving girl gave one last glare to Ed before she walked away.

Liam pushed the plate of bacon closer to Ed. "You're more than welcome to share. It's more than we can eat comfortably."

"You don't have to tell me twice." Ed snatched several pieces of bacon from the plate and wasted no time shoving one of them in his mouth.

"You know," Jorren said between bites, "we are recruiting if you know anyone who wants to join. I've no doubt we'll be treated just like this wherever we stop at towns. And I imagine even better once we win the war. We'll have women throwing themselves at us." Jorren waggled his eyebrows before shoving a piece of bacon in his mouth.

"What's the serving girl's name?" Liam asked Ed.

"Mackenzie."

"What's something you can't get here? Anything they absolutely refuse to serve here?" Liam watched in some disappointment as the other men left. At least there was still Ed they could try to conscript.

"The cook hates okra and won't go near the stuff."

"Mackenzie!" Liam called when he caught sight of her.

She rushed over to him, her cheeks pink. "What can I do for you?"

"Mackenzie." He smiled at her. "I'm feeling a bit homesick smelling all this wonderful food. I wonder if I might get a bowl of roasted okra? My ma used to make it for me any time I was feeling down."

She hesitated. "Well…"

Liam looked at her with sad eyes. "It's been so long since I've seen her, and I don't know if I will again."

"I'll see what I can do." Mackenzie disappeared into the kitchen.

"You're not going to get it." Ed laughed, shaking his head. "They don't even have it in the place."

"Just do it!" They heard Mackenzie screech from the back. She reappeared shortly afterward and smiled at Liam, resting a hand on his. "We'll make sure you feel like you're home here."

"Thank you, Mackenzie." He picked her hand up and kissed her knuckles. "I appreciate you taking such good care of us while we're away from our families."

She blushed and pulled her hand from his. "We've all got our parts to do." She slipped away to tend to other customers.

"I still don't think you're going to get it." Ed crossed his arms over his chest.

"Why don't you wait around and find out?" Jorren asked.

Ed laughed. "You think I'd leave now?"

Liam snorted, clapping him on the shoulder. "Have some more bacon, Ed."

Thirty minutes later, Mackenzie presented Liam with a steaming bowl of roasted okra. "I hope it's just as good as your ma's."

Ed's jaw dropped as he stared at the forbidden food. "You actually got it."

"Women love a soldier," Jorren reminded him, grabbing a piece of okra and popping it in his mouth.

"Where do I sign up?"

 # 13

iam was hastily woken in the morning by Jorren, half-dressed, uniform unbuttoned in the front. Jorren had a wild look in his eyes that scared Liam more than being woken unexpectedly.

"Wake up and get dressed!" Jorren yelled at him.

"What's going on?" Liam sleepily demanded.

"We're being attacked!"

Liam shot off his bedroll and gathered his supplies, following Jorren out of the tent city. He could see the fighting had started not long before he was jolted awake. He could see hardly any dead piled at the side. Lines broken, Salatians and Anatalians intermixed into a hoard of clanging metal. Liam steeled himself and unsheathed his blade, charging into the thick of it, where the sounds of swords and screams surrounded him. He and Jorren were not in the battle long before their swords connected with the enemy.

Liam's heart thudded rapidly in his chest, feeling as though it would burst any second. He could hear the screams of his fellow soldiers intermingling with the enemy's as casualties of both sides fell. Liam screamed himself, the involuntary action giving him a boost of courage as he ran forward to plunge his sword into the last of the adversaries in his line of sight.

Bile rose in Liam's throat as his enemy fell off his sword, turning to reveal a man younger than he. The boy had had so much to live for, but Liam had stolen that from him. He could hold his stomach no longer, the acidity of his regurgitant burning his throat and nose.

Liam struggled to breath, hands on his knees. They had been promised they would see no battles firsthand, clearly a lie told to Lord General Crompton's detail to make them less apprehensive about the war.

"Liam!" Jorren yelled out to him, running to Liam's side. Jorren took a defensive stance, ready to fight off any other attackers that came near the two.

Liam gasped for breath as his stomach continued to lurch, unable to straighten.

"Hurry up and finish," Jorren yelled at him as more attackers came at him.

Gasping for breath, Liam was finally able to stand as a wave of dizziness washed over him. He faltered slightly but was able to stay upright. There were few combatants left, most of them retreating behind their camp lines. The battle was over, most of the fallen men wearing Salatian uniforms. Come morning, Liam was sure there would be a surrender from the enemy's commander, and the Anatalian soldiers would be on their way to Chenalieu in Salatia to take the city in the name of King Sorren of Anatalia.

Oliphant smirked at the pair returning. "Have you quite recovered?"

Liam glared at the pompous lord, whose clothes showed no signs of fighting. No doubt, he had stayed in the back to ensure he did not dirty his hands. Liam stayed quiet, unwilling to quarrel after a long battle. He hadn't the energy for it.

"Would you like me to gather your petticoats?" Oliphant taunted, the smirk deepening on his cretinous face. "Or perhaps find you a lady's maid to put you to bed?"

Jorren grabbed Liam by the shoulder as he turned to confront Oliphant, pulling him toward their tent. "He isn't worthy of a reply."

"You should have let the lady die, Jorren!" the lord yelled after them, his laugh dancing behind them as they retreated.

The men set up camp on the edges of Chenalieu to rest for the night before they waged war on the morrow. Liam helped set up the lord general's war tent with Jorren, weary from a long day of travel.

"Get over here!" The lord general bellowed at the two of them. Crompton wiped his forehead, glistening with sweat from the heat of the afternoon. He had a closely cropped beard that made his cheek bones look severe on his already thin face.

Jorren gave Liam a look and went to their lord general. "Yes, Your Grace?"

"This is the wrong spot," he seethed. "Find somewhere else to set up my war tent."

"Yes, Your Grace," Liam quickly said before Jorren could respond. Jorren had a penchant for letting his mouth run and getting himself in trouble.

Jorren glared at the Duke of Rivack's back. "Arrogant ba—"

"Jorren!" Liam cut him off. Despite Liam disliking their lord general's overwhelming arrogance, he would not hear his fellow soldiers disrespect their superior.

Jorren rolled his eyes at Liam but went to take down the tent nonetheless. He helped Liam bring the tent one hundred feet farther back. The soldiers grunted with their effort to drive the stakes into the ground.

As they finished, Liam wiped his brow with the back of his hand as he stood. "Will there be anything else, Your Grace?"

Crompton curled his lip, looking at the disheveled soldier. "No. Now get out of my sight."

"Yes, Your Grace," Liam said through clenched teeth. He clapped Jorren on the back as he led him away from the lord general's tent. "Let's get some of the slop they call food."

Jorren chuckled and followed Liam to the line for their dinner. They were the last soldiers in line, and it was starting to get dark. Jorren curled his lip at the taste of the swill the military thought appropriate to serve the soldiers. Liam felt the same, but he had to eat. There was little point in starving to death in a war. He could hear others muttering their disgust as they ate their rations.

Liam laughed openly at Jorren as he lifted and dropped the lumpy white substance that landed with a hard plop, causing the rest in his bowl to jiggle. "Do you not like the taste of our gourmet food?"

Jorren dumped the rest of his slop out onto the ground. "Sleep well, Liam, we battle in the morning."

Liam had his back pressed against Jorren's, Salatian soldiers coming toward each of them. He felt Jorren push off first, bellowing as he charged the enemy soldier. Liam charged his own combatant, sword raised. His leather boots splashed through the puddles of blood as he ran, swords clashing against each other. Liam's muscles strained as his enemy tried to overpower him, their weapons grinding heavily as they warred.

The soldiers fought as the sun sank in the distance, many tripping on body parts severed in battle. Liam himself stumbled several times as he made his way toward the oncoming Salatians, letting out a strangled yell when he stumbled on the head of one of his fellow soldiers. He could feel his muscles starting to strain the longer he fought. He came across a Salatian holding a bloodied scythe, one the enemy soldier had more than likely used for harvest. The beast of a man greedily turned toward Liam, bloodlust in his eyes, raising his scythe with a battle cry.

Liam tried to pull back, the bloodied blade catching him in the chest. Pain erupted as blood soaked his shirt. Not without effort, Liam raised his sword to meet the second swing of the scythe, wincing as the weapons met viciously. They battled against each other for a time, neither gaining ground. Liam slowed as his wound throbbed, panic rising when the larger man pushed Liam farther back. He could take little more fighting with his wound draining the strength from his arms.

The Salatian raised his scythe high to finish off Liam. He stiffened as Liam's blade stabbed him.

Liam let out a relieved breath, removing his sword. He looked about the darkened battlefield, hearing both sides call for a retreat. There had been countless losses on both sides; no doubt, the Salatians and Anatalians both needed to regroup before they could continue their battle. The lord generals would call for a truce to last the night so the men could collect their dead and send their spirits to rest as they had the previous nights.

"Jorren?" Liam called out, worry gripping his stomach. He could not find his companion, having lost sight of him during the battle.

"Jorren! Where are you?" He yelled louder, turning around in circles as he searched for his friend.

"Watch where you're going," Oliphant growled when Liam accidentally ran into him. "Now I have to have my servant clean my uniform again."

"Not like it got dirty in the first place." Liam winced in pain as his chest burned with the new contact.

"What did you say to me?" Oliphant shoved him farther away, landing a blow that caused Liam to grunt in pain.

"Not like it got dirty anyway," Liam reiterated with his hand on his sword.

Oliphant rammed his first into the bloody spot on Liam's shirt, causing him to yelp. His chest burned and throbbed from the assault. Liam glared at the noble, clenching his fists at his side.

"Don't speak to me in that tone, peasant." Oliphant turned to walk away.

Liam grabbed Oliphant by the scruff of his neck, throwing him to the ground. He looked over the now-dirtied uniform callously. "You should have paid more attention to your training, Oliphant."

Rubbing his chest, Liam returned to the campsite they had made the previous day. Many tents would be left empty that night. The soldiers who had seen the brunt of the fighting were either dead or severely injured. Liam's own large gash on his chest needed to be sewn back together in order to heal. He would look for Jorren in the healer's tent before he would allow himself to panic.

The healer's tent was over capacity when Liam arrived, many of the men sharing a bed by lying head to foot. His eyes sought out the familiar face of Jorren. Liam had not yet seen him when he was pulled onto a table to have his wound doused with alcohol to sanitize it. His cry of agony joined the chorus of the other men being treated. A healer gave Liam a strip of leather already marred with teeth marks from others to bite on for the pain. He bit down hard as a large hooked needle plunged into his chest to close his wound. The healer finished by rubbing a foul-smelling paste on Liam's wound.

Liam tried to sit and put on his bloodied shirt, but the healer pushed him back down. "You need to stay here and rest," the healer said.

Liam looked at him through squinted eyes. "I'm taking up a bed that could be used by someone in need."

"You need the bed," the healer protested. "You need to wait to see if you have an adverse reaction to the poultice!"

Liam rolled his eyes and waited until the healer was distracted with a new patient before he rose and left the tent. He was able to walk and did not want to take a bed for someone who could not. His eyes searched the crowd for Jorren as he traveled toward their shared tent. Panic gripped him as he thought about the possibility he might not see Jorren again. He could not find his friend anywhere. Liam did not want to admit it was even a possibility his friend could have been slain.

Lord General Crompton was exiting his tent when Liam passed by on the way to his own lodging.

"Your Grace," he called out respectfully.

Lord General Crompton looked disgusted at the sight of Liam's bloodied shirt, his high forehead looking even higher with his brows raised. "Clean yourself up before you speak to me."

"Yes, Your Grace." Liam winced as he bowed, going back to his tent.

He was still anxious to find Jorren. He was really the only friend Liam had. Liam lay in his tent and tried to get comfortable with his wound. He closed his eyes, remembering the day vividly.

The next day of fighting was bloodier than the previous. Liam felt physically sick at the sight. He had taken more lives than he could count. He was covered in blood that was not his own, and the copper tang of it made him want to relieve his stomach of anything currently residing within. Jorren was still nowhere to be found, and Liam had no other choice but to believe his friend was dead, as all the other missing men from their army were presumed to be. Despite their losses, the Anatalian troops still thoroughly defeated the Salatian soldiers as they attacked Chenalieu.

Another halt was called to collect the dead from the battlefield for another massive funeral pyre. Liam searched each face brought in for his missing friend. None of them had Jorren's features. None of them had any features, really; their faces were devoid of any feelings they might have had while they were alive. Liam pushed the heels of his hands into his eyes to fight back his tears.

There were no attacks during the funerals, and the pyres could be seen clearly between the two camps. Liam could not watch for long, his heart sinking at the useless loss of life happening because of this war. He imagined there would be many other occasions that he would see such a sight, but tonight, he could not remain to see the souls depart.

Liam returned to his tent, wanting nothing more than to return to the Duke of Rivack's lands and escape to his parents' home, where there was no talk of war or death, no being forced to murder men performing the same duty to their country he was. Liam lay in his tent with his blanket over his eyes, wishing for sleep to come.

No sleep came, however.

Liam shifted uncomfortably as he tried to relieve the burning in his chest; the wound had reopened in the day's battle. There must be something that he could do to induce sleep. As Liam left his tent to have a look around the camp, he saw Lord General Crompton leaving his own tent without his guard. The wind picked up, and it smelled like rain was about to douse the funeral pyres.

Liam watched the lord general wave away the guards standing at attention around the perimeter of the camp, walking into the woods unattended. The lord general went past the line of camp toward the Salatian side. Liam's brow furrowed in confusion as he followed Crompton. Liam heard another man call out a familiar greeting to the Lord General Crompton. Liam hid behind a large trunk to sneak glances at the two men meeting.

"Lord General Baur," Crompton replied curtly, nodding.

Liam reeled back in shock when he saw that Lord General Crompton was meeting with their enemy's commander. He strained to hear the lord generals speaking, catching enough to gather what was happening. Lord General Crompton was revealing to the enemy exactly where their forces would be over the coming weeks. It was information that would turn the tide of the war against the Anatalians, possibly even cause them to lose. That was not a possibility Liam wanted to entertain.

"Be there in the reserves with your best men," Crompton told the Lord General Baur, a smaller man than he. "I'll make sure my men are worn out before your soldiers take the rest of them."

"Why are you helping us?" Lord General Baur asked curiously, his short hair tossed about by the strengthening wind. "What is it that you hope to gain?"

"Sorren is a disgusting lout who deserves neither to rule a country nor to live much longer. He's more interested in his secret lovers than being a true king.

Anatalia deserves better," Crompton growled. "As for gain, that is none of your concern."

After a moment of silence—clearly shaken by Crompton's words, if Liam had judged correctly—Lord General Baur tossed Crompton the money he was promised. "My king thanks you for your service."

"Tell him there are plans in place for Anatalian men to head for the capital from three different directions."

Liam let out a strangled noise, unable to contain it.

"Who's there?" Lord General Baur demanded harshly, looking at Crompton accusingly. "Is this your doing?"

"No," he clipped. Crompton's back was stiff as he scanned the tree line. "No one is there, my lord. I can assure you, I've been very careful."

Liam sank down as far as he could behind the tree, looking frantically for a route of escape. His heart thudded against his chest as his panic grew. He pressed his body into the wood, almost wishing he could sink into it. There was no route that would not show him plainly to the lord generals. He tried to cover himself with branches as quietly as possible to keep anyone from spying him easily when they left.

Liam waited until he heard the two lord generals retreat before he relaxed. It felt like he was sitting there for hours, but it had likely only been minutes. He let out a breath and pulled the branches away from himself.

"What are you doing spying, dog?" a voice demanded, making Liam jump.

Liam leaped to his feet, unable to hide the guilt from his face. It was Lieutenant Alton Bryant. Liam didn't know what to make of it—was it a plot to trick the enemy, or was it really what it seemed? "I was worried Lord General Crompton would be attacked being out by himself, so I followed...but you would have no reason to worry, though, would you? You're working for the enemy!" Liam thought perhaps he could flush out their plot with an accusation.

The lieutenant rolled his eyes. "Stop acting like a child."

Liam's face scrunched in apprehension. He expected something from the lieutenant, excuses or rebuffing, but none came. He tried again, "You're both traitors to our king."

"You are wrong." Lieutenant Bryant smirked. He took his dagger out of its sheath, pointing it at Liam. "You are the traitor. You came here to meet with Lord General Baur because you hate our beloved king and you want to see another on the throne."

Realization dawned on Liam that he had gotten himself into a situation he couldn't get out of. "But you—"

Lieutenant Bryant cut Liam off with a sharp rap to the temple with the butt of his dagger.

14

Margaret listened to Annalise prattle on about a potential suitor for one of her cousins, telling them all about how he was rumored to have a disfigured spine but that it didn't matter because of how rich he was. Margaret tried not to roll her eyes—somehow rich only mattered if it was old and not new. It was these times that Margaret wished she could shake these girls. Rich was rich, and the Doremises were richer than all of them combined. Who cared about ancient bloodlines?

They circled the great hall, chatting about this and that. Margaret was hardly listening at that point. The court had grown far more boring now that it consisted mostly of women and old men. With the war, the abundance of suitable beaus to flirt with had gone with it.

"Margaret?"

Margaret inhaled deeply, pulled from her thoughts. She looked around to see Clairissa staring at her expectantly. "I'm sorry, what was the question?"

"Have you heard word from your father?" Clairissa asked.

Margaret shook her head. "No. Mama says that's to be expected, though. He'll be busy in Dorcia, rallying the troops."

"That's too bad." Annalise frowned. "We were hoping for some news."

Trying to keep the bitter tone from her voice, Margaret said, "I'm sorry I couldn't be more help." Margaret would much rather be in their positions than hers. None of their fathers had demanded to go off to war, instead sending representatives in their place.

Their dissatisfaction didn't last long as they started in on the next piece of gossip. Margaret was again lost to her thoughts until she caught the view out of one of the windows. Twilight was falling. "I'm sorry, ladies, I need to leave to find my mother. We should have been home by now."

Margaret separated from her friends. She was surprised her mother hadn't found her yet. Now that Papa had left for Dorcia, her mother made sure they were home before it was dark out. For their safety, she said, since they did not have her father there to protect them if anything happened. Her mother didn't believe their servants would protect them if it came down to it. Margaret wandered the corridors, looking for any sign of her mother.

With each coming up empty, Margaret started to look in her mother's usual haunts, the high-ranking noblewomen's chambers. Her mother had tried to ingratiate herself into the highest circles from the moment their family had been ennobled. Her mother had succeeded on occasion with the Duchess Cecily, but not many other ladies had enjoyed her company enough to request it again.

Margaret started to worry when she hadn't found her mother after searching half the palace. Maybe she should wait at the stables with their groom? No. She would get in trouble if she did.

She gasped when she turned the corner and nearly ran into a couple. "My apologies...Mama? Your Majesty!" She fell into a curtsey when she saw it was the king she'd nearly bowled over.

The two separated, and her mother wiped her face free of tears. "Margaret, what are you doing here? Shouldn't you be with your friends?"

"Mama, are you all right?" Margaret looked between her and the king, her brow furrowed. "Are you missing Papa?"

Her mother looked to the king before answering, "I am. His Majesty has been kind enough to console me."

"Your Majesty is too kind." Margaret smiled at him. "I'm so happy we have your support while Papa is in Dorcia."

"I'd be more than happy to comfort you too if you need it, Lady Margaret." The king rested a hand on her shoulder, his thumb rubbing in small circles. "More than happy."

"Thank y—"

Her mother grabbed her arm tightly, pulling her away from King Sorren. "We should not take up any more of His Majesty's time, Margaret." She turned to the king. "With your permission?"

Margaret looked at her mother like she had grown a second head. What was she doing, being so abrupt with the king? She had always demanded the utmost attention paid to the king, and now she couldn't wait to get away from him?

"Of course, I'm sure you're tired after this afternoon." King Sorren nodded to the both of them before leaving.

"You should have waited for me to find you," her mother scolded once the king was out of earshot.

"It was starting to get dark," Margaret protested. "You always want us home before night has settled."

"Next time, don't come looking for me. Just wait in one of the libraries or the great hall until I find you."

Margaret frowned. "Yes, Mama."

She didn't understand her mother's attitude. Had something happened?

15

A sharp kick to his side woke Liam instantly. He inhaled deeply, wincing in pain. He looked around groggily, his head throbbing. He hadn't felt this bad since the last time Jorren had gotten him blind drunk and he'd woken up with a pig sleeping over his middle. He tried to raise his arm to rub his burning eyes, only to have it forcibly stopped by shackles. He was chained to a stake at the center of camp. Liam squinted as light pierced his eyes painfully.

Liam could hear the bustle of the camp surrounding him. It was well into the morning by the *ting*ing of metal utensils on metal bowls as the soldiers ate. Most of the men spoke in low voices in the morning, none awake enough to be boisterous. After several moments of blinking, Liam could finally stand to open his eyes all the way.

"The traitor's awake," Oliphant called out, no doubt the one who had kicked him.

Liam looked around for the traitor, realizing his fellow soldier was speaking of him. "I am no traitor!" He said groggily.

Oliphant kicked Liam once more to silence him. "If Lord General Crompton says you're a traitor, then you are."

"The lord general is the traitor!" Liam pulled against his restraints, trying to stand. When he couldn't, he plopped back down against the post. "He was the one meeting with the enemy!" Liam tried to tell him, but his information fell on deaf ears. Men surrounded him, their eyes hard. He knew these men, and they knew him—how could they think he would betray them and their country?

"Get the lord general!" Lord Oliphant ordered one of the numerous soldiers standing about.

Lord General Crompton came not long after, Lieutenant Bryant following behind. He scowled at Liam. "Stand him up," he commanded.

Two soldiers grabbed Liam under his arms on both sides, reopening the gash on his chest as they forced him to stand. He spat at the lord general, "Traitor!"

Lord General Crompton brought the back of his hand across Liam's face. "Quiet, dog," he growled.

Liam glared at him but quieted nonetheless. He would find the proof the lord general was the traitor. He had seen his betrayal firsthand, and everyone would know. He didn't know how yet, but he would do it.

"What should we do with him?" one of the soldiers asked.

"Kill him!" another piped.

"We'll send him to the capital to be dealt with by the king." Lord General Crompton glared at the soldier who had suggested Liam's execution. "We are still a country upheld by the law."

"I wish to volunteer to take the traitor to Jalmar, Your Grace," Oliphant quickly voiced, grinning sickeningly at Liam. "It would be my pleasure to serve you in this way."

Crompton nodded. "Assemble a guard, and start your journey later today."

Oliphant eagerly obeyed, gathering the men most like him.

"Lieutenant, I want you to ride out within the hour to inform His Majesty of the plot against him and bring the evidence we have to support it."

"Your Grace? Don't you need me here?"

It was the first time Liam had seen Lieutenant Bryant look surprised, and small though it was, it gave Liam a bit of pleasure. Clearly, the lord general didn't keep Bryant entirely in his confidence.

"Take what we have," Lord General Crompton explained slowly, "and bring it to His Majesty to present as evidence. Private Fulton was very thorough in his record keeping. He even managed to hide it from his tentmate."

"Yes, of course he was."

"I'm glad you've remembered."

No he hadn't. What were they talking about? Liam looked wide-eyed between the two. Were they going to use their own records to frame him? As quickly as the crowd had gathered, they disappeared once a decision had been made. There was no one left for Liam to even attempt persuading to help him.

"Is there anything else I can bring?"

Lord General Crompton paused. "I'll write my own message to His Majesty for you to deliver along with the evidence. Now, get ready to leave, and see me before you do."

"Of course, Your Grace." Lieutenant Bryant bowed before he left.

"I can't say I'm sorry it had to be you, Private Fulton. You liked sticking your nose where it didn't belong a little too much," Crompton told him before he, too, left.

Liam sighed and sank to the ground against the post behind him. All he wanted to do was leave his parent's house and have a few adventures before he settled down. He should have listened to his mother and never left. There would have been plenty for him to do on the vineyard, and he was sure there would be a girl he could have been very happy with.

And now all of his hopes were gone.

16

argaret sat at the card tables with her friends. None of them felt like walking about the room; it was too warm for that, and there was no air blowing through the open windows. She waved her fan quickly at her face, trying to cool herself down. If it weren't inappropriate, she'd have her skirts over her knees to let out the hot air gathering around her legs.

"Have you heard anything from your father about the war?" Clairissa asked Margaret.

She shook her head. "He doesn't tell us anything about the war. I don't think he wants us to worry, or he's not getting reports from his lord general."

Ingrid sighed. "Well, that's boring."

"I'm sorry." Margaret shrugged. "I can't give you what I don't have."

"Don't be snippy, Margaret," Annalise snapped.

Elise waved a hand at Annalise. "Don't get mad at Margaret. It's the heat. It's making all of us cranky."

Margaret jumped when the doors behind them banged open. One of the older women rushed in and whispered to her friend. Margaret's brows furrowed when she heard the other woman exclaim and then be shushed. "Do you know them?"

"No." Annalise strained her neck to see them. "But knowing these court ladies, whatever that news is, it won't take long to spread."

"Someone should go over and find out what it is." Clairissa set down her cards and stood. "I'll go." She wasted no time in heading toward the other table.

"What do you think it is?" Margaret asked the remaining group.

"I hope it's about the war," Ingrid gushed, moving side to side to keep an eye on Clairissa.

"Oh, me too!" Elise agreed. "We've been dreadfully deprived of news, and it's been going for months already. Shouldn't it be over by now?"

"It's been two months, and I think war takes longer than that," Margaret commented. "Especially with how far we had to go. It takes almost a month by carriage to reach the Frasisca River from here, and they had to walk there."

They weren't listening to her. Margaret rolled her eyes. They didn't want to listen to anything that didn't suit their need for gossip.

"What's taking so long?" Annalise complained.

"Here she comes." Ingrid said. "She looks excited!"

Clairissa sat with little decorum, her face flushed with excitement. "It's so much better than I could have hoped for."

"Oh, tell us!" Elise grabbed Clairissa's arm, nearly bouncing in her seat.

The other girls joined in, begging for the information.

Clairissa basked in their excitement as long as she could before they brought attention to themselves. "A plot was uncovered."

"You have to tell us more than that!" Margaret groaned. "Don't be a tease, Clairissa."

"One of the soldiers was planning with a lord general from Salatia to overthrow His Majesty!" Clairissa let out a squeal of excitement. "I can't believe it, a plot to usurp the king!"

Margaret gasped, covering her mouth. She briefly uncovered it to say, "No!"

"What's going to happen to him?" Annalise asked.

Clairissa's eyes brightened. "Other soldiers are bringing him here for a trial. The Lord General Crompton's aide de camp brought the news in haste and said the lord general requested they wait until the war was over before he's tried, in the interest of fairness."

"But why?" Ingrid's face scrunched in her confusion. "Shouldn't they have executed him on the spot?"

Clairissa shrugged. "Apparently, the lord general just thinks he was misguided and wanted to make sure he was given a proper trial that anyone else would get if it weren't during wartime."

"That's unexpected." Margaret shook her head. "Lord General Crompton doesn't seem the type for clemency."

Annalise picked up her cards from the table, tapping them on their edges. "Better for us—that means we get to go to the trial and see this traitor for ourselves."

"Oh, we do!" Elise agreed. "How wonderful!"

"I wonder if we'll be able to see him come into the city?" Ingrid asked.

"Of course." Clairissa nodded. "I doubt anyone could keep it a secret when that happens, and we'll have a few days' notice. The streets will be lined, no doubt."

"People will camp out overnight just to see him," Elise agreed.

"I wonder how long it'll take him to get here?" Margaret asked.

Clairissa frowned. "She didn't know, or she didn't tell me so she could have some advantage over others."

"We absolutely *have* to be there," Elise said.

"We'll keep our ears open for any news," Annalise declared, nodding firmly.

"Shall we continue with our game?" Ingrid asked once their excitement died down.

"Yes, yes." Clairissa waved her hands in an upward motion. "Pick up your cards, ladies!"

 # 17

iam stood shackled next to the horse he was to ride for their journey to Jalmar for his punishment. Shepherd Godfrey started to help Liam on to the horse.

"Stop what you are doing!" Oliphant yelled at Godfrey.

"My lord?" Both Shepherd and Liam looked back at Oliphant, confused.

"He will walk." Lord Oliphant gave Liam an acidic grin.

"*Walk?*" Liam asked aghast. "That will take two months!"

"My lord," Godfrey protested, "the lord general wants the traitor in the capital as soon as possible!"

"And the traitor will be." Oliphant attached a long chain to Liam's shackles so he could be held between two soldiers. "I have no intention of slowing our pace."

"My lord!" Shepherd protested.

"Silence!" Oliphant yelled. "You have been given your orders, and they are to transport the prisoner how I see fit. Now move!"

Godfrey let the other two soldiers, Cameron Telcrum and Fletcher Windsor, take Liam's chains. "This will not be on my hands." He grabbed the reins of Liam's horse and led it next to his before climbing atop his own mount.

"Ride on!" Oliphant called, urging his horse into a trot.

Liam was jerked forward when Telcrum and Windsor followed Oliphant. He let out a yelp as the chains pulled him forward, stumbling until he got his footing. The hard metal dug into his hands, threatening to dislocate his wrists if he didn't keep up with the horses' momentum. His chest began to burn as he panted; sweat already beaded on his forehead.

"Slow down!" Liam yelled, stumbling again as the first mile passed. "I can't keep up."

"Slow down, and you'll both join him," Oliphant yelled at Telcrum and Windsor. "Keep on!"

Dread crept into Liam's stomach. He would not survive long enough to make it to the capital if they kept this pace the whole journey. He wouldn't even last the day if he fell and got dragged behind the horses. Swallowing hard, Liam pushed down the vomit in his throat and watched the ground for any holes.

Mile after mile passed before they finally began to slow. Liam's legs felt like jelly under him, and he stumbled at the slower pace. After only a few paces, he fell. Pain erupted in his chest as his wound opened. Dirt filled his mouth, and he coughed violently to expel it; he rolled to his side to keep more dirt from piling in. "Stop!" he yelled.

Relief flooded him when the horses actually stopped.

"We'll break for lunch," Oliphant told them, dismounting. "Tie him to a tree."

Liam was tightly bound to the closest tree trunk, his face scraped and the front of his shirt torn. He didn't care, as long as it meant he was able to rest. He leaned his head back against the rough bark to keep the sweat and blood from pouring into his eyes.

Shepherd Godfrey came to his side with food. "You need to eat," he said to Liam.

"I am not hungry," Liam protested. "I would retch anything that hit my stomach."

Godfrey sighed and let him be. When he rejoined the others for their meal, Godfrey shot Liam frequent looks. Likely to make sure that he didn't die.

Liam watched the others eat and slowly drifted off into a dreamless sleep. He jolted awake with a gasp when his foot was kicked. Liam's whole body ached from just the few miles of travel. He didn't know if he could keep up this pace all the way back to even Anatalia, much less to her capital to be jailed. He looked up at Oliphant with bleary eyes. "Let me rest a while longer."

"You don't get to decide when we leave, traitor." Oliphant spat next to Liam. "Untie him, and chain him to the horses."

"You cannot do this to him, Lord Oliphant," Godfrey complained as Liam was untied. "It's inhumane!"

"Speak again, and you'll join him, Godfrey," Oliphant threatened.

"I'm all right, Godfrey," Liam said as he struggled to stand. He swayed a bit before he leaned against the tree. "Do as he says."

With a sigh, Godfrey climbed onto his horse.

Liam stumbled as Telcrum and Windsor brought him to the horses. He inhaled deeply, steeling himself. He wrapped his hands around the chains to lessen the burden on his wrists, already bruised black from his first run.

"Ride on," Oliphant commanded.

Instead of waiting for the horses to pull him, Liam moved with them. He only lasted a mile before he began to stumble again. His legs burned like fire ants had bitten every inch of them. Another mile passed before Liam fell. He yelled out as he hit the ground.

"Halt!" Oliphant yelled.

Liam sighed, trying to melt into the ground so that it would end. He'd do almost anything to make the day stop. He never should have followed the lord general. He should have minded his own business and— Liam groaned when his hair was gripped tightly, and his head lifted.

Oliphant crouched next to Liam, lifting his head up until Liam could look him in the eyes. "If you cannot keep up," he said lowly, "then you will be whipped until you're bloody."

Liam wasn't given the chance to answer before Oliphant dropped his head. Pain erupted in his cheek—no doubt, it would bruise by the morning.

"Get him up, and let's move," Oliphant commanded. "The king deserves to have the traitor to do with as he will."

Liam closed his eyes tightly, shaking his head to try to clear his weariness. The sky was starting to darken, and he hoped they would not go much longer.

"Onward!" Oliphant commanded.

Liam gasped for breath as he ran, fire burning in his lungs. He could feel blood seeping into the front of his shirt. He would never last this journey. He would certainly bleed out first. Maybe he could play on Godfrey's sympathies to put him out of his misery in the night.

It was not long before Liam started to trip on his own feet. He gripped the chains tightly to stay upright, but even the strength of his arms failed him. He stumbled, not having the will to stay upright. The ground assaulted him rudely, battering Liam as he was dragged behind Telcrum and Windsor. He couldn't bring himself to fight back this time.

"He's fallen!" Godfrey yelled, stopping his horse. "We have to stop."

This time, Liam was lifted from the ground by Oliphant himself. "I told you if you could not keep up, you would be beaten bloody. Chain him to the tree," he commanded.

"You can't do this, my lord," Godfrey said. "You will kill him before we reach the capital!"

"And who is here to tell me otherwise? You?" Oliphant asked. "I don't see anyone else stepping forward in this traitor's defense."

Liam barely registered moving, his arms chained above his head and his shirt lifted to his elbows to expose his back. He heard a jingle of armor before hard leather connected with a crack. Liam was too tired to cry out; he leaned his head against his arm and closed his eyes tightly as each lash came. By the time Oliphant was finished, Liam lost count of how many times he'd been whipped.

"We'll camp here for the night," Oliphant commanded. "Let him down, and set up camp."

Something must have happened in the night.

The day started off with a slow morning, and they didn't leave until nearly noon; he was even tied to his own mount and didn't have to run behind them. Maybe he wouldn't die after all. Liam looked between his escorts and found everyone tensely glaring at each other. He wasn't sure if he was sorry or not to have missed whatever argument had quelled pernicious Lord Oliphant, but Liam was pleased that it had happened.

When they made their first stop for the day, Liam looked imploringly at Godfrey. Godfrey waited until Oliphant was distracted before he said anything. "We told him last night after you fell asleep that if he killed you, we would bring him straight to the lord general and charge him with murder, and drag him back the same way he dragged you here."

Liam let out a single laugh before he groaned. He couldn't do that. It hurt too much. "I wish I had been awake then."

Godfrey shrugged. "We would have waited until you were asleep, regardless, to embarrass him. You know he would have made it worse on you just to spite us if we hadn't."

That was true. Lord Oliphant was more prideful than he deserved to be. He was only a minor lord, after all.

Godfrey gave Liam food and water to have while he rested, and this time, he was only restrained by his middle with one of the soldiers observing him to prevent any escape. It was not like he could—Liam would only make it a couple of feet of clumsy running before he'd be captured.

The rest of the day went easily for him. They all alternated between walking and riding so that they didn't overtire their mounts. Liam was even feeling better by the end of the day. He was still sore, but he at least no longer felt like he would die of exhaustion at any moment.

That didn't last, however.

The next day, Oliphant woke Liam roughly and once again chained Liam between the two horses to run behind them. Each day alternated between an easy ride on the horses and making Liam run for his life. It was almost more torture to give him a day to recover than to keep running ragged.

Liam leaned against the tree, exhausted. They were only a few days out from the capital, and Liam had just finished his *n*th whipping. Oliphant gleefully whipped Liam, mostly with the lord's belt, when Liam inevitably could no longer hold their hard day's pace. The men ate while Liam rested.

"Are you ready for your dinner, traitor?" Oliphant asked, holding his bowl with contents fresh off the fire.

Liam spat at him. "Go to hell."

Oliphant sneered at Liam, throwing the contents on him.

Liam yelled as his chest burned. He glared at Oliphant. If Liam ever got the chance, he would take his revenge on the arrogant lord.

"My lord, if we let the traitor ride the rest of the way, we could reach the capital by tomorrow evening," Godfrey suggested when Oliphant returned to the fire. "And we can finally be rid of him."

Oliphant rolled his eyes. "Stop trying to coddle the traitor, Godfrey."

"We should have been there a month ago—it's already Semonat, for heaven's sake! We're lucky it hasn't snowed and frozen us all to death in the night," Godfrey protested, motioning at the steely clouds in the distance. "I don't want to get a reprimand because you have a ridiculous vendetta against Fulton."

"Would you like to join the traitor, Godfrey?" Oliphant asked, his light tone betraying the deeper threat. "I'm certain a story can be arranged where you are both traitors."

"Lord General Crompton would never corroborate your story."

Oliphant rolled his eyes once more before he turned away from him. "I'll be happy when we're rid of this mewling idiot," Oliphant said to Telcrum and Windsor.

18

"**D**o you see them?" Clairissa demanded.

Margaret shook her head. She pulled her furs closer to her. It had turned cold overnight and, while it was far too early, looked like it could snow any minute with the steel gray clouds billowing in the distance. "Not yet. I can hear other people starting to yell in the distance."

"Well, of course you can," Clairissa snapped.. "Why do you think I'm asking if you can see him, Margaret?"

Margaret rolled her eyes. "If you're so worried about it, why don't you go look for him yourself?"

"Don't be snippy with me, Margaret." Clairissa glared at her. "You want to see him just as much as I do."

"I can hear horses on the cobblestones!" Ingrid declared. "They're coming!"

"Oh!" Elise clapped. "They're getting closer!"

"I can see them!" Annalise had to yell just to be heard over the booing of the crowd.

Margaret was surprised no one was throwing anything at the traitor. She supposed it was because they didn't want to hit the soldiers who were only doing their job bringing the traitor in. They had done nothing wrong, after all. "I wonder who he is?"

"Here they are!" Elise's voice was nearly lost in the crowd.

Gasping, Margaret covered her mouth when the traitor came into view. His clothes were tattered and stained with blood, he was missing a boot, and he stumbled between the horses as he walked. Two soldiers held his arms aloft with rope so that he could not stop moving even if he wanted to. He looked like he hadn't eaten for days, his cheeks hollow with hunger and exhaustion. Nausea bubbled in Margaret's stomach as she watched him stumble. He was saved from falling by the same ropes propelling him along.

"Traitor!" Clairissa screamed next to Margaret. She blended in with the crowd calling the same thing.

He only limped along, his head hung low.

Tears gathered in Margaret's eyes. She knew he was a criminal, but how could he have been so poorly treated on his way to the capital? He looked as though he was seconds from death and wished for it.

A man broke from the crowd and tackled the traitor to the ground. The man flipped him over on his back and began hitting him as hard as he could. The traitor didn't fight as the man hit him; he didn't even cover his face.

Margaret covered her mouth when she saw the traitor's face. She knew him! What was his name? She could not remember, but she knew his face. She had seen him patrolling the city with the Third.

"No!" she yelled at the soldiers. "You have to help him!" She yelled as loudly as she could, but her voice was drowned out by the crowd cheering for the man beating him.

After what seemed like ages, the soldiers were off their horses and pulling the man from the traitor. "Back in the crowd!" one of them bellowed, shoving him in that direction.

Margaret could barely hear another say, "Put him on the horse. This crowd has become too volatile."

The soldiers pulled the traitor on to a horse, and a soldier climbed on behind him to keep him in place. He charged ahead, riding toward the palace. The crowd surged behind him, trying to follow. Margaret was rooted in place as people pushed past her. She had no interest in following. She felt ill, having witnessed the violent scene.

"Can you believe we got to see that?" Clairissa sounded excited.

"We'll have to tell everyone." Ingrid grabbed onto Clairissa's arms, bouncing on her toes. "They'll be so jealous!"

Margaret looked at them with disgust, remaining silent.

19

L iam could hardly believe they had finally reached the capital. He was so worn down and beaten, he was beginning to believe he could die on the spot. His face throbbed from where the man in the crowd had hit him, but it was a welcome distraction from the pain everywhere else. Godfrey had been sent ahead to alert the guards of their presence. No doubt, he would have stopped the man much sooner than the rest of them had. Liam doubted they would have if he wasn't expected. Several sentries and Godfrey were waiting in the courtyard for them.

"We bring the traitor," Oliphant announced to the guards.

Liam fell forward when Telcrum and Windsor let go of his arms, his face connecting with the hard stone. He let out a groan, happy to no longer be forced to stand. He laid his cheek back on the cobblestones, relishing in the coldness they held. It helped ease the pain. He wished he had not survived the journey as his adrenaline wore off and his whole body throbbed in excruciating pain. He could feel each heartbeat in every part of his body. He groaned again and tried to move, but it was too painful.

"What the hell happened to him?" Godfrey knelt next to Liam.

"Your...*care* of the traitor will be duly noted," one of the sentries said. "You may return to the barracks and await your orders there."

The soldiers bowed to the sentry and left Liam in their care.

"Pick the traitor up and take him to his cell," the sentry commanded his men. "And send for a healer immediately."

Liam felt himself raised to his feet, and he groaned in protest. He was taken down to the dungeons. Liam wearily looked around the prison. The palace dungeons had reportedly been well-kept and clean, and while they did not smell of human waste as he expected them to, they were not nearly as orderly as advertised.

The dungeon guards guided him until he saw no more prisoners in the cells. He had been placed in a more secluded area of the dungeon to keep him from interacting with his fellow prisoners and inciting a rebellion. Liam looked around his cell and found a cot for him to sleep on and blankets to keep him warm. For the crime he was accused of, Liam was amazed he was given any such amenities.

The dungeon's smell of wet dirt invaded his senses every time he breathed. It was almost suffocating to be assaulted at every turn with the overwhelming dankness of it. The guards placed him on his cot. Liam let out a groan as his back burned under the weight of him. It was barely longer than he was. He dreaded the time that he would have to spend in the tiny space, but at least it was his alone. On the way to his permanent residence, Liam had seen many of the cells shared with up to four men at a time.

"Sweet Lord."

Liam barely turned his head to see the red robes the palace healers wore. He let out a soft sigh and closed his eyes. "Leave me alone."

"I cannot. My vows wouldn't allow it, and neither would the king's justice," the healer said.

Liam tried to ignore the healer but let out a sharp cry when the healer lifted his shirt. It was in tatters, but the strips were stuck to his skin. "Just leave it, Healer."

"Woolsey," he said. "Healer Woolsey." He cut away what he could of the shirt.

That name was familiar—he was the healer Liam had helped with an amputation. That felt like a lifetime ago now, in an old life that didn't belong to him anymore. Liam let out a sigh when cold cloths rested on his back.

"I'm going to have to debrid it, and it's not going to be pleasant. You've pus and dirt all over your back."

Liam sighed again. "You're not going to leave me alone, are you?"

"No."

Sighing again, Liam said, "Go on, then. There's a wound on the front too."

Woolsey rolled him onto his side and removed his shirt from the front as well. He tugged on the fabric gently, but it didn't move from the wound.

Liam saw the struggle on Woolsey's face before he ripped it off. He let out a shout, clenching his teeth. "You could have given me warning."

"I'm sorry, but there's only so long you can be on your side before your back will begin to hurt, and this will be faster. He wiped the wound quickly with several cloths before putting a salve and a bandage on. Woolsey gently lowered Liam back onto his stomach. "You're lucky that one was hardly pussy."

"It bled quite a lot on the trip."

"The flow of blood likely kept out the dirt."

How lucky for Liam.

"What happened to you?" Woolsey asked.

Liam tensed and gritted his teeth as the healer began wiping his back clean. "I was—" he gasped when a tender spot was lanced "—beaten for not keeping up with the horses."

"You were on foot?" Healer Woolsey demanded. "Has anyone checked your feet yet?"

"You're the first to see me, so no."

Liam felt his remaining boot tugged off and heard retching come from the healer. He could smell the foul stench as well and couldn't blame Woolsey for his reaction.

Woolsey stepped around to the bars of the cell and barked at the guard, "Get me hot water, more bandages, and the case of salves on my workbench."

"I can't leave you alone with the traitor," the guard said.

"What do you think will happen?" Woolsey demanded. "If he tries to stand, he'll likely faint, or I could simply hit him in the back to stop him."

Liam snorted. Was that what he was reduced to? An invalid who would faint if he was hit in the back or stood? The healer might as well put them both out of their misery and give him too much milk of the poppy, lulling him into a sleep from which he would never wake. Or just give him some in general. "Will you not give me something for the pain?"

"I'm afraid we aren't allowed to give the prisoners any milk of the poppy for pain," Healer Woolsey said. "If you're lucky, you'll lose consciousness before we get too far into the process."

If only. If Liam hadn't fainted during his beatings, he doubted he would during the cleaning of his wounds. "Let's get this over with."

"I'm going to give your back a break and work on removing the dead skin from your feet. You don't want it to become gangrenous," Woolsey said. "I'm surprised they aren't already. This is going to be several layers deep, and you won't be able to stand until they've healed enough."

"How am I to relieve myself if I can't stand?" Liam asked. He doubted after the debriding of his back and feet he'd even want to try to stand.

"A servant of mine will be sent in throughout the night to check on you and help with your needs, and I'll be here during the day to change your bandages and reapply any salves and poultices you may need," Woolsey told him. "You'll be sick of all the help you'll get by the time you've healed, honestly."

Liam tried not to cry out when Healer Woolsey scraped the skin from his feet, but he was unsuccessful on many occasions. The guard returned with a servant in tow and opened the cell. Liam wasn't sure if he should be insulted or worried about his condition when the guard didn't even bother closing the cell door. He let out a relieved sigh when a cool, creamy substance was rubbed on his feet before they were tightly bound.

"Now, back to your back, unless you need a break," Woolsey said.

"No, just keep going. I want to be done."

"You're lucky to be alive, you know," Healer Woolsey said, "an infection like this, left untreated, will kill you."

"I know."

When Woolsey finished cleaning his back, he thickly applied a cold substance and said, "I will have to come daily to cleanse the wounds and reapply the poultice. Several times a day, actually. I don't want you to get a blood infection."

Liam remained silent, turning his face away from the healer.

"You'll also need to have daily draughts to help restore you to your full strength."

"What would be the point?" Liam asked acerbically, turning his head to look at the healer directly for the first time. "I'm going to be put to death as soon as I have a trial."

"You are currently in my care, and I say that it's important," Healer Woolsey told Liam firmly. "I want to see you healthy."

"Just let me die, Healer. Don't waste your time."

"I said no. You are my patient, traitor or not, and I will not disgrace myself by letting you die out of convenience," Healer Woolsey snapped. "Now be quiet, and take your treatment."

Liam sighed and turned away from the man.

Liam was sitting against the craggy wall of his cell, his eyes closed, when Healer Woolsey came to his lodgings.

"I see you're feeling better today," he said happily. "At least, well enough to be sitting up."

"Your poultices and draughts are working, Healer Woolsey," Liam informed him. "Despite my wishing that they wouldn't."

"I should hope so," he boasted, "herbal remedies are my speciality."

Liam let a hint of a smile show on his face. "What do you have in store for me today, Healer?"

"The same as always," Woolsey answered, handing Liam his draught.

Liam grimaced as he smelled the familiar potion, choking it down. He sputtered, putting the back of his hand to his mouth. The draught always made him feel like retching after he shot down the liquid, even after a month of drinking the same tonics day in and day out.

"Go ahead and lie on your stomach," the healer instructed.

Liam complied, pulling off his shirt before he rested facedown on his cot. He felt Woolsey peel the now dried paste off his back. He let out a hiss when Woolsey peeled away bits of the healing skin.

"It seems you'll have minimal scarring."

"How wonderful that my chances of staying attractive are high," Liam quipped. "How will I ever fight off all the women?"

Healer Woolsey chuckled, laying down the fresh paste. "Same as before, wait to put on your shirt until it dries."

"Understood."

"Tomorrow will be my last visit," Healer Woolsey informed Liam. "You are doing well enough that you don't need me anymore."

"Thank you, Woolsey, for everything." Liam earnestly thanked him. Despite all his protests, Liam truly did appreciate all of the healer's efforts.

Healer Woolsey nodded to him before he left.

20

"Your Grace," Alton Bryant called as he galloped into the camp. He dismounted and walked up to Lord General Crompton with a sealed parchment bearing the royal crest. "You have a summons from His Majesty."

Crompton took the letter from the soldier and waved him away. He quickly read the summons. He was to return to the capital as soon as possible to appraise the king of what had happened with the traitor. Crompton furrowed his brow. What *had* happened to Fulton?

If the traitor's escorts were being held for something he needed to answer for, that would explain why the contingent hadn't returned.

"Saddle my horse," Crompton commanded one of his guards. He went to his tent and packed lightly. He would set out immediately. Sorren was not the kind of man one kept waiting long. As much as Crompton hated him, the king could still make his life miserable if angered.

"Do you wish for me to return with you?" Alton asked.

"No," Crompton said. "You're needed here."

It took a little over two weeks of hard riding to reach the capital. Crompton went to the chambers always held for him in the palace and made himself presentable for the king. He waited in the king's library for the monarch, sipping an amber liquor.

"Cousin," Sorren said when he finally entered the room. "I'm pleased you could get here so quickly."

"Your letter said with all haste, Your Majesty," Crompton reminded him.

"So it did." The king poured himself his own drink. "I want you to tell me about the traitor."

"Liam Fulton," Crompton said, "farmer's son from Rivack, with no apparent ties to Salatia nor hating Anatalia and its king. I couldn't tell you how or why he would have betrayed us."

"And where were you during this?" Sorren asked, his brows raised.

Crompton shifted. "Lieutenant Bryant found the traitor in action not long after he snuck away from the camp and apprehended him as Lord General Baur escaped. I was in my war tent, preparing the next day's strategies."

"I see…and was it by your command the prisoner was beaten and tortured nearly to death?" The king's brows seemed to try and rise higher, but they were unable to do so.

"I would never!" For all Crompton's faults, he was not a sadist.

"The prisoner was brought here barely alive. He had been forced to run alongside the horses for almost the entire journey, and if he couldn't keep pace, he was beaten and rarely fed," the king told him. "Your soldier Godfrey told us all about it when he was sent ahead to alert us of their arrival."

"I would never have allowed Oliphant to lead the prisoner escort had I known he would treat him as such," Crompton said. "There is no excuse for that behavior, and I can assure you, he will be punished accordingly."

"You will also be punished accordingly." Sorren took a drink of his liquor. His eyes were gelid as he watched Crompton. "You are being reassigned to a new command here in Anatalia."

"Your Majesty, I can serve you more effectively in Salatia!" Lord General Crompton tried to keep his frustration off his face. "I am of no use to you here."

"You'll be plenty useful here, Tobias." His cousin smiled at him. "Now go; you have other matters to attend to. Oliphant and the rest of the escort are in the barracks."

"At least allow me to return to my regiment to turn command over to Lieutenant Bryant," Crompton said.

"Fine." The king waved his hand. "Return with all haste for your new assignment when you finish."

Crompton found the men in the barracks, playing a game of cards, coins strewn about the table. It looked like they had been at the game for some time.

"On your feet, dogs!" Crompton yelled, pleased to see they jumped out of their chairs.

"Lord General." Shepherd Godfrey bowed deeply to him. "Have you come to bring us back? We were told to await your arrival."

"Get out, Godfrey," Crompton growled. "This doesn't concern you."

"Yes, Your Grace." Godfrey bowed out of the barracks.

"Lord General, what is this about?" Oliphant asked, looking at Telcrum and Windsor.

"Do not speak to your betters with so little respect, Oliphant," Crompton ordered. "This is about your treatment of prisoner Fulton while transporting him."

Oliphant glared but stayed silent, waiting for Crompton to continue.

"You are all stripped of your ranks and privileges and will be serving in food preparation and service until the end of the war," Crompton said to the three red faces.

"You can't do that to us!" Oliphant yelled in protest.

"Latrine duty for you, Oliphant," Crompton countered.

"Latrine duty!" Oliphant's face was beet red. "You—"

"Would you like for me to make it a permanent assignment, Oliphant?"

"No, Your Grace," Oliphant seethed.

"Good," Crompton turned to leave, "Oliphant, you will be leaving with me so I can assure you don't pass your duty off on someone else."

Crompton leaned against the neck of his horse, weariness dragging him down. The camp was within sight, and he could not wait to get to his tent and sleep. The king had delayed him with a month's worth of tasking, and a snow storm had come in Omonat, earlier than any other year he'd seen. Being stuck, the king saw fit to give him even more tasking to last him through the winter. He'd ridden hard to make sure he didn't miss more than he already had. With how fast things changed in war, he couldn't be away from the front for long.

He slid from his horse when he got closer to his tent in the center of camp. He handed off his mount to the man who came to greet him. "Make sure he's watered thoroughly and wiped down. He's had a rough time of it."

"Yes, Your Grace!"

"Someone find me Lieutenant Bryant," Crompton called to whomever was within earshot before going into his tent.

Alton joined him not long after Crompton had removed his dust-covered coat. "Your Grace, welcome back. How was your trip?"

"Oliphant nearly killed Private Fulton." Crompton threw a boot to the ground. "He's lucky he didn't."

"Wouldn't it have been better if he did?" Alton asked.

"We have a law system for a reason, Lieutenant." Crompton looked at Alton, his face weary. "No matter what we are trying to do here, we don't want to throw Anatalia into lawlessness."

"Yes, sir."

"What's happened in my absence?"

Lieutenant Byrant stood at attention with his hands behind his back. "Our friend has been apprised of your departure and instructed to wait until we send him word for our plan to begin again. He's kept us up to date with his movements so we can adjust our plans as needed, since it would be suspicious for him to remain in one location for an undetermined amount of time."

"Good. Very good."

"Will there be anything else?"

"No. I don't want to do anything until tomorrow, after I've had a chance to rest."

"As you wish. I'll have a meal sent to your tent, Your Grace," Alton said.

Crompton nodded. "Tomorrow, we'll need to work fast. I have orders to return with all haste to the capital for a new assignment."

"Do you think Private Fulton told them anything?"

Crompton shook his head. "Even if he did, he was in such poor condition, they would think he was hallucinating. The evidence we provided when you alerted the king of this treachery would be damning enough that no one will believe him anyway."

"Very good, Your Grace," Alton said. "I'll leave you to eat and rest."

21

Margaret grabbed a money purse and smiled, remembering the scolding she'd gotten from her father when she'd sewn her pockets shut to avoid carrying money. She'd ripped the stitches from her pockets after he left for Dorcia, knowing it would make him happy upon his return to hear she'd been doing as he'd like.

"Mama?" Margaret called into the drawing room.

"What is it, Margaret?"

Margaret stepped into the room, grabbing a fan off one of the side tables. "I'm going to the market to get some flowers. Do you want any in particular?"

"Why don't you let one of the servants do that?" her mother asked. "Isn't that why we pay them?"

"I like doing it. Papa used to go with me as often as he could when he was here, because it reminded him of home," Margaret said. "It helps me miss him less."

Her mother sighed. "Take someone with you, at least. I'm sure one of the servants can be dragged away."

"I can take the groom. He doesn't have any duties today since we aren't going to the palace."

"All right. Hurry along, then. Wear a hat; no man wants a woman who looks like she works in the fields."

Margaret sighed. "Yes, Mama."

When she left the drawing room, she went to the back of the house, where the stables were. "Hanson?"

Hanson stood at attention when he saw her. "Yes, my lady?"

"If it isn't inconvenient, would you escort me to the flower market?"

"Of course, my lady. Would you like to take the carriage or walk as your father did?" Hanson asked.

Margaret smiled. "It's a nice enough day out; would you mind walking?"

"Not at all, my lady." He grabbed his hat from the wall and placed it on his head before offering an arm to Margaret. "Would you do me the honor of taking my arm?"

Margaret smiled again, taking his arm. "Of course, thank you, Hanson."

He led them forward, keeping a slow pace she could easily keep up with. They made idle chatter as they walked. Hanson pointed out places he would visit with his family as a child before he came to work for Margaret's family.

Margaret was fascinated. She had very few memories of the city before Hanson worked for them, and she couldn't imagine anything different. She was glad to have his company. It was a long walk to the flower market from her home, and it was nice to have the time occupied.

The market was crowded when they reached it, and Hanson moved in front of Margaret to make a break in the crowd. "We're almost there, my lady," he called over his shoulder.

"Thank you, Hanson." Margaret inhaled deeply and briefly closed her eyes. The Amonat breeze picked up tendrils of her hair, blowing them across her face. The flower market was not as crowded as the other sections, which Margaret was happy about. "To the left, please, Hanson. That's where my favorite flowers are."

Margaret browsed the flowers until she came to what she wanted: the hydrangea. It was her and her father's favorite. She smiled, inhaling deeply. She began pulling several stems from the groups of colors. "Oh, frog nuggets! I forgot to bring my basket. Will you hold them for me?" she asked Hanson.

Hanson laughed. "Of course, my lady."

Margaret piled several colors into his outstretched arms, holding some in her own when his grew too full. "I think this should be enough."

She walked toward the vendor, barely able to see over the pile of blooms. Margaret turned the corner, nearly dropping the flowers when she ran into someone. "Oh, I'm sorry!"

"Lady Margaret?"

Margaret lowered her arms to clear her view. "Mr. Luther?" She hadn't seen him in ages with her father in Dorcia. He looked just as good as the last time—better even.

Charles bowed his head to her. "What are you doing here?"

She lifted her arms briefly with all the flowers. "Getting flowers for Cerule House. Papa would be disappointed if we stopped putting out flowers just because he's gone."

A woman came to stand at Charles's side. She cleared her throat, looking up at him.

"My apologies, Lady Margaret, may I present Miss Charlotte Lebrack? Charlotte, this is the Lady Margaret. I work for her father, the Count of Dorcia, with his business."

"It's a pleasure to meet you, Lady Margaret." Charlotte curtsied to her.

Margaret examined her. She had blonde hair that shone in the sun, glowing wherever the light hit it. "The pleasure is all mine, Miss Lebrack. How do you know Charles?"

Charlotte blushed. "We're courting, my lady."

"Oh!" Margaret plastered a smile on her face, though she felt like dropping the flowers and clawing the golden woman's eyes out. "How wonderful for you both."

Charles looked pleased. "Thank you, my lady. I was hoping to introduce her to your father, but I fear it would be too dangerous to travel with a lady during the war."

Margaret's face fell at the mention. "Yes, of course. It's easy to forget there's a war happening when there's no trace of it here."

"All too true, my lady," Charlotte agreed. "I was the one to suggest traveling to your father; Charles just adores him."

Color crept up Charles's pale neck. "Charlotte—"

"My father feels the same about you, but he would want you to stay where it's safe." Margaret nodded as she spoke. Margaret thought if she nodded any faster, she would nod her head right off. She had to leave; she wasn't far from making a fool of herself.

"We should let you go about your business," Charles said. "It was wonderful to see you, my lady."

"It was a pleasure to meet you." Charlotte bowed her head respectfully.

It certainly was not a pleasure. Margaret kept a tight smile on her face. "I hope to see you both again someday soon."

Once the couple had left, Margaret turned to Hanson. "I think I would like to take a carriage back, if you would be so kind as to fetch one for us?"

"Of course, my lady. Are you not feeling well?"

"No, I'm not."

Hanson hurried away, and Margaret sighed when he left. She knew it was inevitable that Charles would find a woman he would be interested in, but she had hoped it would be her. Margaret paid for the flowers as fast as she could. She wanted to be home, away from here. She didn't want to be anywhere she could run into Charlotte again. Now she wished they had taken the carriage initially; they never would have met the couple, and Margaret would be blissfully unaware of Charles's new relationship.

Now her happy day was ruined irreparably.

 **22**

Liam's two usual guards appeared at his cell door. "Morning, traitor," one said.

Liam sighed. "What do you want?"

"Two thousand dead this month," the other said.

"I have been in this cell for six months—if I were the one causing us to lose the war, don't you think the numbers would go down?"

"You probably inspired other traitors, scum," the first said.

When the door to his cell opened, Liam looked at the guards, confused. "What's happening?"

"You're going for a walk," the second guard told him.

Liam apprehensively rose from his cot. "A walk to where?"

The first guard slapped manacles on Liam and took him into the garden. He squinted as the sun painfully stabbed his eyes. It was the first time he had been out of the dungeon since he had arrived six months prior. That last time had been cold and cloudy, and the sun's warmth was almost too much for him.

"You have twenty minutes," they instructed, giving Liam some distance.

He looked around in wonder, deeply breathing in the fresh air. Liam almost couldn't remember what fresh air smelled like. He looked around at the garden in full bloom, unsure of what to do with all the space. Liam closed his eyes as the wind blew, caressing his skin with a gentle touch.

He looked back at his guards, trying to discern whether he was being tested or not. He would not run; he would be killed immediately if he did. Maybe that's why they were doing it—the guards had never been kind to him. Liam stayed in their line of sight, delighting in being in the open. He put each flower and leaf to memory. Liam was unsure when or if he would ever see such things again. Once his trial happened—whenever the war finally came to an end—it would be the end of him. Maybe Liam would get lucky and the flowers would still be in bloom when he was executed.

"Time is up," the guard told Liam, grabbing him by the arm and leading him back toward the dungeon.

Liam looked longingly back at the lush garden, sucking in his last gulp of fresh air before he was led back into the dungeons. The dank air suffocatingly coated his senses once more. Liam reluctantly returned to his tiny quarters.

An older man, hunched with a bundle of papers under his arm, approached Liam's cell. His hands shook with age as he waited for the guard to arrive with his stool. This was the first new person Liam had seen since Healer Woolsey and his assistants had stopped coming to treat him a year ago.

"My name is Cedric Barrows. I am to be your counsel if you so wish it." The older man gave Liam a once-over.

"Am I even allowed counsel for my alleged crime?" Liam asked tartly. He didn't think alleged traitors were allowed counsel. And, if they were, why was he just now receiving it when he'd been here a year and a half already?

The older man brushed off his comments as he sat on the stool provided for him. "His Majesty has deemed you will stay in the dungeons until the war is over. At that time, the lord generals will testify either for or against you, and the king will make his decision based on their testimony."

"I am not the traitor," Liam seethed, "Lord General Crompton is the one giving away tactical positions to the enemy. He is the one who should be tried for treason!"

"Whether that holds any truth or not," —Cedric tilted his head down to look at Liam over his spectacles— "it does not bode well for you that it is the king's cousin accusing you. And that you are accusing him."

"And you think there is no chance for me," Liam stated more than asked.

"No."

Liam unconsciously stepped back. He knew the answer was no, but to have it said so bluntly was shocking. "Surely, His Majesty feels the same way you do," he protested, "and if he does, then there is no point to having counsel."

"You may choose to dismiss my service, or I can continue to help you develop your argument." Cedric gave him a bored look, putting his papers down on his lap. "I am paid either way."

Liam nodded with a sigh. "I suppose it won't hurt to have your help."

"Do you have any evidence in your favor?" Cedric looked at Liam over his glasses again.

"Only my word."

"I see… Can anyone corroborate your word?"

"No," Liam sighed. There was no evidence he could give. There hadn't even been time to gather any if he wanted to—he'd been imprisoned since discovering the treason. He did not have a chance at winning this trial. "Why won't the king just try me now for treason?"

Cedric took off his glasses, looking at Liam like he would a child. "We cannot afford to pull the Lord General Crompton away from the war effort to testify against you. The king has decided to wait until the fighting has ended."

"But why wait at all?" Liam grew as frustrated as Cedric looked. "Treason is an executable offense. Why not just execute me on the battlefield instead of bringing me here? Why not just let me die when I arrived? I certainly wanted to."

"Because no one is above the law, not even the king. After an untried mass execution by King Reuben of House Platiri a little over a hundred years ago, his son King Reuben II enacted a law that required a trial for any crime where the punishment was death," Cedric told him.

Liam sighed. "I suppose I should be thankful to him, then."

"Shall we go over the evidence Lord General Crompton and Lieutenant Bryant have against you?"

"How do they even have incriminating evidence against me?" Liam demanded. "I did nothing wrong."

"They allegedly have an unsent letter written in your hand to Lord General Baur with troop movements, and several of his letters telling you where to meet and the amount of payment owed to you with promises of sanctuary in Salatia once the war has been won."

"That can't be real!" he cried. "I've never been in contact with Lord General Baur, much less gotten any money from him."

Cedric dug through his papers, pulling out a folded parchment with a broken seal. He handed it to Liam through the bars. "This is just one of the letters. Is this your writing?"

Liam started when he saw his writing but unfamiliar words. "I didn't write this!"

"But is it your writing?"

Hesitating, Liam said, "Yes. I don't know how they could make this. I didn't write this. I *wouldn't* write this!"

"All right." Cedric held out his hand for the letter.

Liam was tempted to rip it up. He handed it over reluctantly.

"Is there anything they could have found with your writing to make a facsimile?"

"We all sent letters home to family to assure them we weren't dead yet," Liam said, "but the last letter I wrote was the week before we hit Chenalieu."

Cedric nodded, pursing his lips. "It's possible the letters were not yet sent and they copied your writing."

"That can be the only explanation—the first time I ever saw Lord General Baur was when he spoke to Lord General Crompton. I don't know if I'd be able to pick him out of a crowd if I were asked."

"That will be our defense, then," Cedric said. "I'll be back in a few weeks to go over anything you can think of that will help your case."

"Is there any end in sight to the war?" Liam asked.

"Radovan, Mekhor, and Frasisca have joined the fighting, so it should be over soon."

Cedric shuffled in front of the bars to Liam's cell. His breathing was heavy, and sweat beaded on his forehead. He sat wearily on his stool and dug in his satchel. "How are you today, Liam?" He coughed heavily, the sound wet.

Liam came to the bars, gripping one in each hand. "Well, I'm here. Better than you, probably. You don't sound good."

"It's these cells," Cedric told him. "The damp isn't good for my old bones."

"I'm not sure it's your bones you should be worrying about."

Cedric waved a dismissive hand. "I thought you could send out a few letters to your family. Your parents have been sending you letters, and you aren't returning them."

"I can't write to them." Liam went back to his cot and collapsed onto it. "They would be ashamed to hear from me."

"I doubt it, since they keep sending you letters, Liam." Cedric slid a stack of ten letters through the bars. "Just read them, and then see how you feel about sending them a letter in return."

Liam didn't answer, but he did pick up the letters.

"I'll leave you some writing supplies." He pushed blank parchment with a quill and ink through the bars. "I'll come back in a few hours."

Sighing, Liam cracked one of the seals from the letters. He set it down when he saw his mother's writing. Tears welled in his eyes, and he pressed the heels of his hands into his eyes. He didn't want to look at them. He didn't want to read them. He didn't want to read about their worry, their shame, or their adamant refusal that he was guilty.

"Pull yourself together, Liam," he scolded himself, pulling his hands away from his eyes.

He pulled the letters out, forcing himself to read them. They were everything he expected them to be, full of sorrowful prose and hopes he would be found not guilty because they knew he was innocent. They knew he could never have done what was being said.

Liam wrote them a letter telling them of a hope he didn't have so their own fears would be assuaged. He told them of his lawyer and how Cedric had high hopes that they had enough evidence to prove he wasn't guilty. He wanted to make them feel better, even if he had to lie to them to make it happen.

He folded the letter when it was finished and put it at the door to his cell so Cedric could grab it without disturbing him. Liam didn't feel like talking to anyone after that.

23

"**D**o we have to go, Mama?" Margaret whined, plopping onto the sofa behind her.

Her mother gave her a flat look. "Yes, we do. His Majesty has personally invited us tonight."

Margaret sighed. "But the prince has grown so insufferable. He thinks he can just boss me around as he likes."

"He can, Margaret. He's the Prince of Anatalia, and its future king." Her mother grabbed her shawl from the back of the couch. "And you had better start being more receptive if you want him to keep his attention on you."

"But I don't."

"Well you should," her mother snapped. "Do you know how many other girls have been trying to get his attention, and you've just been shoved into his view? You could be the queen one day!"

"I don't want to be the queen, Mama," Margaret told her. "I want to find someone who appreciates Dorcia as much as I do and would be happy to be there instead of here."

Her mother rolled her eyes. "Would you forget Charles already? He's a commoner, and he isn't for you."

"That was unkind, Mama." Margaret looked away from her. "You married Papa when he was a commoner."

"That was different. Your father was a merchant with a promising company, and I was in the same class. You are the daughter of a count and need to marry within your rank or higher. You have a duty to this family."

Margaret remained quiet, still not looking at her mother.

"Now, get in the carriage before I command Hanson to put you in it himself." Her mother walked away, heels clicking angrily against the hardwood floors.

Margaret dragged herself off the sofa with a groan. "I still don't want to go."

"I don't care. You're almost seventeen and marriageable—start acting like it."

Margaret scowled over her wine. Prince Gareth was well into his drinks by the time the dinner started and flat-out drunk by the time the meal ended. "Come with me," he slurred, grabbing Margaret's arm and pulling her to her feet.

"Where are we going?" She dug her feet into the floor, but it was futile. He was too strong and continued pulling her along.

He grinned. "You'll see. I want to show you something."

Margaret reluctantly followed him; she'd end up tripping if she didn't. "What is it?"

"It's a sup—" he hiccupped "—surprise!"

Dread curled in her stomach. "I'm not sure—"

"You'll love it; it's a secret."

Margaret looked over her shoulder to see if there was anyone she could call upon for help if things went in a direction she was uncomfortable with. The servants passing them refused to make eye contact with her for more than a second, quickly looking down until they had passed. Her stomach curled. No one would help her. He dragged her into a library she'd never been in before—which was odd as she thought she'd been in all the palace had to offer—and let go of her arm. He searched the farthest wall, pulling books off left and right.

"What are you doing?" Margaret cried, looking at the scattered books.

"I'm looking for the trigger," he said as if it were obvious.

"What?"

"To move the bookcase!"

Margaret furrowed her brows. "I don't think the palace has—"

"Aha!" Gareth grinned as the bookcase opened. "See?"

She went to the opening and looked inside. "Where does it go?"

"Come on." He grabbed a candelabra off one of the tables before he grabbed her arm and led her down the corridor. The walls were rough carved stones, the crags easily deep enough to bloody her arms if she tripped. It smelled of mildew, and somewhere far off, the sound of water dripping echoed.

They traveled for what felt like forever, Margaret having to constantly duck spider webs. "I don't know if I like this."

"I found this a while back," Gareth explained. "It was quite the find, if I say so myself."

Margaret felt the hairs on the back of her neck rise. "I don't feel comfortable, Your Highness. I want to go back."

"We're almost there." Gareth looked at her over his shoulder and sloppily smiled. "Almost no one knows what I'm going to show you. Aren't you excited, Margaret?"

A chill ran down her spine. "No."

Gareth paused only a moment before continuing on. "No matter. What I want to show you is just around the corner."

Margaret sighed. "Your Highness, please, I want to go back."

"Wait here." Gareth let go of her arm. "I'll be right back." He opened a door and went through, closing it behind him.

"Your Highness!" Margaret cried when the dark enveloped her. "Please, come back!"

She clung to the wall, the darkness making her feel like she could not stand up straight. Her breath came faster. Margaret closed her eyes. If her eyes were closed, it was only a normal dark, not the oppressive, frightening dark surrounding her.

"Gareth?" Margaret called out timidly. "Please come back!" She opened her eyes and noticed light coming from the bottom of the doors. She walked toward it, clinging to the craggy walls in case she tripped over something.

They opened, and light washed over Margaret.

"Come on, then," Gareth said, exasperated. "Stop whining like a baby."

Margaret launched herself at the prince, wrapping her arms tightly around his middle. "Don't leave me like that!"

"I was gone only a few seconds." Gareth wrapped his arms around her, his fingers pressing tightly into her back. "You're all right."

"Can we go into the light, please?"

Gareth led Margaret into the secret room by the hand, closing the door behind them. The room was piled with books, furniture, and things that Margaret could not identify.

"What is this place?" Margaret asked, moving toward the piles of books.

"It's the Triburn room," Gareth told her. "My great-great-grandfather had this room built after he conquered Anatalia."

"Triburn? I don't think I know that name." Margaret picked up one of the books. The leather was cracked with age, and the date on the book was several hundred years old.

"You wouldn't have. My great-great-grandfather had every book with their name in it burned or collected, every portrait destroyed, and every member of the family killed."

Margaret fumbled with the book in her hands. "I beg your pardon?" She looked at him with wide eyes.

"The Triburns stole our throne," Gareth said, his eyes dark, "so we took it back and made sure they could never usurp us again."

Margaret looked around the room again. It was far more ominous now than it had been seconds before. Now it was a mausoleum for the long dead's possessions. "Why are you telling me this?"

Gareth stepped closer to Margaret, cupping her cheek in his large hand. He stroked her cheek, smiling at her before saying, "Because, Lady Margaret, I want you to know what our family does to families who displease us."

"I don't understand where this is coming from, Your Highness." Margaret's voice shook as she backed away. "Our families get along very well."

"I want to make sure it stays that way." Gareth turned from her. "When families get too powerful, they tend to set their eyes higher than they should. Usually on the throne."

"Your Highness," Margaret started, "all my father wants in life is to run his business, care for his family, and ensure his people are safe."

"The *king's* people."

"I'm sorry?"

"They aren't your father's people. He goes on and on about 'his people,' but they aren't his. They're ours," Gareth seethed. "He only has his position because we gave it to him."

"I must disagree, Your Highness." Margaret furrowed her brow. What was she doing, arguing with him? It was too late now; she had to finish what she started. "My father bought the land from other peers long before His Majesty was kind enough to grant my father a title. The land is his, and the title gives him the duty of caring for the people who reside on that land."

"It is Anatalian soil, Lady Margaret. Purchased or not, we can take it from him at any point, and it will be our right as the royal family."

Margaret's mouth formed a flat line. "Your Highness, I think we should return to our parents."

"Yes, and you can let your mother know she can stop pushing you on me," Gareth said. "Yours is not a family that will ever marry into royalty. She should know her place, and so should you." He motioned to the room. "Or else this is what will happen."

"I assure you, Your Highness, death would have to be threatened before I would marry into this family."

Margaret barreled down the steps. "Mama!" she yelled. "Mama, is he here yet?"

"Not yet." Excitement brightened her mother's eyes. "He won't be here for a few hours yet."

Margaret groaned. It had been forever since she'd seen her father. He'd been gone for almost three years with the war effort and hadn't been able to come home, because it was unsafe to travel. They had received his letter out of the blue that he was coming home and would be there by the end of Mamonat. And finally, it was the end of the month.

"Can't we go out to the gates of the city to wait for him?" Margaret asked.

"No, Margaret. He's going to want to rest when he gets home and sees us, not listen to your prattle all the way home."

She groaned again, throwing herself on a couch.

"Stop acting like a child, Margaret," her mother snapped. "No one appreciates it."

Margaret rolled her eyes. "I'm not acting like a child, Mama."

"Aren't you?" She snapped her book closed. "You're throwing yourself on the furniture, you're whining, and you're rolling your eyes. That sounds childish to me."

Crossing her arms over her chest, Margaret looked away. "I'm just anxious to see Papa."

"I am too," she said softly.

Margaret shot to her feet when she heard horseshoes on the cobblestones. "He's here!" She picked up her skirts and ran to the door. She threw open the door and stepped outside, shielding her eyes from the sun.

Her father was sliding from his horse, his clothes rumpled and dusty. Bags hung heavily under his eyes, and his hair was messy. He turned when Margaret called out for him, and a smile spread across his face. He bounded up the steps and took Margaret in his arms and spun her around. "By Theotes, you've grown!"

"You've been gone a while." She buried her face into his chest.

He took her by the shoulders and held her at arm's length. "Let me have a look at you." He looked her over, studying her face for a long while. "You look exactly like your mother when she was your age."

"His Majesty has said on many occasions how similar we look," Margaret told him with a smile.

Her father was about to reply when her mother walked through the door. He let go of Margaret and pulled his wife into a tight embrace. "I missed you both so much."

"We've missed you too, Papa."

"Let's get you inside." Her mother's voice was thick. "You look tired."

"The horse—"

"I'll go tell Hanson to take care of him," Margaret said. "Go and rest."

Margaret sat curled into her father's side. He had an arm wrapped around her, holding her close.

"So the war is almost over?" her mother asked.

"It won't be more than a month or two before it's all finished. Salatia is all but beaten, and our armies are putting down small rebellions rather than waging battles against armies," her father told them. "I don't think Salatia expected Frasisca, Radovan, and Mekhor to join the fight. Glessic adamantly refused to join either side, but especially not ours. Salatia was surrounded on all sides by the end."

"Then, why did it take so long?" her mother asked.

"Radovan and Mekhor didn't join until the last few months," her father said. "I don't think they wanted to, but they were starting to hurt from the length of the war."

"Either way, it'll be over soon, and we can all go back to normal." Margaret shifted, sweeping hair away from her face. "I can hardly wait to stop hearing about how frightened all the ladies of the court are."

He looked down at her. "Weren't you frightened?"

Margaret shook her head. "Anatalia has the best army in the world. There's no way we would have lost to Salatia. They don't even train their soldiers!"

"I hope you at least showed your peers some support," he said.

Margaret nodded. "I didn't tell them how silly they were being, at least."

He sighed. "At least you did that."

Margaret stood between her mother and father in the great hall of the palace. The peers had been called for a meeting by the royal family. She looked around curiously. The other nobles whispered to each other, obviously wondering what they were there for. There'd been no gossip circulating as to why the meeting had been called, which was anomalous.

She was uncomfortable with this lack of knowledge. Margaret did not like surprises, especially not when the royal family was concerned, after Prince Gareth had surprised her with the Triburn room.

The royal family came into the front of the room, and the peers bowed or curtsied to them. King Sorren lifted a hand to release them from their positions. "Thank you for coming. We have some news that should please everyone here greatly."

The peers started to whisper again, and the king lifted his hand again to silence them. "My lords, my ladies, I am pleased to announce that the war with Salatia is over." He grinned. "We have won!"

A cheer erupted in the room.

Margaret smiled, looking around at all the happy faces. It was nice to see unadulterated joy for the first time in years. She was happy too; she would not have to spend her time worried about a war and what that might mean for her family.

"There will be a feast this evening," King Sorren said, "along with every night this week, in celebration of our victory."

24

Crompton dreaded reaching the Salatian capital. The countryside where he traveled was still war-torn; broken and burned buildings littered the fields. Half of those fields themselves were burned.

What a waste.

What an awful waste.

Had he known the war would have gone on this long and done this much damage, he never would have suggested it as an option. He would have just found a way to kill Sorren himself. Most of the battles of previous generations had lasted only months, if not weeks, for the sake of human life, but this war had taken none into consideration.

And he would have to live with himself and the part he had played in it.

The familiar Salatian palace came into view when his party crested the hill, its white walls gleaming in the hot Jumonat sun. Armed soldiers lined the entirety of the city preceding it. Crompton couldn't blame them. He would do the same if a party were to arrive at Jalmar after the war.

Crompton lifted his hand to halt the party. "Only myself, Lieutenant Bryant, Ambassador Beaumont, and one man will continue on from here. We don't want the Salatians more on edge than they already are."

"Your Grace," the ambassador said, "is that a good idea?" His beady eyes peered into Crompton's, wider than they normally were.

Crompton leveled him with a hard stare. "You know these people, Ambassador. They were generous enough to send you with the message of war and allow you to return home rather than keeping you prisoner. Do you really think they would hurt you now that we're brokering peace?"

The ambassador looked away. "No."

Crompton turned back to the men. "Set up camp here, and we will send word daily on our progress to ensure that we have not become prisoners for better negotiations." Crompton inhaled deeply, patting his horse on his neck. He would be lucky if his part in the war wasn't brought to light. "Men, ride on."

When they drew closer to the city, ten of the Salatian guards filed into two rows to escort them to the palace. Crompton's neck prickled, and he glanced about, finding several of their escorts glaring at him. These would likely not be the only people to throw vitriol his way.

At the least, he deserved it.

Upon reaching the palace, they were immediately escorted to their rooms. There were only two of King Peralta's counsel to greet them, which was more than Crompton expected. The ambassador was reinstated in his old chambers, and Crompton was given a suite where Alton and the solitary soldier, William, could stay with him.

Crompton motioned Alton into the bedchamber and closed the door behind him to keep William from hearing what he had to say. "When I am in meetings with the king, I want you to find as much evidence with my name on it as you can and hide it until we've left and can decide what to do with it."

Alton furrowed his brow. "Why not just burn it?"

"There might be something in there to protect me later if King Peralta tries to charge me with war crimes." If he did, Crompton would take him down with him.

"I will do my best, Your Grace."

"Good." Crompton clapped him on the shoulder. "Now go clean yourself up. We likely won't leave this room until dinner, and the negotiations won't start until tomorrow."

"What in the hell happened?" King Peralta yelled, throwing his paperweight against the wall. It shattered, small pieces spraying across the floor. "This war was supposed to be ours."

"I was taken out of Salatia and reassigned to the capital. Your Majesty—there was nothing I could do without bringing suspicion on myself." When Crompton saw the king's enraged look, he quickly added, "And you. What do you think would have happened to us if Aratia found out we both brewed up this war? We would have been executed!"

Peralta sighed, sitting heavily across from Crompton. "All those people."

"I know."

"It's our fault."

Inhaling deeply and releasing it slowly, Crompton repeated, "I know."

The king poured them both a drink of dark amber. Crompton started to refuse, but the king cut him off, saying, "We both need one. I don't know about you, but I haven't been able to stop since I realized we wouldn't win."

"It doesn't mean much," Crompton said, taking the drink, "but I'm prepared to offer far more than we would in a normal negotiation."

"You're right, it doesn't mean anything," Peralta snapped. "Hundreds of thousands of my people are dead!"

Crompton took a long drink before he responded. "You could have conceded at the end of a few months, Your Majesty, not waited until three years had passed when other countries got involved." He pulled his lips in to form a flat line before he said any more.

"My pride was at stake!"

"So were your people, and ours. And Sorren is not one to back down." Crompton stood, straightening his jacket. "I should leave before we get heated. I'll see you at the negotiations, Your Majesty."

Crompton wearily sank into one of the plush chairs of his sitting room. A week of negotiations, and they were no closer to having a treaty. Faulting the Salatian king for his part in keeping the war going for so long had been ill-advised, and now the king was taking it out on Crompton. He rubbed his face roughly with both hands, hoping the vigor would scrub away his weariness.

He pulled his hands away from his face when the door opened. Alton entered, looking equally tired.

"Have you found anything yet?"

Alton shook his head. "There's nothing to find."

"Keep looking." Crompton sighed heavily. "We're going to be here a while."

25

L iam mindlessly tossed the cloth ball he had constructed from old clothes into the air. Nothing had happened in quite some time. He didn't even know what day it was. He didn't care what day it was, really. Time meant nothing in this hellscape, his daily feedings blurring together as the hours passed unending. Nothing mattered much to him anymore. There was no point to anything, especially when he already knew what would happen now the war was over.

He'd seen the evidence that Lord General Crompton and Lieutenant Bryant had gathered against him over the last two and a half years. It was extensive and thorough. It would have even Liam believing that he was guilty if he didn't know better. There was no way his judges would find him not guilty.

"Liam?"

Liam jumped, fumbling to catch his ball. The despondent tone scared him more than the sudden appearance of another person. Cedric stood at his cell door.

"Cedric? What are you doing here? Is there something new with my case?"

Cedric shook his head. His shoulders drooped more than usual, and his eyes were full of sympathy. "I'm not here about your case."

Standing, Liam went to the bars. "Then, why are you here?"

"I…" Cedric grabbed the bars as if he needed support. "I'm here about your parents."

"Are they okay?"

"Liam…"

Liam backed away from the bars, a sinking feeling consuming his stomach. "No."

"Liam, I'm sorry. Your parents—"

"I don't want to hear this, Cedric." Liam shook his head. He didn't want to hear anything to do with the tone Cedric had. It wasn't going to be good news.

Cedric hesitated before he said, "Your parents have both passed on. With the high body count of the war, there have been more diseases being spread, and I'm afraid they succumbed to the plague."

Liam shook his head, tears coming to his eyes. His nose burned until he scrunched it. "No. I don't accept it. My father was healthy, and my mother was too scared to leave the house. How could they get the plague?"

"I'm sorry, Liam," Cedric said quietly. "They were buried two weeks ago on the property, and no will was found."

"They didn't have one. We didn't own anything to pass on."

"Do you need anything?"

Liam shook his head, wiping his face. "No."

"I'll leave you, then, to let you grieve." Cedric let go of the bars to his cell. "I'll check on you tomorrow."

Closing his eyes, Liam sat on his cot. This couldn't be happening. His parents were supposed to be safe. They were supposed to outlive him until their hair was white and their joints grew sore with arthritis.

His lips trembled, and he clenched his fists. Tears slipped down his cheeks, and Liam stood once again. Liam paced the small cell, needing to let out his emotions. He didn't know how to feel. He let out a yell and hit his fists against the craggy walls until they were bloody.

Liam collapsed onto his cot, letting out one choking sob.

At the very least, they wouldn't have to see him executed.

Liam watched Cedric sort through his papers, sighing as he waited. He had plenty of time to wait, but he wished Cedric would hurry up.

"Well, I've asked around several places, but it seems like everyone from your old unit in the war—excepting several lords who refuse to talk to me—was killed during battle, so that avenue ended poorly," Cedric said. "I've asked within the city guard where you served before the war, and no one there will listen to me past your name before they start cursing you."

"Should I really be surprised?" Liam asked.

"No." Cedric shook his head. "No, you shouldn't be surprised. No one likes a traitor, guilty or not. And you, my friend, look very guilty at the moment."

"I'm not."

"I'm not here to pass judgment on you, Liam," Cedric assured him. "I'll support whichever claim you make, because that's what I do."

Liam sighed and leaned back against the wall.

"Now, on to your court date. With the war over, the king has requested your court date be set. The next available date is in four weeks, so we have until then to try to find someone who will testify on your behalf."

"The people you've already asked would be the only ones who would support me, and they've already said they wouldn't."

"I'll keep on trying until the day of your trial, but I want you to know it isn't looking good for you," Cedric said.

Liam shrugged. "I didn't expect it to. I'm supposed to be a traitor, after all."

"As long as you know and you won't get your hopes up." Cedric pulled his glasses down his nose. "It makes it easier."

26

Margaret ran down the stairs, holding her shoes in her hands. "Papa!"

"What is it, Mar— What the hell are you wearing?" her father demanded, setting down his paper.

Margaret spun, a grin on her face. She was dressed in one of her most impressive gowns, accentuating her small waist and ample bosom. She had her corset cinched in further than she normally would have. Her kirtle was a deep crimson, a color even the queen rarely dared to wear due to the expense of the dye, opening up to a golden skirt underneath.

The cut was lower than she was usually allowed to wear, barely covering her full figure. She paired the dress with a ruby necklace that had seven stones all told—six medium sized and the largest one dropping down in the center. It was an extravagant outfit; it would show off not only her assets but her wealth as well.

It was past time where she was to be courted and married, and she wanted every man to notice her. She did not want to go for another year without a man asking for permission from her father to court her. Margaret had turned seventeen weeks ago and was disappointed that her mother had already been married for two years by her age, and she was not.

"Do you like it, Papa?"

"No, I do not!" Her father stood, throwing down his paper. "What do you think you're doing, dressing like that?"

"Mama had the dress made for me." Margaret frowned "What's wrong with it?"

"You look like you're about to become a courtesan."

Margaret's mouth dropped open "*Papa!*"

"Where are you planning on going?"

"I want to go to the trial. It's today, and all my friends are going to be there," Margaret told him, crossing her arms under her chest.

"Don't cross your arms like that!" He yelled, averting his eyes and waving a hand in her general direction. "You're not going, and that's final."

"Papa! That's not fair. It's the social event of the year! I must attend this trial, or I'll be the absolute laughingstock of all my friends!" Margaret even stamped her foot to provide the proper emphasis she felt needed to persuade her father.

He raised his brows and looked like he would start counting like he had when she was a child.

"Don't look at me like that! I can hear Ingrid now: 'Oh, little Margaret, your Papa not let you come again? How you must feel for missing all of this!' With her snide little giggles, laughing at me behind my back!" Margaret could feel the heat crawling up her neck. "It would be embarrassing not to be there."

"No." Her father shook his head, picking back up his paper. "Absolutely not."

"Mama said I could go," Margaret complained. "That's why I even have this dress. Mama said it will help me find a husband."

"I don't think you'll find the husband you want, looking like that."

Margaret pouted. "I don't care. It's embarrassing, Papa. All my friends have received at least two proposals, and I can't even get a man to look at me."

It wasn't as if she did not have her own small fortune for her dowry to attract at least a few suitors. Margaret knew it was because they considered her a parvenue, even though she had come to court at a young age and learned everything they had. She noticed the sneers her father had gotten when they were first invited to dine with houses that had held titles for hundreds of years, whereas the Count of Dorcia was a new title.

Her lack of attention had gotten to the point that her friends began to take pity on her and tried to bring her along on some of their long walks to get their suitors to turn their attentions upon Margaret instead of them. It had only added insult to injury after she had lost Charles Luther as a prospective husband.

Her father sighed heavily. "Fine, you can go, Margaret. But you walk away from anyone who makes you feel uncomfortable."

Margaret squealed, kissing him on the cheek. "Thank you, Papa!"

She dropped her shoes and slipped her feet in. Margaret was not waiting for her father to change his mind before she left, and she ran out the door. She had Hanson take her to the palace. It was already crowded, and the trial wouldn't start for several more hours. Margaret looked for her friends, standing on her toes.

They were next to the witness box at the front of the courtroom. Margaret grinned. They had said they wanted to sit there, and they had probably beat people off with their fans just to get to that spot. Margaret rushed over to them and heard their squeals as she approached.

"Sit down, sit down!" Ingrid squealed. "Come on, before someone tries to take it."

Margaret slid onto the bench next to them, her face bright with excitement. "When did you get to the courtroom to be able to get these seats?"

"Hours ago," Elise said. "What took you so long?"

"Papa almost didn't let me come."

"Doesn't he know this is the event of the season?"

"He doesn't like the way I'm dressed." Margaret motioned to her clothing.

Her friends looked her over, shaking their heads. "You'll be certain to catch a husband in that dress," Annalise said.

Margaret nodded, a coy smile on her face. "That's the intention."

Ingrid laughed. "It'll be about time you get some attention."

"Oh, stop." Margaret shook her head. "I've had some attention."

"Oh, yes." Elise chortled. "An ambassador asking you where he can find the kitchens is grand attention."

Margaret glared at them. "That should change today. I've heard there will be several second sons here who would be happy to make my acquaintance."

"All right, Margaret."

"His Grace, the Duke of Rivack, Lord General Tobias Crompton," the herald called out as the Lord General Crompton entered the room.

The king sat with two other judges at the head of the room. King Sorren watched him cross the length of the hall. Margaret was told by one of her friends he would have the main voice in the ruling, but the other judges could at least keep him from making any rash decisions.

Daniel Hershire, the judge to King Sorren's right, stood and cleared his throat. "We are here to hear the case of Private Liam Fulton's treason. His Grace, Lord General Crompton, will be the first to address the court with his testimony." The judge nodded to the duke to start his testimony.

Margaret looked around the room. Why wasn't the traitor there to hear the charges against him? She had never been to a trial, but she thought he should be there for the entirety of the testimonies.

The lord general looked at the crowd. "The traitor was found on the twenty-eighth day of Jumonat, in the year of our Lord 2271, speaking to the Lord General Baur of the Salatian forces. He was giving away tactical positions to our enemy in an attempt to turn the tide of the war in favor of the enemy."

"Do you have any proof of this?" Thomas Wilburn, the judge to Sorren's left, asked.

"When we searched his belongings, we found coded correspondence from the Lord General Baur, going back to before the war started in Fiorar. Many explained what Fulton was supposed to find and the timeline the Salatian's needed the information by," Crompton told the judge and the court. "We even found some of my paperwork and orders directly from the king in his possession. There did not seem to be any rationale behind the traitor's willingness to help the enemy. The evidence has been given to you for your examination."

"How would he have gotten the correspondence?" King Sorren asked, resting his head on his hand.

That was a good question. Margaret looked to the lord general.

He looked taken aback by the question, like it was one he hadn't expected. "Presumably the same way any of our other soldiers received correspondence, through our currier system, which regularly delivered correspondence between soldiers and their families." Crompton pulled his lips into a flat line. "None of the letters had any names in it, other than addressing them to Private Fulton, so he could have even had them passed by enemy soldiers who knew who to look for."

King Sorren narrowed his eyes. "And did you have no one set to look for odd messages and activity?"

"What reason would I have had?" Crompton demanded. "My men were loyal—or so I thought."

"And how did you find him?" Judge Hershire brought the questioning back to the alleged traitor.

"Lieutenant Bryant informed me that Private Fulton had snuck away, and we searched the area he had last been seen. Lieutenant Bryant found him meeting with the enemy, informing him where the troops were going to be next. The Lord General Baur escaped while Lieutenant Bryant apprehended the traitor."

"Are you aware that he says you are the traitor instead and that you were the one meeting with the opposing lord general?" King Sorren leaned forward, looking at Crompton intently.

Margaret looked back and forth between the two—each one stared hard at the other. It looked almost like the king was questioning the lord general instead. Did he suspect that something wasn't all that it seemed?

"I am," Crompton said. "He's been saying it since we found him. It is a weak ploy to call my loyalty into question so that he has a chance of escaping punishment."

"Thank you, Your Grace," Judge Wilburn nodded to the duke. "You may step down."

"We would like to call Lieutenant Bryant, who informed you of the traitor's departure," Judge Hershire announced, looking around the room for a man to stand.

Margaret looked around the room as well. The crowd looked eager to hear whatever the lieutenant had to say. Lieutenant Bryant stood, straightening his uniform before he went to the witness box. The dark blue suited his pale skin, Margaret thought, though it did nothing for his smarmy face.

"Lieutenant Bryant, could you tell us what happened the evening you found Private Fulton?" Judge Wilburn requested.

"Of course, Your Honor. I observed Private Fulton sneaking away from the camp approximately thirty minutes after the sun had set. We'd been having problems with Fulton for the duration of the march, and we now know that was because it was more difficult for him to get his information out to the Salatian lord general." Lieutenant Bryant shifted in his seat, looking around the room. His tone was clinical, as though he'd practiced his speech several times.

"I proceeded to follow Private Fulton into the forest. Once I'd followed him for a while, I found the traitor meeting with the Salatian lord general, and by the end of it, the Salatian was giving Private Fulton a coin purse for giving him our troop movements."

"And did anything result from the passing of that information?" Judge Hershire asked.

"Nearly our entire troop was slaughtered. They were waiting for us at the next city we planned on taking."

"And you didn't think to change your plans after learning Private Fulton had allegedly been giving away troop movements?" Judge Wilburn asked.

Lieutenant Bryant leaned forward. "We were delayed through the winter taking the traitor to Jalmar and then waiting for Lord General Crompton to return from his summons from His Majesty. We thought that it would be safe enough to take the town as planned and that the Salatians would have figured we changed our movements to accommodate the breach."

"And where did you find the evidence?" King Sorren asked.

"We searched his tent after we captured Private Fulton and found the evidence presented hidden in his travel pack."

"Thank you for your testimony, Lieutenant Bryant. You are dismissed." King Sorren said.

"We will take a short recess to review the evidence and testimonies presented," Judge Wilburn said as the three judges stood.

Margaret looked around the room again. The people were whispering to themselves, some of them looking as apprehensive as she felt. All of the testimony felt either too practiced or unprepared. Why wouldn't the lord general have been watching for any sort of odd behavior in his men, and why wouldn't he have noticed if someone were sneaking into his camp?

 **27**

he day of the trial came almost three years to the day of his imprisonment in the royal dungeons. The guards sent in a manservant to help Liam clean and ready himself for being in the king's presence. He was shaved and given a demure version of his military uniform, but without any of his accolades or decoration. It was not quite the apparel he would have expected to be put in, but he was not complaining as it was not the same coarse cotton uniform that he was put in for his day-to-day life in prison.

"Where is Cedric?" Liam asked, looking around for the hunched old man. "He told me he would be here when the trial came."

"He won't be here." The guard urged Liam forward.

"What do you mean he won't be here?" Liam demanded, refusing to walk.

"He died last week." He pushed Liam forward again.

What? Liam had an unexpected pang shoot through his chest. They weren't friends, but they had at least been friendly when Cedric came, and he was Liam's only outside company. "Why didn't anyone tell me? And why wasn't I appointed new counsel?"

"I couldn't tell you that," the guard told him. "Now move."

They probably hadn't told anyone he no longer had counsel to ensure that he would be found guilty. They hated him with a passion. The guard took Liam to a courtroom already filled to the brim with nobility. There was a group of pompous-looking young girls behind where he was to be seated. They whispered to each other while looking at him, vicious excitement in their eyes. It was obvious they wanted a show that only his trial would produce. One of the young girls wore a crimson-and-gold gown that made her more noticeable than the rest. He watched the young woman in red as he was brought to his seat. She was the only one who did not actively whisper to the others. There was no condemnation in her eyes, unlike everyone else in the room.

Liam turned as everyone stood.

"His Majesty, King of Anatalia, King Sorren!" a herald cried out.

The king entered the room. There was an arrogant look on his face, a single eyebrow raised as he walked the length of the courtroom to join his fellow judges. His brown hair and beard were streaked with white, and his eyes looked heavy with the weight of his office. All bowed before him; the king barely glanced at his subjects.

"You have been brought here to answer for the charge of treason," Judge Wilburn started.

"What is it that you have to say for yourself?" The king asked.

"I am not guilty of this treason, Your Majesty," Liam said emphatically.

"Do you have any proof of that?" The king demanded.

"I have no proof but my own word, sir," Liam said slowly, "I am loyal to this country, and I am loyal to you, as loyal as the day I swore my oath of fealty when I took on the mantle of service."

King Sorren leaned on his elbow, his chin in his hand. "Tell us your side of the story. We've already heard His Grace, the Lord General Crompton's side and the testimony of Lieutenant Bryant."

"Yes, sir," Liam said. "I was unable to sleep because of my wounds" —Liam unconsciously rubbed his chest where his wound had been, his brow furrowing— "and I was going for a walk through the camp when I saw Lord General Crompton sneaking away from his tent, an uncommon occurrence for him, especially at night. It would do us no good to lose the lord general on a careless stroll.

"I followed the Lord General Crompton to make sure that he would be safe while he was on his own," Liam told the crowd, adding quickly that he had not taken his guard and that there had been a surprise attack at another battle, making Liam feel uneasy that the lord general would do something so careless. He described the night in detail, talking of the weather and the unease he felt. "I saw him go into the woods, and then I heard him talking to another person."

Liam looked at Lord General Crompton, shaking his head. Crompton didn't look the least bit ashamed of what he had done—of what he was doing to Liam. "I didn't understand until I heard what they were talking about. The lord general was telling Lord General Baur of our strategies and our movements." Anger tightened Liam's shoulders as he glared at the lord general. "And he did it for a few gold coins."

Whispers erupted in the room, shock clear on the people's face that he had accused Lord General Crompton of treason for monetary gain. All eyes went to Lord General Crompton.

He remained calm; he didn't even look bothered that Liam had accused him of trying to overthrow his cousin. Lord General Crompton stood to address the crimes that Liam Fulton had accused him of. "And you believe this traitor? He weaves a catching tale, yet he has no proof. He describes his own story but changes the key characters, as you can tell based on Lieutenant Bryant's testimony."

"His Grace, the Lord General Crompton, wants your throne, Your Majesty," Liam told the king plainly. "He wants to be the next King of Anatalia. He said,

'Sorren is a disgusting lout who neither deserves to rule a country nor to live much longer,' to the Lord General Baur."

The court fell silent, all eyes on the king.

King Sorren sat for a moment with his chin cupped in his fingers, contemplating Liam's testimony. "I have heard what you have to say, but it is my decision that you are indeed the traitor in this event."

Liam looked at him incredulously. "Can you not see Lord General Crompton is the traitor?"

"You will remain silent," the king commanded.

"How can you not see that Crompton is lying to your face? How he fabricated evidence against me to cover his tracks?" Liam demanded. Heat traveled to Liam's face, his cheeks burning, the angrier he became. "Are you so blind that you cannot see the snake in your own garden?"

King Sorren stood, his own face red. "Guards, remove this man. Liam Fulton, you will be executed for treason!" The king yelled as he was taken out of the courtroom.

"He is the traitor!" Liam yelled as he was dragged by the arms. "This is not justice!"

The guards threw Liam into his cell with disgusted looks on their faces. "Good riddance, traitor."

Liam put his face in his hands. How could this be happening to him? He was no traitor; he was loyal to his country. He could not be put to death for a crime that he had not committed. Liam would not allow this to happen. Surely, there was something he could do to right the situation.

28

Margaret covered her lips with her fingers. She could still hear Liam yelling in the corridor. She looked around the courtroom and saw the other ladies looked much the same as she did.

"That was invigorating!" Ingrid's eyes were bright with excitement.

Elise nodded. "I knew he was guilty."

Margaret would have to disagree. Someone who had sat in a cell and maintained his innocence for three years couldn't be guilty. Could he? She didn't think so, but the evidence was compelling, even with the rehearsed feeling from the Lord General Crompton and Lieutenant Bryant. Standing with her friends, she started to file out of the seating. "We should go," Margaret said. "I want to get away from here."

"Why?"

Margaret shuddered. "I can still hear him screaming. It was such a horrible sound."

"All right, we can go." Ingrid stood on her toes, looking around the room. "People are starting to leave, anyway."

Following them, Margaret kept her head down as she walked. She gasped when she ran into someone. "My apologies!" Margaret finally looked up and blushed.

He smiled, his white teeth gleaming. "No apology necessary, my lady. It was my fault."

"Oh, no." Margaret put a hand to her chest. "It was mine. I wasn't looking where I was going."

"I'm glad that you weren't." His bright blue eyes roved her face. "What's your name, my lady?"

Elise came up behind her, linking arms with Margaret. "This is the Lady Margaret, daughter of the Count of Dorcia. And you are?"

"Elise," Margaret whispered, "I can handle a conversation by myself, thank you."

"Lord Nicholas, son of the Baron of Marcel." He picked up Margaret's hand and gently kissed her knuckles. "It's a pleasure to make your acquaintance, my lady."

Margaret blushed and pulled her hand away. "It's nice to meet you, Lord Nicholas."

"May I escort you home, Lady Margaret?"

"You may," Ingrid said for her. "She lives in Cerule House."

Margaret's jaw dropped. "Ingrid! Shouldn't I be the one to answer?"

Lord Nicholas linked arms with Margaret. "I would love to get to know you better, my lady. Won't you let me?"

Her cheeks warmed. Wasn't this what she wanted? Margaret looked between her friends, who all looked back at her with bright eyes and excited smiles. "It's a very long walk from here."

"The longer, the better," Nicholas answered, grinning at her.

"Go on, Margaret!" Ingrid nearly shoved the pair toward the door. "We'll talk to you tomorrow."

"Shall we go, my lady?"

Margaret didn't know why she was hesitating. Her whole goal of the day was to find a suitor, and there was finally one standing in front of her. She smiled up at him. "I suppose we shall."

Nicholas grinned back at her, patting her hand on his arm. "Would you like to go a more direct way…or the long way?"

Margaret swallowed. "The long way, please."

Nicholas was quite handsome, Margaret had to admit. He was taller than her by a few inches, but he did not tower over her, and she did not need to strain her neck to look at him. His eyes reminded her of her father: kind and soft. He had a strong jaw only lightly dusted with stubble. Margaret wondered what it would feel like against her cheeks.

"As my lady commands." He led her from the palace. "How is it that I've never seen you before?"

Likely because Margaret had never worn something so daring. "I don't know, my lord. Perhaps it was the war?"

Nodding, Nicholas said, "It would have to be. I doubt I would pass up such a pretty face without vying for your attention."

"Were you in much danger?" Margaret asked, her cheeks warm. "In the war, I mean."

"I fought alongside the Lord General Crompton in the war—we were fortunate to have a very elite force."

"Does that mean that you served with Private Fulton?"

Nicholas's face darkened, his dark brown brows furrowing. "Unfortunately so. We did not get along, I'm afraid."

Margaret looked up at him, worrying on her bottom lip. "Do you think he could do such a thing?"

"I do, without a doubt," he said quickly. "There was plenty of evidence against him." Nicholas paused their walk. "Do you not?"

Margaret shrugged slightly. "I don't know. I don't know if I can believe any of our soldiers could wish ill on Anatalia."

Nicholas let out a short laugh. "If only we could all have your innocence, Lady Margaret. We would be a better world for it."

Margaret blushed, looking down at the road. "Surely, you don't believe everyone has ill intent, my lord?"

"I believe that you don't," he said. "And that is a wonderful thing to see."

They walked for a while in silence, the cool air urging her closer to Nicholas. She should have brought a shawl with her, not only to cover up, but to keep herself— Margaret started when she felt a heavy coat fall over her shoulders. She looked at Nicholas, now without his woolen uniform jacket.

"You were shaking so hard, I thought you would break your teeth, Lady Margaret," he said. "Unless, my presence is making you shake?"

Margaret pulled the jacket tighter around her, smiling at him. His pleasant smell enveloped her, warming her cheeks as thoroughly as his jacket did. "It's the cold, I assure you. It's unusually chilly for Semonat."

"Good. I would hate for this to be our only encounter." He grinned at her, showing his pearly white teeth sitting in straight rows.

They talked companionably the rest of the way to Cerule House. Margaret turned to him when they reached her front door. "Thank you; I've enjoyed this."

"May I see you again?" His dark brown hair fell into his eyes, and he swiped it away with a small smile.

"You...want to see me again?" Margaret almost laughed. No one ever wanted to see her again.

"Of course I do." Nicholas smiled at her. "I've had a very good time with you."

"I don't think my father would be opposed to my seeing you again." Margaret pulled his jacket from her shoulders and handed it to him. She loathed to give up its warmth, but by now, he needed it far more than she did. "Why don't you come calling some time next week?"

"I'm already looking forward to it." He bent forward, kissing her hand.

Margaret smiled at him as he walked away, rushing inside quickly after.

"How was the trial?" Her mother asked.

"It was emotionally charged." Margaret sat across from her in the library. "I almost wish I hadn't gone."

Her mother laughed. "Don't tell your father that."

"I won't." Margaret looked to her mother with a small smile tugging on her lips. "I have a gentleman caller coming next week."

Her mother set down her book. "Really?"

Margaret nodded. "I met him today at the trial. He was a soldier in the war, and he's the son of a baron."

"A baron?" Her mother frowned. "I'm not sure that's appropriate for you. At least try for the inheriting son of a duke."

"Mama, he's the first man to show any interest in me," Margaret whined. "The only way I'd even get close to a duke is being a courtesan."

Her mother looked her over slowly. "Well…"

"Mama! I will not become a courtesan!" Margaret stood, her fists clenched at her side.

"You're the one who brought it up, Margaret."

Margaret glared at her. "I can't believe you'd even consider it."

"It could be very lucrative for you."

"Ugh!" Margaret stormed out of the room, running up to her room and slammed the door. How could her mother prefer her to be a whore than be involved with someone below her rank?

A gentle knock sounded on Margaret's bedroom door. "My lady?" her maid called. "Your gentleman caller is on his way."

Margaret unceremoniously tossed her book on her bed and ripped open the door. She'd lost hope that Nicholas was going to come—it'd been two weeks since they'd met, and she hadn't heard from him since. She was beginning to believe that, like all the others, he'd lost interest in her after their initial meeting and moved on. "He's coming?"

Her maid nodded. "Yes, my lady."

Margaret squealed and pushed past the maid. She went down to the library, where they received visitors, and sat impatiently in a chair by the window. She wanted to look her best when he arrived.

Her father came into the room, paper in hand. "I understand you're to have a visitor?"

Margaret nodded. "The gentleman I met at the trial, Papa."

"I should like to meet the man who makes my daughter so excited," he said.

"He's very handsome."

"I'm sure that he is."

"And he seems intelligent," Margaret added. "And kind."

He smiled. "Kind is good."

Bruggen entered the doorway, clearing his throat. "Lady Margaret, a Lord Nicholas to see you."

Margaret smiled brightly, standing. She smoothed her skirts and clasped her hands in front of her. Nicholas wore his uniform, the dark blue bringing out his eyes. His hair was perfectly combed, not a hair out of place.

Her father was the first to reach him, hand held out. Nicholas grasped it firmly and nodded respectfully. "My lord."

Margaret joined them, letting Nicholas pick up her hand. As he kissed it, she said, "Papa, may I present to you Lord Nicholas Oliphant?

 **29**

It had been two weeks since he had been thrown back into his cell to wait for the executioner. Liam lay in wait for the guards who were coming to take him to his execution. Today was the day the king had set for him to die, and he was having none of it. Liam had loosened one of the stones of his cell and held it in his hand under the coarse blanket on his cot. He had to prove his innocence; he would not be put to death for something he had nothing to do with except the misfortune of witnessing it.

Liam's heart pounded as he heard the guards approaching his cell. They were laughing as they came up to him. "Are you ready to be quartered?" One of them asked gleefully.

"Or burned?" The other asked.

"Or both," they chimed together with a chuckle.

Liam felt sick as they joked so flippantly about his death. He waited for them to open the door to his prison cell, his heart pounding harder. Liam waited for them to come in the small room before he attacked behind the small wall of privacy in front of his cot, stone raised high. He hit the first guard with the full force of his strength. A sickening crack sounded, and the guard went down with a gush of blood over Liam's hand. He started at the felled guard—he thought he'd killed his last man in the war.

Liam yelled when he was tackled from the side. He was flipped onto his back by the other guard, and Liam raised his hands to his face to shield himself against the rain of punches coming down. He didn't have time for this.

He kicked out to get the guard off him. Liam was tempted to run out of the cell, but he had to make sure the guard wouldn't follow and recapture him for his execution. Liam came to his feet and steeled himself. It was him or the guard, and he chose the guard. He grabbed the guard by his hair and beat his head against the floor until he stopped moving.

Liam wiped the blood from his hands before poking his head out of the cell. There were some advantages to being in a cellblock of his own—there were no other guards coming to help the fallen. Now he needed to figure out how to get out. He looked at the guards, contemplating taking one of their uniforms, but both were drenched with blood. They would raise more suspicion than if he just walked out.

He'd heard there were sewers running under the palace that dumped out into the ocean a few miles away. Looking around, there wasn't much choice. He could either go further into the dungeons to find this sewer, or he could try to sneak out from the surface.

Inhaling deeply, Liam turned to go further into the dungeons. The surface would only get him killed, and he hadn't murdered two guards just to die now. He didn't have any other choice but to find the sewer, and fast. If he didn't, he'd go down in a fight with the guards. He would *not* be paraded in front of the people as a traitor before he was killed. The walls got darker as he went further down, and Liam grabbed a torch from the wall hook before he risked coming across a corridor without any light.

After descending several more levels, Liam could follow his nose to find the sewer. The smell was overpowering once Liam came to the end of the hall. He held his torch farther out in front of him to see what came next—there was no closing wall at the end of the hall. Instead, there was a platform and a murky river beyond it. Liam grimaced before he spotted thigh waders. He settled the torch in one of the wall hooks before slipping on the boots. He didn't want to think about what was on them, what he would walk through in only moments.

Liam grabbed the torch from the wall again and followed the stairs down into the murk. He gagged as his steps stirred the smell. It was worth it. The smell was worth it. His freedom would be worth it.

He scowled at the sucking sound his legs made as he walked.

It was worth it.

The smell was worth it.

His freedom would be worth it.

Liam kept those three thoughts at the forefront of his mind as he followed the flow of the filth. The river got higher on his legs the farther he went. He couldn't tell, but he thought the ceiling was getting lower.

It was.

It was getting lower, and Liam soon had to stoop to avoid his head scraping the ceiling. He supposed it was willful ignorance for him to think that he would have an easy walk right out into the ocean. He wasn't in the gardens; he was in the sewers. Sewers probably designed to only allow waste to escape.

The ceiling continued to fall, and soon liquid spilled over Liam's stolen boots. "Ugh," he groaned, stomach turning and threatening to empty.

It was worth it.

The smell was worth it.

His freedom would be worth it.

Liam spotted a small light at the end of the tunnel and reluctantly dropped his torch. There wasn't much room left to hold it, anyway. When the ceiling became too low, he dropped to his knees and crawled the rest of the way. As the end came nearer, he had to lie on his stomach and pull himself through the muck—and occasionally his own vomit.

It was worth it.

The smell was worth it.

His freedom would be worth it.

His hands gripped the lip of the end of the tunnel. Liam inhaled the fresh—or at least mostly fresh—air and let out a whoop. He was almost there. He just needed to—

His stomach fell. The drop below him was at least sixty feet. No wonder there were no bars at the opening. Who would climb this height and crawl through a river of shit just to invade the palace? There were better ways, and the builders knew it.

Gripping the lip tightly, Liam pulled himself carefully out of the tunnel. He would try to climb down instead of jumping straight into the Bragasso Ocean. He just had to keep his grip from slipping before he—

Liam yelled as he fell back.

He had to turn.

He couldn't land on his back. He would break it and drown, and then all of this would have been for nothing.

Liam barely got his feet down before he hit the water. He tried not to yell, but his mouth filled with water anyway. He clawed his way to the surface and sputtered, gasping for breath. He swam until the water was clear, rinsing his mouth of the foul taste of sewer.

He'd done it.

He'd escaped, and he'd survived.

Liam's clothes had stains on them that would not come out in the salty water. Liam would need to find a place where he could get new clothes, and fast. He would head for the Salatian border to escape from the soldiers who would soon be searching for him. After the war, they would not be welcome in Salatia. Once he crossed the border, he would travel down to Glessic.

He waded in the water until he could no longer smell the waste. He would travel eastward toward Reung and Dorcia. Dorcia would be the place for him to gather lasting supplies until he could get to Glessic. Like his fellow soldiers, he wouldn't be welcome in Salatia as an Anatalian, and he did not intend to stop near people.

Liam trudged onto the sandy beach and lay in the sun for a moment. He wouldn't have long to rest, but he wanted to bask in the sun. Just for a moment.

When he was finished, he took off his boots and dumped the contents, scrunching his nose. Liam washed them out in the waves, his legs and feet included, before he made his way along the coast to the forested area. He would be safer once he had more cover. He felt vulnerable in the open.

Night would fall soon, and he would rest until then. He planned on traveling through the dark to get ahead of the inevitable search party.

Liam felt tension leave his shoulders when his parents' home came into view. He knew they wouldn't be there, but he could visit their graves, at least. He wasn't sure he wanted to go to the house, but his mother had kept a bag under the floorboards with clothes for all of them and money in case they ever had to leave in a hurry. He'd thought her crazy for it—he still did if he was honest with himself—but he was thankful for it now.

As Liam got closer, he saw the garden was overgrown and browning, and the grapes in the fields were swollen to near bursting. No one had taken the place of his parents yet—good. No doubt, people were still reeling from the war and hadn't had time to fill the position of a single viticulturist.

Steeling himself, Liam opened the front door.

Everything looked the same as the last time he had been there, except for the rotting food in the kitchen. Liam was a little surprised the house hadn't been ransacked for supplies. He went to his parents' room, pausing to take it in. He thought of taking the marriage quilt his mother had made from the bed, but if his parents had died of plague, he should touch nothing other than the bag under the floorboards.

Liam knelt on the floor near the corner, pulling at boards until they started to lift. He pulled out the pack and removed his mother's clothes before changing his mind and putting them back. He could use his mother's skirts as a blanket if there was a chill in the night.

As much as Liam wanted to stay, he shouldn't linger anywhere long. He went to the back where the graves would be. They were side by side under one of the trees. He wasn't quite sure how to feel; he'd thoroughly mourned them while he was in prison; their passing held a distant sorrow for him now. They were better off where they were, without having to live with the shame that not only was their son accused of treason, but was also now a murderer.

"I'm sorry." He rested his hand on the raised earth. "I love you."

Liam looked over his shoulder, eyes wild. He'd spotted soldiers on the road and darted into the forest to the left. He hoped they hadn't seen him, but he lost hope when he heard shouting behind him.

"He's over there!"

Liam let out a curse and broke into a run. He held his arm in front of his face to keep any low-hanging branches from hitting him. He tripped on a high root, going down hard. Liam gasped, curling into himself. He couldn't stay there long. They would catch him if he did. He groaned as he uncurled and stumbled to his feet, trying to run again.

He was tackled from behind soon after, falling on another root. Liam gasped for breath, wiggling against his assailant.

"You're under arrest, Private Fulton," one said. "You're to be taken back to the capital for execution by order of His Majesty."

"No!" Liam yelled. "I'm innocent!" He struggled to get out from under the soldier. "You can't take an innocent man to his death."

"You're not an innocent man, Private. You murdered two men in your escape."

The two other soldiers pulled Liam up, holding him between them. Liam ripped his arms from the soldiers and took off at a run. He left the forest and went to the road for a faster run. It would be easier to find him, but he was close to the Salatian border. Anatalian citizens were permitted to cross over the border, but no Anatalian soldiers were permitted to enter the country. It was the safest place for Liam at the moment.

"Stop him!" One of the soldiers yelled, slightly out of breath. "He can't cross that border!"

Liam urged his legs to go faster. The border was in sight. He had to get to it, or he'd be dead. He could not see any Salatian soldiers patrolling the border, which could be either good or bad for him: good, that he could get through the border with no question; bad, because so could the soldiers in pursuit of him. Liam hoped they were more afraid of the consequences of going into Salatia than they were of not catching him when they had the chance.

Breathing hard, Liam pounded over the wooden bridge poised over the Frasisca River separating Anatalia and Salatia. He chanced a look over his shoulder and saw the soldiers had stopped at the bridge. Liam grinned, leaning over and resting his hands on his knees. He wanted to revel in this moment, but he knew if he gloated too much, he would be welcoming them to Salatia.

"Watch your back, Private. We'll be waiting for you," one of the soldiers called over the bridge. "And we won't let you get away next time."

Liam only nodded and turned around to walk further into Salatia. He was free. For now, at least.

30

Margaret walked into the great hall on Nicholas's arm. "I wonder what's going on?"

Nicholas shook his head. "I'm sure we'll find out soon enough with your friends."

Laughing, she searched for them. "What's going on? Why does everyone look like they want to run from the hall and go home?"

"The traitor escaped last night. He killed his guards when they went to bring him to his execution, and fled," Ingrid said. "No one can find him."

"*What?*" Nicholas demanded. "Have they formed a search party?"

"One immediately after, and more are forming now," Ingrid told him. "The men are gathering in the courtyard."

Nicholas left without a word, and Margaret frowned at him. "Goodbye, I guess."

"He just wants to help," Ingrid said. "Come here with the rest of us. We're trying to figure out who this traitor really is. No one here knows anything about him."

"He was a city soldier before the war," Margaret said. "I saw him patrolling with the Third—he was the one who was chasing after that thief when I hurt my arm."

"Why didn't you tell us this before?" Annalise demanded.

Margaret shrugged. "It wasn't important, and you were there the same time I was. Everyone knew he was a soldier."

"But you knew who he was before anyone else did."

"I've never even spoken to him." Margaret shrugged. She didn't understand why having seen him on the streets was a revolutionary thing. If they had been paying attention, they would have seen him too. "I wouldn't have had the opportunity."

"But you recognized him," Ingrid complained. "That's better than everyone else in the room."

"That's all I know about him," Margaret said. "I swear. I don't know anything else. What are the other ladies saying?"

Annalise spoke up before anyone else could. "He's apparently from a poor family in Rivack, and he joined the army to support them, if anyone here is to be believed."

"Then how did he have such clear speech?" Elise asked.

"Maybe his parents paid to have him sent to a lord's house for etiquette lessons?" Ingrid asked. "It's fairly common."

"That's certainly a possibility," Margaret said. "He was very well-spoken."

"You said you didn't know anything else, Margaret!" Ingrid complained.

"I don't! You heard him in court too; you know how he speaks," Margaret fired back.

"I wonder where he'll go?" Elise asked.

Ingrid laughed. "Far away from here, if he's smart."

"What do you think His Majesty will do?" Annalise asked.

"I can ask Nicholas when he comes back. He's still in the army," Margaret said. "He might have an idea where Liam might go. He served with him during the war. They didn't get along very well."

"Margaret, I swear, if you hold anything back again, we're leaving you behind," Ingrid said.

"I promise, that's all."

"We've never sat this close before," Margaret said as they were seated in front of the head table.

"Well, my dear, the king likes us," her father said.

"Then, why haven't we sat closer before?" Margaret asked. "We've always been a few tables back."

"Because we have to follow protocol, Margaret." Her mother sighed. "We have to let our betters come before us."

"But Papa is one of His Majesty's closest friends," Margaret complained. "And you're good friends with him too."

"And that's why we're as close as we usually are," her father said. "You're going to be a maid of honor to the queen, and that will also help elevate our status."

Margaret opened her mouth to ask another question, but her mother cut her off. "Enough questions, Margaret. We're sitting closer, and that's that."

The meal began, and they waited patiently for food to be sent to them. One of the footmen brought a platter of salmon to their table. "From the queen, with her regards," he said, serving the fish on to their plates.

"Salmon?" her mother asked, her voice raising, looking to the head table.

Queen Lillian raised her glass to them, a smile on her face.

Her mother glared at her before turning to her father. "I hate salmon. Her Majesty should know this after the last time it was served and I got sick," she said not too quietly. "Perhaps she should work on her memory."

The crowd around them quieted and looked to the queen. She was glaring directly at Margaret's mother, her cheeks red.

Margaret looked between her mother, the queen, and her father. Her father's face was pale, except for his cheeks. He looked equal parts livid and mortified. He stood, the cutlery clanging against the plates as he took her mother's arm in his hand.

"What are you doing?" her mother demanded.

"You're leaving," he whispered harshly. "Get up, now."

"Papa?" Margaret asked.

"Stay there, Margaret. I'll be back in a moment."

Her father escorted her mother from the dining hall, his back stiff. The hall was silent as they walked out. Margaret looked around the room and saw everyone was staring at her parents. She turned her gaze back to her plate, her face as red as her wine.

Slowly, the room filled with conversation again. About them. That had not been a wise move on her mother's part, and Margaret hoped it wouldn't keep her from being a maid of honor for the queen. She wanted to bring honor to her family.

When her father returned to the hall, several eyes followed him. She and her father ate in silence and left as soon as they were able. "I'll speak to the king tomorrow, but we should likely stay away from court," he said as they climbed into the carriage. "At least until Charles's wedding at week's end."

Margaret sighed. She didn't want to see Charles married to another woman. She had Nicholas now, yes, but Charles was her first love. "Papa, do I really need to go to that?"

"Yes, you do, Margaret," her father said sharply, "and I want that to be the last I hear of that."

"You're going, Margaret, and that's final," her father said from her doorway. "Now, get dressed in the dress your mother had made for you, and come downstairs."

"I don't want to go!" Margaret whined. "I don't want to see Charles get married to that—that woman! She's horrible for him, and we both know it."

Her father rolled his eyes. "Charlotte is a fine woman, and I happen to like her. You're just upset that Charles didn't marry you like you wanted."

"That's not fair, Papa." Margaret crossed her arms over her chest, the black and gold brocade waffling under the pressure.

"But it's why you're acting up."

Margaret glared at him. "You're starting to sound like Mama."

"Get changed into your new dress and out of this black thing, and come downstairs," he commanded.

She threw herself on her bed with a groan. She knew it was silly to pout over Charles marrying someone he loved. He wasn't obligated to play into her fantasies, no matter how much she wanted him to. It was not as if he'd ever shown her any sort of interest over the years, but she had still held out hope.

Margaret changed her dress with the help of her maid and went downstairs. "Are you happy now?"

"I'd be happier if you lost that attitude before we got to the church," her father said. "I don't want you to ruin this day for Charles. He's very important to me."

"Aren't my feelings important to you?" Margaret whined.

"Not right now, no."

Margaret crossed her arms and glared at him.

"Come on, then," he said as he walked toward the door. "We're going to be late if we don't leave now."

"What about Mama?" Margaret asked. "I don't see her."

"She was already in the city and is going to meet us there."

Margaret sighed and walked out the door.

Hanson was already waiting with the carriage door open. "Good afternoon, Lady Margaret." He offered her his hand.

She took it as she got into the carriage. "Thank you, Hanson."

"Take us to Saint Germaine's chapel, please, Hanson," her father said as he got into the carriage.

"Very good, my lord." Hanson closed the door to the cab and climbed into the front bench.

It didn't take long to get to Saint Germaine's chapel. Margaret wished it would have taken longer and that they were late for the wedding. She didn't want to see him marry. At least, not anyone but her.

Her father escorted Margaret into the church, finding a seat on the groom's side. Margaret paused when she saw Charles at the front of the church. He looked better than she had ever seen him. He was in his best suit, his strawberry blond hair shining golden red in the light.

He grinned when he saw them and came to their sides. "My lord! Lady Margaret, I'm so glad you could make it today." Charles clasped her father's hand, his smile still large.

"We wouldn't miss it for the world," her father told him, and meant it.

"Of course," Margaret agreed reluctantly. "We only want to see you happy."

Charles gently clasped Margaret's upper arm, squeezing it. "Soon we'll see you marry and go out on your own."

Margaret's smile fell from her face. "We'll see."

Music started from the back of the church, and Charles made his apologies to them before returning to his appointed spot. Margaret looked to the back of the church and fought the urge to scowl. Charlotte looked beautiful in her gown, her blonde hair shining gold in the light spilling through the doorway. Margaret looked back toward Charles, and his jaw was slack, and tears were gathered in his eyes. She'd lost him, she knew.

The ceremony was kept short, lasting no more than fifteen minutes. Margaret was glad for it; she felt sick to her stomach, watching them express their love for each other. "Papa, do we have to go to the reception? Mama didn't even show up for the wedding."

"Yes, we're going." He herded her toward the door. "And you have to stay for the whole thing."

"But, Papa!" Margaret stopped at the door, turning to face him. "This is miserable for me."

"You're acting like a child, Margaret. It's unbecoming of a young lady of your station," her father scolded, pulling her away from the people starting to stare. "I want you to keep quiet and pretend like you're enjoying yourself for my sake and for Charles's sake. Besides, you have Lord Nicholas to keep your attention, or have you forgotten all about him in your childish tantrum?"

"Fine." Margaret turned on her heels and stormed out of the church. Shame heated her cheeks. She was being selfish; she did have Nicholas, and he was good to her, and here she was still hoping Charles would see her blossomed before him and abandon his wife.

31

The farther Liam traveled toward Glessic, the more his stomach filled with dread. Shouldn't he at least try first to find some evidence on his behalf that he was innocent? He slowed his pace, sighing. He would have to turn back.

Liam made his camp outside of Chenalieu. The area hadn't changed much since he had last been there, and the horrors he had seen and done haunted him still. They would always haunt him, he suspected. He found himself unconsciously looking for Jorren in the surrounding area.

Rubbing the scar on his chest, Liam looked away. Jorren wasn't there—he wouldn't be there. Even if he had somehow survived that battle, nearly everyone except some of the noblemen in his unit had been killed. It pained him, knowing Jorren had gotten them both assigned to the lord general's unit only to have both of their lives cut short. Liam hadn't lost his, but his life would never be the same.

Once his camp was set up, Liam went in search of his dinner. He could find fish in one of the streams easily enough. He pulled out his small rod, which was simply a stick with a line and a hook tied to it. He didn't need much more for the type of fishing he would do.

He let his mind wander as he waited. Was he doing the right thing, going straight in and looking for evidence? For all he knew, he'd be captured here and returned to Anatalia for his execution.

He sighed heavily. He could start a new life somewhere else with a new name and a new background. He could be a farmer like his father. That had been enough for him—why couldn't it be enough for Liam?

But he knew.

He knew why it wasn't enough. Liam's name and reputation were everything to him, and he couldn't live with himself without clearing it. And he couldn't live with himself killing his guards to escape if he wasn't going to do anything with his second chance.

Liam approached the city of Chenalieu cautiously. He kept his head down, avoiding eye contact with most people. He wasn't quite sure what he was doing or where he'd find information, but he would still try. He searched for the nearest pub and looked for the area with the most men. He'd found that all military men liked to commiserate with each other over a drink or two.

He let out a single laugh when he saw a group of five men in the corner, with several empty pints between them. There was an empty seat close to the bar that Liam took up. He didn't want to go straight to their table; that would be suspicious. Liam couldn't afford suspicious. Not now, not for the rest of his life.

Liam lifted a finger at the barkeep and waited for his pint. He inhaled deeply, rubbing his eyes.

"Ye all right, son?"

Liam looked around, expecting the barkeep to have spoken. When the barkeep pointed behind Liam, he turned around. It was one of the men at the table.

"I'm all right, thanks."

"D'ye serve?" the bulkiest of the men asked.

"I did," Liam said hesitantly.

He waved Liam over. "Come sit with us old folk an' tell us about yer time."

Liam smiled slightly. He could always depend on old military men wanting to talk. He grabbed his pint and pulled up a chair to his table. "I did like the rest of my countrymen and fought. I can't say I was too happy with the outcome."

"None of us were, son," the eldest said, "none of us were."

Liam raised his glass. "To the fallen."

The other men raised theirs as well before taking long drinks. If there was anything that either side could agree on, the loss of life was to be grieved. By the look on the men's faces, they had lost an equal amount to Liam.

"Where'd'ye serve?"

"I was lucky to be further north, by the river." Liam hadn't gotten many reports in his cell, but he had heard that a group had broken through the border in the north, over the Frasiscan River, near the end of the war. They had occupied a town and, at the end of the war, left at the first request and without bloodshed.

The eldest grunted and crossed his arms, clearly unimpressed. "Buncha lily-livers that lot."

Liam smiled and took a long drink. "But living lily-livers."

The bulky one laughed, slapping Liam on the shoulder. "That ye are. What brings ye here?"

"I'm going to see my sister," Liam lied. He thought about adding more detail, but keeping it simpler was better. "Did you serve here?"

"Aye." The bulky man leaned back. "We got lucky too. Weren't for the Hero of Chenalieu, we'd've had much worse."

Liam furrowed his brow. 'The Hero of Chenalieu'? "Who's that?"

"That Anatalian who fought with Lord General Crompton." The elder man looked incredulously at Liam. "Without 'im, we'd've been slaughtered. They stopped the fightin' after that to deal with 'im, and we were able to use the information he gave Lord General Baur to kill every Anatalian here."

So it was him. He was the hero for betraying his people in their eyes. The ale in his stomach turned sour. He forced himself to finish his pint and stood. "As much as I'd like to stay and talk more about the war, I should be on my way."

Liam left, sick to his stomach. Clearly, getting help to clear his name in Salatia was going to be much harder than he thought.

Liam pulled his hood further down his face to obscure his identity. He wasn't sure why he'd returned to Anatalia. He knew his return could mean his death. After a year of being gone, the siren call of his homeland had been too much for him, and he'd crossed over the border a few weeks ago. He'd stopped in a few of the smaller villages to beg for food and had been fairly successful in getting it, even if it was just a loaf of bread shoved through the cracked door.

He'd seen soldiers on the road, but Liam hoped that, having grown his hair and beard out, he would be harder to identify than when he'd escaped. Especially since it seemed Lieutenant Bryant and Lord General Crompton still blamed him for their own crimes and hadn't stopped since Liam's escape a year ago. It seemed they were very well connected with the seediest people.

Another village was coming into view, and his stomach growled uproariously. Liam would stop for a bite to eat and nothing more. He didn't want to risk bringing the wrath of the soldiers on the innocent people of the village. Since the Lord General Crompton had continued his crimes in Liam's name, the king had updated Liam's warrant to say that anyone found helping him would be executed right alongside him. After that, he'd avoided people as much as possible and only came close when game was sparse.

Liam went to one of the last houses he could see on the village street and knocked on the door. It opened not long after, and a burly man appeared in the doorway.

"What do you want?" he asked.

"Do you have any food to spare?"

"I don't think—"

"I don't want much, even some spare bread would be enough," Liam said. "I don't even need a full loaf."

The man sighed. "Wait here." He disappeared from the doorway and reappeared with a quarter loaf of bread. "This is all we have to spare."

"Thank you, truly." Liam held the bread up with a smile. "It will be a feast."

Liam left before the man could say anything else. He didn't want to be seen here if soldiers were following him. There was a forested area not too far away, where he could hide and eat in peace. He stuck mostly to the forests anyway; it was an easier place to hide, especially now that he only wore earth tones and could easily blend in with the woods.

He found a nice shaded area to sit with his water skin and newly acquired meal. Liam sighed, relaxing against a wide tree trunk. It wasn't where he'd expected to be by now, but it was better than dead. There were many times he wanted to give up and settle in another country, but he couldn't rest until he cleared his name. His conscience wouldn't allow it.

Liam shot from his sitting position when he heard yelling. He moved to the treeline and saw soldiers in the village.

"Where is he?" one asked.

"Who?" a villager asked.

"The traitor, Liam Fulton. We saw him enter this village less than an hour ago."

"No one new's been here all day."

"Get everyone out here," the soldier commanded. "We want to talk to everyone. Someone must have seen him and where he went."

Liam climbed up a tree to get a better view of the village and to keep out of the soldier's eyeline in case they searched the forest. The three other soldiers began beating on doors and pulling people out of their homes, pushing them toward the center road. The first soldier waited until everyone was gathered before holding up a parchment. Liam felt sick to his stomach. He shouldn't have gone into the village when he saw the soldiers. He should have stayed in the forests and tried harder for game.

"This man was seen less than an hour ago, entering this village. He is wanted by the king for treason and the murder of two men," the soldier said. "His appearance will have changed—we believe he now sports a beard and longer hair. Have any of you seen him?"

The villagers remained silent, looking between each other, waiting for someone to speak up. Liam hoped when no one did, the soldiers would leave them alone. Only one person had seen him, he thought, and that was the man he'd asked for bread.

The soldier walked down the line. "Any person found helping the traitor will also be executed, but we don't think that's fair. You might not know it's him. If you have helped him, we won't follow that order. Have you seen this man?"

The man in front of the soldier shook his head.

The soldier moved to the next man, and the next, and the next, with similar results. The longer this went on, the sicker Liam felt. He shouldn't have pushed his luck.

Finally, the man who gave him bread spoke up. "I gave a man some bread when he came to the door. He looked like a beggar, not a traitor."

Liam's stomach tightened. He hoped the soldiers would keep good on their promise of leniency.

"That's more like it," the soldier said. "Now where did he go?"

The burly man shrugged. "I didn't pay attention past him leaving my front door."

The soldier hit him in the gut, doubling him over. "That's not good enough. You know where he went, and you're going to tell us."

Once he'd gotten his breath back, the burly man said, "I don't know where he went, and I don't care where he went."

The soldier hit him again. "Wrong answer."

Liam felt sick with each wrong answer the burly man gave the soldier, who in turn hit him again. He didn't want to watch any longer, but he couldn't stop. He needed to know what happened.

The burly man was now lying on the ground, face bloodied. "I don't know where he is." He struggled with each word.

"I don't know why you're doing this to yourself." The soldier kicked him in the face. "You're just going to get yourself hurt." The soldier kicked him again. "And I'm real tired of you lying to me, because I know you know where he is."

Liam watched in horror as the soldier kicked the man until he no longer moved.

"Take this as an example," the soldier said to the remaining villagers. "If we come to you again asking about a traitor, you will tell us the information we want, or this is what will happen to you."

It was time to go back to Salatia and onward to another country from there. Liam waited until it was dark before he came down from his perch. He would be hunting for his food from now on—or just go hungry.

32

Margaret grinned and put down her last card. "I win!"

Elise sighed. "This is why we don't like playing with you, Margaret. You always win."

Margaret shrugged. "I'm sorry that I'm better at cards than you."

"And you're a sore winner." Annalise rolled her eyes.

"Have you heard the latest on the traitor?" Clairissa leaned forward, her face bright with anticipation.

Margaret shook her head. "I wasn't here this morning."

"Right...well—" Clarissa cleared her throat "—there was another sighting of him about three weeks back. The villagers wouldn't give him up, and one of them ended up dead. They're adding a third murder charge to his list of crimes now!"

"Really?" Margaret could hardly believe it. "Why would they add another murder if he didn't actually kill the villager?"

"Because he was the reason that villager was beaten to death, Margaret," Ingrid said. "This is why we don't tell you things. You just pick it apart until no one is having fun."

Margaret frowned. "But I still don't understand why the soldier wasn't charged with the murder instead."

"Because he's working in the service of his king to bring in a traitor?" Ingrid huffed. "Can we change the subject now?"

Elise dealt a new hand.

Margaret picked up her cards and smiled. She had three eights—she would win again. "Fine. What do you want to talk about?"

"Why haven't we seen Lord Nicholas around?" Annalise asked.

"He's been busy. He's trying to get added to one of the search parties for Private Fulton, but no one will take him." Margaret didn't understand why; he was incredibly eager and willing. "It's put him in a foul mood ever since."

"He's been trying for months now, then." Ingrid put down a card. "Why doesn't he give up?"

Margaret shrugged. "Pride, likely. He hates that Private Fulton escaped."

"Doesn't everyone?" Annalise asked.

Margaret wasn't too upset over it. She was disappointed he'd murdered his guards—she did have trouble accepting that—but it never would have happened if he hadn't been accused of treason.

They finished three more games of cards before Margaret grew tired and excused herself to go home. She'd barely made it up the stairs when her father called from the bottom, "Margaret, come down here."

She flitted down the stairs. "Yes, Papa?"

"I know your birthday isn't until next week, but your present has arrived, and it's not something that can be easily hidden." Her father grinned excitedly.

"What is it?" A thrill ran up Margaret; her father's excitement was contagious.

"Come on, then, I'll take you to it."

Margaret bounced on her toes. "It's so big you have to take me to it?"

"Yes," he said. "Now come along." He ushered her to the back, toward stables.

Hanson stood with a horse Margaret didn't recognize, holding the reins loosely. Her dark brown coat shined brightly from fresh brushing.

"Is...she mine?" Margaret turned to her father, her mouth hanging open. "Papa, this is too extravagant!"

"Nothing is too much for you, my darling." He wrapped an arm around her shoulders. "You deserve it."

"Can I ride her?" Margaret asked, moving closer to the horse.

"She's already saddled for you to do just that," he said. "I knew you'd want to ride her as soon as you saw her."

Margaret gently touched the horse's nose. "Hello, you. What shall we call you, hmm?"

The horse blew air through her nose at Margaret, lipping at her arm.

"I think Duchess." Margaret smiled when Duchess lipped at her hair. "I feel like one, getting you for my birthday."

"Would you like for me to go with you?" her father asked.

Margaret shook her head. "I'm going to surprise Nicholas and visit him at the barracks to see if he'd like to go on a ride outside the city with me."

He frowned. "I don't like that boy. Something's off about him, but I can't tell what."

"I like him, Papa." Margaret frowned at him. "He's kind to me."

"And what about to everyone else?"

Margaret's brow furrowed. "What about them?"

"Do you want someone who only cares for one person?" he asked. "Someone who makes you forget about other people?"

"I wouldn't have anyone if he didn't want me," Margaret complained.

"I'd rather you be alone than become a selfish person like that man."

"Well I'd rather not be alone," Margaret snapped, going to the step stool to help herself on to the horse. "And I know you don't want me to be alone."

"No, I don't want you to be alone, but I don't want you with him either." He followed to help her keep her balance on the steps.

Margaret sighed. "Papa, you're going to have to learn to like him. I don't have any intention of calling off our courtship."

Her father sighed. "I don't want you gone more than a few more hours."

Margaret kissed his cheek before mounting her mare. "I'll be home before dark, I promise."

She urged Duchess into a slow walk and went to the royal barracks to find Nicholas. The courtyard was busy with activity, trainees and soldiers alike doing their assigned tasks to keep everything orderly.

Margaret tied Duchess to one of the holding stations for visitors who wouldn't be there long, gently stroking her nose. "Be a good girl. I'll be back in a moment."

Margaret found Nicholas in the dining hall, and the men he sat with stood when she approached. Only Nicholas remained sitting. Her father's words about not liking the way he treated people rose in the back of her mind. She smiled at him anyway, even though she felt a little miffed. "Will you come for a ride with me?"

Nicholas wiped his mouth and tossed down his napkin. "If it'll make you happy."

"It will." Margaret frowned at him. "Papa gifted me a horse today, and I'd like to stretch her legs."

He stood while saying, "Gentlemen," and escorted Margaret from the hall. He took her over to her horse and helped her up before he led her to the stables. "I don't know why you didn't put her here in the first place."

"I was excited to get to you," Margaret said. "I didn't want the hassle of the stables."

Nicholas shook his head as he saddled his horse. "Where do you want to go?"

"I thought a ride to the cliffs would be nice," she said. "I haven't seen the ocean in a while."

"All right, then." Nicholas mounted his horse. "Come on."

"Is there something the matter?"

Nicholas furrowed his brow, looking confused. "What do you mean?"

"You're acting out of sorts." He never treated her this way. Margaret didn't understand his behavior. "Did something happen?"

"No." He clicked his horse forward without another word.

Margaret followed him, wishing she'd taken her father up on his offer instead. At least he would want to be there.

It didn't take long after they'd left the city gates to reach the cliffs. Margaret let out a contented sigh. The water expanded as far as the eye could see, a deep blue that soothed her. She could see small peaks of white here and there as the surf broke. "It's beautiful here."

"This is where the traitor escaped, you know," Nicholas said gruffly. "Climbed right out of the sewers and jumped into the ocean."

"How do you know?"

"It's the only exit from the dungeon that isn't the surface, and he never came out the entrance."

Margaret made a noncommittal noise. "There was another sighting of him."

"I heard. It's a shame the people protected him." Nicholas pushed the hair from his face.

"The soldiers killed a man, and you're upset they didn't know more?" Margaret's eyes went wide.

"Any person caught helping a traitor gets a death penalty as well, Margaret," he snapped. "That man got what he deserved."

"If he even is a traitor," Margaret mumbled.

"What was that?" Nicholas asked sharply.

"I said I'm ready to go home." She didn't want to get into a fight with him now. Not about Private Fulton, where he would get exceptionally testy if she disagreed.

"I'll escort you." He turned his horse toward the city. "Your safety is paramount, Lady Margaret. We wouldn't want you to encounter the traitor and let your delicate sensibilities get you killed."

Margaret inhaled deeply, setting her shoulders. He was going to force her to argue. "So what if I don't think he did it?"

"You should keep your opinions to yourself," Nicholas growled. "You're the only one who thinks that."

Margaret waited until she was in front of the house before she slid from Duchess. "I don't know what you want me to say, Nicholas. I'm not going to apologize for having an opinion on things."

"You've got a real smart mouth on you," Nicholas said. "And that needs to change."

"Oh, Nicholas, calm down. You're verging on the hysterics of the court ladies, the way you talk about Private Fulton." Margaret straightened her skirts and laughed. "If you don't, I'll have to make an appointment with my seamstress for your new skirts."

Nicholas stormed toward her, his hand raised. "You—"

Duchess stamped her front hooves and lunged toward Nicholas, her teeth grabbing onto his arm.

"Call your horse off, you stupid bitch!" Nicholas yelled, trying to pull his arm back.

Margaret glared at him. "I think—"

"What did you call my daughter?"

Margaret looked over to see her father storming from one of the stalls in the stables. His face contorted, his cheeks mottled red as he came toward Nicholas. Her father grabbed him by the front of his shirt and got in his face. "What did you say to my daughter?" he demanded.

"I called her a stupid bitch because that's what she is, siccing this damn horse on me," Nicholas spat, still trying to rip his arm from the horse. "Get this future glue off me!"

Her father hit Nicholas square in the jaw, knocking him to the ground. Duchess held onto his arm, a loud rip echoing as he fell. "I got her off you; now get yourself off my property, and don't come back."

"Papa!"

"Margaret, go inside," he commanded. "I don't want you anywhere near him."

She hesitated, looking between Nicholas and her father.

"*Now*, Margaret!"

Margaret went as far as the door, hovering at the back entrance to the house. She couldn't leave them both there while they were fighting.

"If I ever see you near my daughter again, I will personally see that you're reported to your commander, and His Majesty will hear all about how his soldiers don't have the training to treat women properly." He picked Nicholas up by his shirt front and shoved him toward his horse. "Now go."

Nicholas clumsily got on his horse, clutching his arm to his chest. "You'll be getting my bill from the healer," he spat before he rode off.

Her father left Duchess with Hanson. He stopped short when Margaret came away from the door. "I don't want you to ever see that man again."

"Papa, he didn't mean it," Margaret said. "He was just upset."

"I don't care how angry he was; he should never speak to you that way." He ran a hand through his hair. "He is not allowed here—ever, Margaret. And you are forbidden from seeing him."

"But, Papa!"

"No, Margaret. I've given you an order, and you're to follow it," he said, "and if you don't, there will be severe consequences for you."

Margaret crossed her arms over her chest. "Fine."

"Margaret, come in here, please," her father called from his office.

"What is it, Papa?" Margaret asked, going into his office. "Is there something wrong?"

"What are you all dressed up for?"

Margaret hesitated. "I'm going to see Nicholas."

"I thought I told you you were never seeing him again?" He leaned back in his chair, crossing his arms over his chest. "You are not going."

"Papa, I'm going to see him. It's been months. He wants to apologize," Margaret said. "And I'm going to let him."

"You are not, and that's final, young lady." He stood, his face determined. "I will lock you in your room if you try to leave this house."

"I am seeing him!" Margaret yelled. "I don't care what you say!"

"You are not." He moved toward her but stopped short. He grabbed the back of his oak chair until his knuckles turned white. His eyes grew far away and stared at Margaret blankly.

"Papa, what's wrong?" Margaret's stomach dropped, cold running through her. "Papa?" she asked timidly.

He fell to the floor and began to shake uncontrollably. Her stomach knotted with fear as he jerked and writhed, knocking down anything in the path of his flailing limbs; the crashing noises added to Margaret's horror.

By the time Margaret reached him, his shaking had subsided. She collapsed onto her knees in front of him, taking him by the shoulders. "Papa, Papa! What's wrong?"

He looked at her, his eyes still far away. He didn't respond to her calls or when she shook him. His eyes followed her wherever she moved, but nothing else happened.

"Mama!" Margaret screamed, leaving her father's office. "Mama, it's Papa!"

Margaret found her mother in the drawing room, having tea. She seemed unconcerned until Margaret grabbed her by the wrists. "Mama, you have to come. Papa collapsed and had a shaking fit," she said hurriedly, dragging her mother toward her father's office.

"What?" She ran ahead of Margaret, and they found him still lying on the floor.

He had a hand to his head and his eyes closed tightly shut. "What happened?"

"You collapsed." Margaret's voice shook. Tears gathered in her eyes as she put a hand to her mouth. "You wouldn't respond to anything I said, and you looked so far away."

He shook his head and groaned from the motion. "Send someone to get a healer, Margaret."

Her mother knelt on the floor next to him and pulled him into a tight hug. "Are you all right?"

Margaret didn't get to hear the rest of the conversation as she went in search of Hanson. He would be able to get to the healer the fastest with one of the horses. She commanded him to go with all haste and went back into the house.

"Bruggen!" she shouted.

"My lady?" he asked, coming up one of the flights of stairs from the servant's quarters. "What's happened? We've heard shouting."

"Help Papa get up to bed; he's collapsed and isn't feeling well," Margaret said. "He's in his study."

Bruggen barely nodded to Margaret before rushing to the study. She followed close behind and was happy to see her mother had her father at least sitting up.

"Papa, Hanson is on his way to get a healer for you, and Bruggen is going to help you up to your room for you to rest more comfortably."

"Thank you, Margaret," he said weakly.

Margaret grabbed a piece of parchment from her father's desk and scribbled a quick note to Nicholas to let him know what happened and that she would not be coming to see him. She couldn't even think of leaving now, not after what happened. Margaret did not want to leave her father's side in case he needed anything or her mother needed support.

On the way up the stairs, Margaret caught one of the maids and handed her the note. "Please make sure this gets to Lord Nicholas Oliphant at the royal barracks so he knows not to wait for me."

"Right away, my lady." She hurried down the stairs and out the door.

Once her father was on the bed, Margaret and her mother helped pull off his shoes and loosen his neckerchief so he could breathe easier.

"How are you feeling now, Papa?"

"A little better." He leaned back into the pillows and closed his eyes. "If you don't mind, I think I'll rest my eyes a bit while we wait for the healer."

"Of course, dearest." Her mother kissed his forehead. "We'll come back when the healer arrives."

Margaret wrapped her arms around herself, going down to the library. "What are we going to do, Mama?" she asked when her mother joined her.

She collapsed onto the couch, putting her face into her hands. "I don't know, Margaret."

33

L iam reached the final village, Marbon, before the Salatia-Glessic border. He had tried to cross the border at a different spot each time so he would not have a recognizable pattern of travel. This was his first time going through Marbon, a small fishing village with a little farmland. The main part of town was a single road with shops lining it. It seemed a metropolis compared to some of the other villages he'd been through.

Tempting as it was to stop, Liam ignored his growling stomach when he smelled the bread coming from the bakery at the end of the street. He would fish for his dinner tonight, not stop at any stores. It didn't take long to walk around the main part of the village and into the farmland not far outside the village limits.

He passed a worn house on his way to the river, noting a few shingles missing from the roof. His hands itched to fix them as he would have when he had lived with his parents, but it was not his home and not his business. Liam needed to go to the river, catch his dinner, and move on. The village was separated from Salatia only by the Frasisca River, and Salatia was his next destination. Some of the smaller farming villages in their neighboring country were much more welcoming to farm hands, even if they were from Anatalia, than the larger towns. He'd been to a few of those already and quite enjoyed their relaxed atmosphere. They always reminded him of his father on the vineyard.

Liam stopped at a branch of the river for easier fishing. The water gurgled lazily compared to the rushing waters of the wide Frasisca River that cut through almost the entire continent. He found an empty dock and went to the end before getting out his twine and hooks. He'd set a few hooks to the pilings so that he could relax. Once they were set, Liam lounged back on his elbows and breathed in the fresh air the river brought.

It wasn't long before Liam was lost in his own thoughts. He longed to be able to settle and live his days in peace, if only he weren't wanted by the crown. If only he could find the evidence he knew was out there to clear his name. If only this, if only that—he'd had many thoughts that started out that way, but in reality, he was the only one preventing himself from having those "if only"s. He could easily find a town where no one would care who he was in Glessic or Salatia, where Anatalian soldiers weren't welcomed, and spend the rest of his days there, but he couldn't seem to stay away from Anatalia. He didn't understand it. He should want to stay away, but she called to him whenever he was out of her borders, and he could not help but return. Even if he had to hide his face and live as a beggar, he could not stay away.

"Philip?"

Liam jolted, his foot dipping into the river. He grimaced and looked behind him where the voice sounded. An older gentleman with gray hair around his temples stood at the end of the dock, clutching a fishing pole with white-knuckled fists.

"I'm sorry, I'll leave." Liam pulled his empty lines from the water.

The man shook his head as he moved closer to Liam. "You can stay. It's not my dock to tell you to get off."

Liam settled back down and took off his boot to dump the water and let it dry out.

"Any luck?"

"Nothing yet," Liam said. "I haven't been here long, though."

The man's mouth pursed. "The river's higher than usual, and the current looks stronger. I don't think you'll get much today."

"I'll give it a while longer. I'm tired of squirrel and berries." Liam placed new bait on his hooks. The little bastards had snuck up and taken the food without having the decency to get caught. At least one of them was going to get to eat, and it better be him.

After a long pause, the man said, "Why don't you take supper with us tonight? My wife would like to see you...you look so much like our son Philip when he was your age."

Liam hesitated. "I don't know if that's a good idea."

"I won't take no for an answer." He held out his hand. "Aram Gollack."

Looking around for anyone near them, Liam shook his hand. "Liam."

"Do you have a family name, son?"

He took in a deep breath and swallowed hard. He didn't want to lie to the man and have him end up like the other villager. "Fulton. I'm Liam Fulton."

Aram shook his head. "I've not heard the name. Have you been in the area long?"

Liam almost laughed—someone hadn't heard of him! He was the most wanted man in the whole country, and this small little village had no idea. And if Aram had no idea, that meant soldiers didn't come frequently to Marbon. Liam's shoulders relaxed a bit, and a small smile formed. He could afford to stay for a dinner. "I'm just passing through."

Silence passed between them for a while, the river bubbling on.

"You look like you haven't had a good meal in a while," Aram said finally. "You'll enjoy my Beth's cooking"—he patted his larger middle—"she feeds me like a king."

Liam smiled. "You're a lucky man."

"Indeed I am, son. Indeed I am."

It was nice to be called son again. Liam closed his eyes and enjoyed the moment while it lasted. By the time they were done at the river, they had only four fish between them. It didn't matter much; it would be enough. They were decent in size.

"Come along then," Aram said as he walked away. "Beth'll be pleased with the haul."

Liam looked around again and saw no one. He'd barely even seen villagers when he passed through. Had they been ravaged by the war and not recovered? As they walked, they came close to the home, and Liam noticed it was the one with missing shingles. If these people were already suffering on their own, Liam couldn't let them welcome him into their home without giving them the full story.

"Aram, wait." Liam stopped on the front porch.

Aram turned, his brows furrowed. "What is it?"

"I don't think I should go in," Liam said. He didn't know why he had let himself get carried away. He shouldn't have accepted the offer in the first place. He'd gotten someone killed over some bread in the last place he had talked to someone—even if the soldiers didn't come often, he shouldn't risk their lives.

"Nonsense!" Aram harrumphed, pulling him inside. "You're welcome in our home."

"Aram, I—"

"Who do we…" The woman speaking trailed off, her eyes wide. "Aram?"

Aram went to her side, kissing the top of her head. It was easy for him; she only came to his shoulder. "I found him by the river, Beth. Meet Liam." He motioned to Liam, then back to his wife. "Liam, may I introduce my wife, Elizabeth?"

Liam looked between the two before slowly saying, "It's a pleasure to meet you, Elizabeth."

Elizabeth looked expectantly toward Aram, her brows rising.

"I invited him to stay for dinner," Aram said. "He looks as if he hadn't had a proper meal for weeks."

"About that—"

"He does look thin." She looked him over, turning her head this way and that.

"I don't know—"

"Go on and wash up," Elizabeth said as she grabbed the fish from Aram.

Liam looked between the two. He had to tell them before they bowled over him the entire night. They seemed nice enough, if a little chatty. "I—"

"Do you—"

"I'm wanted by the crown!" Liam's cheek's colored when they fell silent and stared at him.

"What?" Aram turned to him, confusion coloring his face.

"I've been trying to tell you," Liam said shyly, "but I couldn't get a word in."

"What's your crime?" Elizabeth asked.

"Treason and—"

"And?" Aram demanded.

In a small voice, Liam said, "Murder."

Silence hung in the air before Elizabeth asked, "And did you do it?"

"Only one of the crimes," Liam said. "I killed my guards to escape so I wouldn't be executed for treason. I was the fall man for one of the lord generals during the war, and he forged information to use against me during my trial."

"But you didn't do it?" Aram asked.

Liam shook his head. "I love Anatalia too much to betray her."

"If it hadn't been for your treason charge, would you have killed someone?" Elizabeth asked.

Liam looked her over. She didn't look fearful, only curious. "Only if I had no other option."

Aram and Elizabeth looked at each other.

"Wash up for dinner, will you?" Elizabeth said before she walked into the kitchen with the fish. "Food will be on the table in a short while."

Liam furrowed his brow. "I shouldn't stay. The penalty for helping me is death. If soldiers found—"

"Son, soldiers haven't been here in over a year," Aram said. "As soon as the war ended, we were left to ourselves, and they haven't taken a second glance our way. They likely think we're all gone. There're hardly any of us left, anyway."

Liam sighed. "Where do I wash?"

One night turned into two; two nights into a week; a week into a month.

Liam stared at the ceiling. He rubbed his hands over his face in frustration. He'd been at the Gollacks for too long, but it was so easy to fall into a life with the Gollacks. It was like he had parents again; they reminded him so much of his.

Sighing, he got out of bed and packed his things. He'd leave today. He couldn't let himself slip into bad habits.

When he reached the main room, he found Elizabeth sewing a shirt that was far too small for Aram. "Beth," he greeted.

Her smile dropped when she saw his rucksack in his hand. "Are you leaving?"

"I really shouldn't have stayed so long in the first place." Liam set down his bag. "You and Aram have been so kind to me, but I can't take advantage of that kindness."

"You're not taking advantage," she countered, "you've been helping us more than we've helped you."

"Beth…"

"Please stay, Liam," Elizabeth begged. "It's like having Phillip here again."

Liam sighed heavily. "Beth, it's not safe for me to stay."

"You've been here for a month already, and we haven't seen a single soldier from either Salatia or Anatalia." She put her sewing into her lap, a determined look hardening her face. "Be honest, how many times have you *actually* encountered people searching for you since you left?"

Liam frowned. "Two." It felt like it'd been more than that. Had it really been only two in a year?

"See?" Elizabeth looked defiant, her mouth set in a line. "I don't think you're being searched for as hard as you think you are." She pulled the sewing from her lap and stood, grabbing onto his arm. "Please stay, at least through the winter. It's already Semonat. It's going to start getting cold soon, and you shouldn't be outside on your own."

Liam sighed heavily. "All right—just through the winter. I can help make sure you have enough wood for the colder months."

Patting his cheek affectionately, Elizabeth grinned triumphant. "Good. I'm glad to hear it." She returned to her seat, picking up the shirt she was stitching. "I'll have this finished for you by the end of the day."

She was making him a shirt? Liam swallowed hard. The last time anyone had made him anything was his mother. "Thank you, Beth." He swallowed again before saying, "Where is Aram?"

"Outside, dear. You can help him with the fence."

34

argaret linked her arm with her father's. It had been a long while since he had felt well enough to take the long walk to the palace. She smiled up at him. It was nice to see him outside. "It's nice out today." Margaret turned her face toward the sun.

"It is," he agreed, patting her hand.

"Are you sure you want to walk all the way there, Papa?"

"We can send for Hanson if I get tired," he said. "You and your mother have been keeping me cooped up since my last attack, and I want out."

"The healers said that you needed rest, Papa."

"They also said I needed to live normally."

"People have been asking about you at the palace." Margaret smiled up at him. She knew dwelling on what the healers said would only put him in a bad mood.

Her father grinned. "Then they'll be happy to see me there."

Margaret deliberately walked slower than her normal pace so her father would not tire quickly. It took them almost double the time it would to get to the palace than before his attacks began. Margaret looked at the steps leading up to the palace with dread. "You've walked all the way here, Papa. Are you sure that you want to go in and spend the day?"

"I'm not an invalid, Margaret," he snapped. "Not yet, at least, and I plan on living my life until that happens."

Margaret sighed, giving in. "All right, Papa. We'll go in."

They took the stairs even slower; her father's balance was not what it used to be, and he had difficulty climbing them without getting dizzy. When they made it to the entrance, her father led them to a bench rather than entering.

Margaret squeezed his arm sympathetically. "We can stay here for a while if you'd like."

"I think that would be a good idea."

"Lord Dorcia?"

Her father popped up with ease, and Margaret followed suit, linking her arm in his when he swayed. He leaned against her to steady himself.

"Lord Crawford, it's a pleasure to see you," Margaret said.

"It's been too long, Lord Dorcia," he said. "I'm glad to see you out and about again. Gossipers were making their rounds, saying you were on death's door."

Her father smiled tightly. "No, not quite. I'll be back to myself in short order."

"Good to hear it." Lord Crawford tipped his hat to them.

Wearily sitting down, her father said, "Call for Hanson, Margaret. I'd like to go home now."

Margaret put a bundle of herbs the healers had requested for her father's draughts in her basket. Her back was to the street as she paid the vendor.

"Poor girl," she heard someone say.

Margaret looked around to find the child being spoken of.

There were no young children.

"I heard her father's fallen out of favor with the king because of his illness. Did you hear he got lost on the streets and no one could find him for hours?"

Margaret's face burned hot. Her father had gone out by himself on a day where he was feeling like his old self and had an episode on the streets. Some poor guardsman had to practically carry him back to Cerule House when they finally figured out who he was.

"I heard the queen thinks they're cursed by Theotes because they tried to climb too high. Haven't you heard how Lady Catherine spoke to the queen? It's audacious!"

Margaret turned around and glared at the women. How dare they! The women were too engrossed with their conversation to notice her or her glare.

"Undoubtedly, she thinks Lord Dorcia's reputation will protect her."

Margaret could stomach no more of their talk. She purchased her wares and went home. She was greeted by her mother pacing near the stairs in the foyer, fear clear on her face.

"Margaret!" she cried.

"What's wrong? What's happened?" Margaret asked, dropping her basket and hurrying to her mother's side.

"He—your father—he-he's gotten worse." Tears slid down her cheeks as she held back a sob. "He's had another episode."

"Why are you down here, then?" Margaret demanded, hitching up her skirts and running up the stairs.

Her father lay on the bed, eyes distant. Spittle ran down his chin, and his clothes were slightly disheveled.

Margaret turned when she heard someone behind her; it was her mother. "How long has he been like this, Mama?"

Her mother wiped her cheeks free of tears, but they were immediately replaced. "Half an hour at least. I've called for the healer, but he's not come yet."

Margaret picked up a cloth and wiped her father's face. She sat on the edge of the bed next to him. "It will be all right, Papa. We'll take care of you."

After an hour, the healer arrived. He immediately went to Margaret's father and took several tools from his bag.

"You have to make him better," her mother commanded. "He can't get any worse."

"If you would, my ladies, leave me to my work."

Margaret glared at him, but she left with her mother. "Is that a new healer?"

"Healer Witman must be busy," her mother said. "I'm sure he knows what he's doing."

"If you say so, Mama."

She covered her face. "He can't die. Without an heir named, we could lose our lands. The queen will petition for our title to be taken after that incident in the dining hall, and we'll be ruined."

How could that be the only thing that her mother thought about? Her father was dying, and she was worried about her lands! Before she could say anything to her mother, the healer appeared in the doorway.

Margaret stood, asking, "How is he?"

"He's resting as comfortably as he can, but he might have some difficulty coming out of it. He had two more episodes while I was with him, and his condition hasn't changed much," the healer said. "You should prepare yourself for him not to be quite the same when he begins speaking again."

Margaret covered her mouth, tears coming to her eyes. How could this be happening?

Bruggen entered the library and bowed his head to Margaret. "My lady, Lord Nicholas to see you."

Margaret furrowed her brow. Nicholas? They had sent the occasional letter to each other after he had profusely apologized, but she still obeyed her father's wishes in not seeing him. "What is he doing here?"

"I couldn't say, my lady." Bruggen pursed his lips. "Shall I turn him away?"

Margaret knew the rounds had been made in the servants hall about what had happened between them. Clearly, Bruggen disapproved as much as her father did.

"No, I'll see what he wants." She set down her book and went to the foyer, where he waited. "Lord Nicholas, is there something I can help you with?"

"Come with me." Nicholas held out his hand to Margaret. "You've been trapped in here for too long."

"I've been forbidden to see you, if you remember," Margaret said slowly. "And you've been forbidden from coming here."

Nicholas sighed, his hand still outstretched. "You know I didn't mean the things I said, Lady Margaret. Will you not come with me and let me prove it?"

Margaret hesitated. She still felt a flutter in her stomach when she looked at him, and she had missed being in his company all these months. "Where are we going?" Margaret slipped her hand into his.

"Don't worry, it's nowhere dangerous." He led her toward the door.

Margaret hesitated. "I don't know if I can leave my father for long."

"You have servants who can help him."

"He isn't doing well, Nicholas…he'd want his family around him."

"You deserve an evening to yourself." Nicholas pulled her along. "I've planned a feast in your honor."

Margaret smiled slightly. "That's kind of you."

When she and Nicholas arrived at his father's home, Margaret was surprised to see her friends in the dining room. "What are you doing here?" she asked.

"Lord Nicholas invited us," Elise said. "He said it would be a very special evening for you."

Margaret turned to Nicholas, smiling at him. "What have you done?"

Nicholas waved his hand to a servant, and a small orchestra was led in. "I had a few pieces commissioned for you especially, to express my love for you."

"Did you?" Margaret smiled brightly. She was pleased that, even after all this time, he still had feelings for her.

"I did." He lifted her hand and kissed it. "Shall we sit? I'm sure the others are famished."

Margaret nodded, letting Nicholas pull out her seat. When she sat, the music started. It must have cost him a small fortune to not only hire the singers and orchestra, but commission brand new pieces for her.

Nicholas clapped his hands, and footmen poured into the room for each side, each plate more extravagant than the last. She saw game pies decorated to perfection, stacked in intricate patterns. She gasped when a croquembouche taller than she's ever seen was carried in by two footmen and placed in the center of the table.

"Your chefs have outdone themselves!" Margaret said.

Nicholas gave her a mischievous grin. "I've had three extra chefs brought in just for this dinner."

"What's so special about this occasion?" Margaret asked.

"You'll find out before the champagne course, my dear."

Margaret's eyes went wide. "What aren't you telling me?"

"I'm not going to ruin the surprise for you," he said.

Margaret grew anxious as the dinner went on. It was now well dark out, and she did not want to be away from her father; certainly not as long as she already had. Everyone seemed to be enjoying themselves still, and she didn't want to ruin their fun, but she was ready to leave.

"Nicholas," she whispered. "How much longer until this dinner is finished?"

"Did you really just ask me that?" Nicholas asked, throwing down his napkin.

Margaret frowned. "It's been hours, Nicholas, and I told you I couldn't be away for long."

"Do you want your surprise now, then?" he snapped, standing abruptly. "Fine. Get up."

The room went silent, and Margaret awkwardly stood. She looked around the room, and her friends looked as uncomfortable as she felt. "Do we need to do this now? Can it not wait?"

"No, you're in a hurry," Nicholas snapped. He grabbed her hand roughly and shoved a ring on her left ring finger. "Do me the honor of being my wife."

Margaret looked down at the ring, then back up at him. She'd dreamed of the day someone would propose to her, and this was not it. She should have listened to her father—Nicholas was selfish and arrogant and cared for only himself. She should have ended their courtship entirely the moment her father had his first episode fighting over her relationship and not entertained his letters. She shouldn't have even come. He was causing stress on her family, stress on her, and he was not worth it.

"No." She took the ring off and set it on the table. "I'm going home, where I'm needed."

"Margaret!" Ingrid's eyes widened.

Margaret ignored her and stepped away from the table.

"Don't you walk away from me!" Nicholas yelled.

Margaret ignored him too and exited the dining room. She heard him raging all the way down the hall. She'd made the right choice, and she felt the tension flow out of her with each step.

Margaret wiped her father's forehead with a cold wet cloth. He'd had another episode that morning, and he'd been left sweating in bed. Margaret hadn't seen her mother for several hours, but she didn't want to leave her father's side to find her. She pulled the velvet rope next to the bed and waited for her father's valet to appear.

"What can I help you with, my lady?" he asked when he entered the room.

"I was wondering where my mother was," Margaret said. "Has anyone seen her?"

"I believe she went into the city, Lady Margaret."

"Does anyone know why she's been gone so long?" Margaret frowned. It seems that her mother was gone more often than she was home. Why wouldn't she want to be with her husband?

He shook his head. "I'm sorry, my lady. She only said that she had business there."

Margaret sighed heavily. "Thank you. Could you have the cook send up broth for Papa?"

"Right away, my lady." He bowed before leaving the room.

Margaret sighed again, looking at her father. His face looked worn; his cheeks hollow with exhaustion and dark circles settled permanently under his eyes. White that hadn't been there before his episodes appeared at his temples, and his hair was no longer as thick as it had been even a few months ago. Despite all the concoctions and draughts the healers had given her father, nothing seemed to work. Margaret had yet to lose hope, but lately, it seemed harder to keep her spirits up. Her father's episodes were becoming more frequent than she or the healers were comfortable with. They were almost daily now.

Her father no longer was able to leave the house for fear of having an episode in public, where no one could help him after the last time. Margaret was happy for that, at least.

"Where is that broth?" Margaret asked herself, irritated.

"Sweetheart," her father said wearily, "why don't you go rest? One of the servants can help me, or I can wait until your mother gets home."

"I don't want to leave you, Papa." Margaret moved to sit on the edge of the bed, brushing hair off his forehead. "And we don't know when Mama will be home—she never is anymore."

"I'll be fine, Margaret," he said. "You need to rest yourself. You've been here all day."

"Papa—"

"Listen to your father, Margaret," her mother scolded from the doorway. "You never obey commands."

Margaret stood from the bed, clasping her hands in front of her. Of course she would show up when Margaret was talking about her. "I'm sorry, Mama. I didn't want him to be alone."

"A servant could have sat with him." Her mother took the chair next to the bed. "Now go away. Your father wants you to leave, and I'm here now."

Margaret hesitated. "Yes, Mama," she said finally, heading toward the door.

"You don't have to be so cruel to her," her father said when she was almost out the door.

Her mother scoffed. "I'm not cruel. I'm preparing her for whomever she marries."

"She will not marry someone like that," her father said firmly.

Margaret was happy she was out of earshot for the rest of their conversation. She did not want to hear more about how her mother did things for her own good without care for anyone else's feelings. She went to her room to lie down before dinner was served for herself and her mother.

"Margaret! Margaret, wake up!"

Margaret groaned, swatting at whoever was shaking her. "Go away."

"Margaret, your father is having another episode."

She shot from the bed, eyes wide. "What happened?" she asked her mother.

"He was eating when he suddenly had another attack." There was fear in her mother's eyes as she gripped onto Margaret's arms.

"Have you called for the healer yet?" Margaret asked as she quickly walked to her father's room.

"No," her mother said as they reached the doorway.

Margaret whirled on her. "That should have been the first thing you did!" she yelled before storming to her father's bedside.

He looked pale, spit-up spilling down his cheek. One side of his face looked slack compared to the other, and he struggled to speak. He reached toward Margaret but collapsed back, his eyes fearful.

Her nose burned as she fought back tears. Margaret grabbed his hand and squeezed it tightly, pulling it to her mouth. "It's going to be all right, Papa. Mama is getting the healer."

The healer arrived after what felt like ages, and Margaret was shooed from the room despite her protests. She was kept out until late in the evening and then forced to go to bed instead of checking on her father.

Margaret poked her head into her father's room in the morning and saw he was sleeping, so she went to her mother's room instead. They needed to have a talk about her mother's behavior now that her father was even worse than before. She stopped short when she saw it. Everything was strewn about the room, clothes, sheets, jewels—everything that could be on the floor was. "Mama?"

She moved further into the room. Almost all of her mother's jewels were missing, but none of her clothes were. "Mama?" Margaret called again, her voice higher as she started to panic.

She moved toward her mother's closets and found her wedding ring on the floor. Margaret's eyes welled with tears, rapidly spilling over. She ran to the call rope and pulled it urgently before collapsing into a chair. She put a hand to her chest to calm her fluttering heart as she took long deep breaths. What had happened?

"My lady—" Her mother's lady's maid stopped short when she saw the room.

"Where is she?" Margaret cried.

"Lady Margaret?"

"Where is my mother?" she demanded.

"I-I don't know, my lady." The lady's maid looked as panicked as Margaret felt, her eyes wild and darting about the room.

Margaret pulled herself out of her chair, wiping furiously at her face. "How can you not know she's gone? You're her lady's maid!"

The lady's maid looked as much at a loss as Margaret. "Her ladyship didn't say anything last night, Lady Margaret…she only said she wanted to sleep late in the morning after his lordship's ordeal."

"Find out from the other servants if they saw her leave this morning or if she asked one of them to help her."

"Yes, my lady." The maid rushed from the room. She hadn't even curtsied in her hurry.

Margaret picked up the ring, staring into the deep blue sapphire. "Mama, what did you do?"

THE ANATALIAN SOLDIER

After her mother disappeared, Margaret was the sole caretaker for her father. She had no inkling as to the first thing to do. Her mother had been gone for three weeks now, and Margaret almost never left her father's side. The servants helped where they could, but there was only so much she would trust them with. She'd tried everything she could think of, consulting herbalists, healers, and priests. She even started to consult the alchemists—despite their admonishment by the church as a black art and a sin against Theotes—in her desperation to help her father.

The last healer they would try was on his way now. He was one of the most famous healers in Aratia. His Majesty had wanted to keep him on retainer, but he could not afford to keep him for more than a year. As it was, Margaret was paying him enough to feed a village for three months for him to come all the way from Glessic. There was no price she wouldn't pay to help her father if she could.

Margaret poked her head into her father's bedroom to check on him and found he was sleeping. She decided instead of waiting for the healer in her father's room, she would wait in the library and hope to ply him with sweets and tea to allow her in the room for his examination. Only one out of the six healers she'd brought to see her father had allowed her in the room.

She went to the kitchens and saw the cook pulling scones out of the oven. Good. They would be still warm when the healer arrived. That would be a nice touch. "Please make sure the kettle is on the fire so that tea will be ready when the healer gets here at noon," Margaret told the cook.

"Yes, m'lady," the cook responded, not taking her eyes off her task.

Margaret nodded, satisfied—not that the cook could see it—and went to the library to wait. The sun shone through the windows in sharp beams, lighting the room effortlessly. The library had become her refuge since her mother left—it was a place she could escape her own reality with the stories others had written. She went to the shelves, running her fingers along the spines until she found a favorite of hers: *The Adventures of Sir Donehugh the Great*. She most enjoyed the tales of chivalry and adventure. She brought it to one of the chaise lounges in front of the windows and relaxed with a sigh.

She'd just gotten into the story when Bruggen entered the room. "Healer Dellis to see you, my lady."

Margaret stood quickly, setting the book on the chaise. "Let him in."

Bruggen bowed, opening the door to let the healer in. He had bronzed skin with a mess of black hair that curled at his forehead. He was younger than Margaret expected—when she'd heard of his reputation, she'd expected a man older than her father, not someone younger than him.

"Healer Dellis," she said finally, "thank you for coming. Would you care to take some refreshments before you see my father?"

"I understand that he has been seen by many others?"

Margaret furrowed her brow. He was straight to the point. "Yes, he has. He's seen everyone from priests to alchemists."

Healer Dellis looked surprised. "Those charlatans are worthless, my lady. They likely did more harm than good."

"I was desperate," Margaret admitted.

"Might I see him?"

"Yes, of course." She walked toward the door, extending her hand in the direction she would go. "Please follow me." She headed toward her father's bedroom. "He's been too weak to get out of bed for three weeks now."

The healer looked at her sharply before asking, "Have you moved him at all?"

"The servants help him sit up or stand to make it to the chamber pot on a regular basis, but he doesn't seem willing to do any more than that."

"At least he has that. Have you noticed any bed sores when you bathe him?"

Margaret shook her head. "No, he hasn't had any of those. He gets bathed once in the morning and once in the evening to keep him clean enough not to get them."

"That's not the only way one would get bed sores, my lady, but you moving him so often will help keep him from developing them."

Margaret smiled as she opened the door to her father's bedroom. "Papa, there's someone here to see you," she said cheerfully.

Her father barely turned his head in their direction, his hollow cheeks looking deeper in the midday light. His mouth twitched as he tried to speak, and he soon gave up, sighing. Margaret went to his side, turning down the bed to give the healer better access in his examination. She did a quick examination of her own, checking to see if there were any changes from the last time she had sat with him that morning.

"Papa, I've brought the illustrious Healer Dellis all the way from Glessic to see you," Margaret told him gently as she brushed his thinning hair off his forehead. She decided she wasn't going to give him a choice in whether she stayed and nodded toward the chair in the corner, saying, "I'll be right there if you need me."

"Thank you, Lady Margaret," Healer Dellis said.

The healer helped her father to sit up, putting his ear to his back and tapping several areas before straightening again. He laid her father back down and repeated the process on his chest. Healer Dellis snuck a quick look to Margaret. "Has he always been this thin?"

She shook her head. "He started losing weight after his worst episode a few weeks ago. He barely has any appetite."

"Does he have any trouble swallowing?"

"Sometimes."

"That's probably why he's been losing weight. If he can't swallow, he can't eat. Are you feeding him solid food or soft food?"

"A mix of both."

"Have your cook mash his food as one would for a babe."

"I will do that as soon as you're finished here," Margaret assured him. She could kick herself for not thinking of that before.

"Good."

Healer Dellis went back to his examination, poking and prodding her father more than she was comfortable with, but he was the best healer money could buy. And he certainly knew more than she did on the matter. He asked her father to do several tasks, like push his feet against his hands and squeeze his fingers, but the reason why escaped her. None of the other healers had looked at him for more than five minutes to examine him, and Healer Dellis was closing in on half an hour.

At last, the healer straightened and turned toward her. "Lady Margaret, I'm afraid that I don't have hopeful news for you and your father."

Margaret stood, clasping her hands tightly in front of her to keep them from shaking. "What is your prognosis, then?"

Healer Dellis looked first to her father, then to Margaret. "I'm afraid my Lord Dorcia has had a stroke and has developed a palsy along with it."

Margaret put a hand to her mouth. "Was every episode a stroke?"

"It's possible, though without having seen him before, I couldn't say one way or the other, my lady." Healer Dellis pulled the covers back over her father. "The only thing that can be done for him now is to make sure that he has a balanced diet, good water, and fresh air."

Margaret sank back into her chair, her stomach sinking with her. "There's truly nothing else I can do?"

"You can try the mineral waters from Bomack's springs. They're alleged to have healing properties that might replenish him enough to show some improvement, but he will not return to the way he was, my lady."

Margaret stood, smoothing out her skirts to hide her trembling hands. "Thank you, Healer Dellis…I'll see you out if there's nothing else?"

"Thank you, Lady Margaret. I am truly sorry I don't have better news for you."

35

Margaret looked around her home sadly. This was her last day in it; there was hardly any furniture left that hadn't been covered by white sheets. She felt rather like a failure, really, but she could no longer keep up with the house and her father's business on her own. Even with the move, they would only take a few servants with them to help with the few things Margaret couldn't do on her own.

Tomorrow, she and her father would leave for Silvica. Her father had a small home in the countryside he had built when he was first granted his title, where he enjoyed spending his time away from court. That was where Margaret chose to take him for his recovery. When Margaret asked why he hadn't built in Dorcia, he'd said that he wanted to be where no one knew his name. He enjoyed having a conversation with someone who wanted nothing from him and spoke for the pure joy of bonding with another person. It reminded him of when he was young and just starting to grow his business. She thought he would be most comfortable there, deciding that was the best place to retreat. It would hopefully make his episodes less frequent if he was away from any stressors, and the fresh air would do his soul well. Margaret would also have mineral waters shipped from the springs in Bomack suggested by Healer Dellis, no matter the costs.

Before they left, Margaret called for a meeting with Charles, her father's right-hand man in the company. She knew nothing of business dealings, try as she might, and it would do her father's legacy no good if she destroyed it. She waited in her father's office for Charles to arrive; she wanted to at least look like she knew what she was doing. Margaret sat in her father's overlarge chair, looking around his untidy study. She awkwardly aligned the items on his desk in neat piles.

A light knock sounded on the door before Bruggen poked his head in. "Lady Margaret, Mister Charles Luther is here to see you."

"Thank you, Bruggen." Margaret felt her stomach flip. "Send him in."

"Very good, my lady," Bruggen bowed his head deeply before leaving.

Margaret put her hands atop the desk and found they were trembling. She quickly put them in her lap to hide her fear when the door was opened, Charles Luther being let in.

"Little Margaret," Charles said with a smile. Despite the stern look on Bruggen's face, he kissed her on the cheek before he sat.

174

She smiled, her face red. She had missed seeing him more than she expected. He looked well; marriage clearly suited him. "Charles, it's wonderful to see you again."

"And you." He leaned back into his chair. "What is it that I can do for you?"

Margaret cleared her throat, gripping the leather-clad armrests until her knuckles were white. "As you know, we will be moving Papa out into the country for his health."

"Yes." Charles looked at her sympathetically. "I had heard."

"As such, we will need you to take a larger part in the running of the company." Margaret quickly added, "As you've already been doing, though on a more permanent basis."

"I see." Charles leaned forward on his elbows, steepling his fingers in front of his mouth. "You have no hope of your father's recovery?"

Margaret looked down, her mouth pursed. "Healer Dellis has said that he won't return to the way he was before, and we can only hope that there might be slight improvement. I wish for you to be left in charge and that you provide updates I can read to him."

Charles gave Margaret a half smile. "Charlotte will not be happy about this. She already thinks I work too much as it is."

Margaret frowned at the mention of his wife. "You will be monetarily compensated for your additional work. The financial branch of the company has already been given instructions on how to proceed in the matter. She'll have no complaints when she sees the money."

"When will you be leaving?" Charles asked. "I would like to say goodbye to your father."

"Tomorrow," Margaret told him as she stood.

Charles stood in response. "I will make my goodbyes now, then."

"Thank you for all that you're doing, Charles," Margaret told him with a smile. "I'll have a contract drawn up by our lawyer to make everything official and have it sent to you. I look forward to hearing from you soon."

Charles nodded to her before leaving.

Margaret collapsed into her father's chair, amazed she had not stumbled or been rendered unable to speak as she often was in his presence. He had made her heart flutter every time he came into the room, no matter how many times she'd seen him.

Margaret pulled the curtains from the carriage to look out the window. She sighed as she saw the city pass her by. "This is it, Papa. We'll be outside the city limits in a few minutes." She looked to her father, who leaned against the corner of the carriage, a blanket covering his withering legs.

He looked back at her with a twisted mouth. It was nearly his constant expression.

Margaret sighed again. This would be a long journey. "Perhaps you'd like for me to read to you to pass the time, Papa?"

He nodded wobbly, his lips parting slightly, and an unintelligible noise passed them.

Margaret dug through her bag and pulled out one of the few books she had with her, *The Corners of Aratia, a Definitive History of Monarchy*. Her father loved histories; he couldn't get enough of them. It wasn't her favorite, but she would read them as long as he could listen. They rode with only the sound of her voice for hours before their chauffeur, Hanson, stopped for them to lunch.

Hanson helped both of them out of the carriage, supporting all of her father's weight until he was seated in an armed chair brought from home. He pulled Margaret aside before she could sit next to her father. "My lady," he said, his brow furrowed, "I'm not sure you've thought this through. What will you do if one of us has to leave? There should be more than two of us to help you after everything is settled."

"I'll manage, Hanson." Margaret worried her bottom lip. "I'll build up the strength with the two of you."

"What if he falls when we're running an errand?" Hanson asked. "Then what will you do?"

Margaret paused, looking between Hanson and her father. She straightened her shoulders before saying, "I will pick him up, and we will carry on."

Margaret smiled when she saw their cottage come into view. It was just as she remembered it, though the varied brown stones looked more weathered than the last time they were there. Soon they could settle and move on with their lives. "Papa, we're home."

She saw the slump of his shoulders as he let out a contented sigh. At least he was happy they were there. Hopefully, being able to rest in surroundings that reminded him of his childhood would help him gain some sense of peace.

The carriage door opened, and Hanson offered Margaret a hand. She took it, happy to stretch her legs after the last leg of their trip. She watched the four servants they'd sent ahead of them scurry out of the front door to greet them. Her father's chair was brought around by Hanson before helping him out of the carriage.

"Shall we go inside, Papa?" Margaret asked as she wheeled him through the front door.

The servants had done a wonderful job cleaning the cottage—it had been years since any of the family had been back. The home smelled of fresh-cut flowers, likely the wildflowers that surrounded the house. The garden had died while they were gone, but that could be revived in due time.

"How about we give you a bath and let you rest?" Margaret smiled at her father. "It's been a long day for you."

Margaret hated speaking to him like a child, but with him being unable to answer, she didn't know how else to talk. It was almost as if he were a child again, relying on her for his every need. Margaret left her father in front of the fire to warm him; the weather was growing colder by the day as the autumn ended, and the stone of the cottage kept it even cooler inside. She went to their bathhouse to light the fire to warm the water and looked around helplessly. She'd never lit a fire before.

"Frances?" She called. "Frances, will you come light the fire?"

Frances appeared by her side and gave a quick curtsey. "My lady, would you like me to light it, or would you like me to teach you how?"

Margaret hesitated. She should learn, but she was tired. "Maybe tomorrow."

"My lady…may I speak frankly?"

"Yes, of course you may, Frances." Concern coiled in Margaret's chest.

"Without more help, your days are going to be long, and they will be hard. You'll be tired, but you'll have no other choice but to carry on since you'll be the one primarily caring for his lordship." Frances looked up at her. "You need to learn now, even while you're tired, in case Hanson or myself aren't here to help."

Margaret swallowed hard. She knew this, but hearing it so frankly was unsettling. She squared her shoulders—anything for her father. "All right, then," Margaret said. "What do I do?"

"Follow me to the wood stacks, my lady," Frances said as she walked from the room.

Margaret followed her and was shown where the basket for carrying wood was, and instructed to load it herself and carry it back to the bathing house. Frances walked her through the steps of using the kindling, not overloading the fire, and feeding it until it was strong.

"Now what?"

"You have to wait for the water to heat, my lady, and then pump it into the bath."

Margaret nodded, hands on her hips. Even those small tasks had formed a sheen of sweat on her forehead.

"My lady?"

"Yes, Frances?"

"How will you be getting your father into the bath?" She gestured at the high walls of the tub.

"I…I don't know yet," Margaret said. She hadn't even thought of that. "I suppose I'll just have to wash him in his chair for now. I won't be able to lift him in and out of the tub today."

Margaret pulled the covers over her father before she wiped her forehead. She'd done it. She'd bathed and clothed him with minimal help from the servants, and she was looking forward to a rest herself. She went into their small kitchen and put the kettle over the fire and sat, putting her feet up.

"My lady?"

"Yes, Frances, what is it?"

"There's still more work to be done. We need to clean the tub, snuff the fire, and gather your father's clothes for laundering," Frances said. "And prepare for dinner."

Margaret slumped, almost groaning. "There's that much more?"

"After that, we have to clean the kitchen, prepare the rooms for the sleep, and get things in place for the morning."

Margaret did groan now.

"You must be prepared and know how to do all this in case we aren't here, my lady."

Margaret couldn't be sure, but she thought Frances was enjoying this far more than she should. "I know." She stood, straightening her skirts. "Let's go, then."

Frances smiled. "Take the kettle off the fire, my lady."

Margaret glared at her but took the kettle off nonetheless.

36

Liam knew his time with the Gollacks was coming to a close. He'd said he'd stay through the winter, but he'd been there too long already—every time he tried to go, Elizabeth would say it felt like having her Phillip home again and he wouldn't have the heart to leave. In the months that he'd stayed, he'd replaced the roof, fixed their fences, and helped Aram repair the dining table. As the weather grew colder and the crops less reliable, he'd seen several soldiers come over from Salatia. Most were harmless, taking livestock and some dried grains, but it was only a matter of time before they came during the day and turned violent.

In the last month, the raids had become weekly, if not more than that. It wouldn't be long before soldiers were called in to protect the border. He couldn't risk bringing the king's wrath on their heads. It wouldn't be fair. They'd only done what was in their nature: care. It was something he'd desperately needed when he arrived, but their kindness had filled him with enough spirit to move on in his search to clear his name. He would come back one day; he always made his way back to Anatalia one way or another.

"Liam!" Elizabeth called from behind the house. "Liam, Aram needs your help."

He made his way to the back to see Aram hunched over the chopping stump. "What's wrong?"

"He's hurt his back again." Elizabeth worried at her bottom lip.

Aram shot her a look, using the handle of his ax to stand up straight. "I have not."

"Why don't you take a break?" Liam asked, holding his hand out. "I'll chop for a while. I could use the work."

"Listen to him." Elizabeth raised her eyebrows at her husband in a challenge for him to disagree.

Huffing, Aram handed over the ax. He pursed his lips into a frown in Elizabeth's direction before storming into the house. She shrugged at Liam before following him.

Liam inhaled deeply before he swung, and a satisfying *crack* and *thud* followed. He would try to get at least three month's worth of wood chopped for the Gollacks before he left; it shouldn't take too long. He and Aram had already portioned out the trees to foot-and-a-half sections the week before. Chopping became monotonous, and Liam let his thoughts wander. Where would he go next?

He'd never been to Mekhor. It was the only country he hadn't been in on the continent. There were ways to get into the country, but cities along the border that accepted anyone other than natives were few and far between. They were a people who believed in isolation and did not take too kindly to strangers, even if they were there to trade. The last time Liam had tried, he'd been turned away at the border and told his people were not wanted. Maybe if he made his way in with a Radovian trading party, he could manage to slip in. Perhaps even if he went by way of Salatia—

Liam yelled out when he was knocked over. He rolled on his forearms and sprang to his feet, looking around wildly. A man in a gray uniform was running toward the house, knife in hand.

"Stop!" Liam yelled, running toward him.

The Salatian soldier barely had time to turn before Liam tackled him to the ground. He raised his arms to defend against the onslaught of Liam's fists and managed to push Liam away with his legs.

"Liam—"

"Stay inside, Elizabeth!" Liam yelled, putting himself between the house and the soldier. He briefly scanned the area and saw there were two more soldiers headed their way. Dread creeped down his shoulders. He didn't know if he could defend the house against all three soldiers at once, not after splitting a cord of wood and wearing himself out.

After hearing Elizabeth close the door, Liam advanced on the soldier in front of him. He stayed slightly crouched, his arms spread wide to block any attempt to run around him to reach the house. "Get out of here before things get ugly for you."

The soldier laughed. "You think you can win?"

"Try me," Liam challenged, his low voice growling. If he were an animal, his teeth would be bared and hackles raised.

The soldier matched Liam's pose, knife held erect in one hand. He advanced cautiously, scanning Liam for any sign of movement. He lunged when he saw none.

Liam grunted when the soldier's body connected with his own, and grabbed for the knife. He would not last long if he couldn't disarm his opponent. His ax was too far away to reach, and Aram had no weapons in the house. He didn't believe in them, he'd said. Grabbing the knife as he went down, Liam allowed the soldier to best him.

The soldier kicked Liam, hitting him square in the ribs. He curled in on himself, waiting for the second kick. Predictably, it came. Liam grabbed his calf, trapping the leg in the crook of his arm while he slashed at the back of his knee with the stolen knife. The soldier screamed, falling to the ground.

That would certainly keep him down and make the fight more fair for Liam.

He rose and waited for the other soldiers to come to their comrade's aid, but to Liam's surprise, they fled the property. Liam turned his attention back to the felled soldier.

He squatted on his heels, toying with the weight of the knife for a moment before he spoke. "Are there any more of you?"

The soldier spat at Liam, glaring at him with a red face as he struggled not to scream.

Liam grimaced, flicking the sputum from his cheek. "Are there any more of you?" he asked again, adding, "Spit at me again, and I'll cut your other hamstring and dump you in the river."

Letting his head drop to the ground, the soldier answered, "It was just the three of us."

"Was this an organized attack or a raid?"

The soldier glared at Liam, reaching toward him.

Liam grabbed his wounded leg, lifting it upward, letting it go when the soldier fell back with a scream. "Answer my question."

"It was a raid."

"Does anyone else know you're here?"

The soldier remained quiet until Liam reached for his leg again. "Just the other two."

"Will they come back to find you?"

Some of the fight left the soldier when Liam asked the question. "No. It's every man for himself."

"Good." Liam stood. "Don't crawl away. It'll be worse for you if you do."

He went into the house, bloody knife at his side. He found Aram and Elizabeth in the common room, a fire poker in Aram's hand and Elizabeth behind him.

Aram dropped the poker when he saw that it was Liam. "What happened?"

"I incapacitated one of the soldiers, and the other two ran away. He says it was a raid, and no one will come looking for him. What do you want me to do with him?"

"What?"

"These are your lands; you make the rules for what happens on them." He was not about to kill a man without the consent of Aram; he wouldn't want to ruin their relationship.

"I don't want to know, Liam." Aram shook his head. "I don't want any details, but he cannot remain here."

Liam's mouth formed a hard line. "I'll take care of it."

He went back outside to find the soldier had crawled almost to the stump where the ax was.

Liam sprinted toward him, stepping on his hand before it could reach the handle. "I thought I told you not to crawl away." He grabbed the soldier by the arm and hauled him up. "We're taking a little trip."

"What are you going to do with me?"

"Does it matter at this point?"

"Just…just make it quick. I don't want to suffer."

"I promise," Liam said, and meant it.

When Liam returned, his breeches were wet from the knee down, and his hair was slicked back. He removed his boots and left them outside before entering the house, not wanting to track mud onto the rugs Elizabeth had laid out.

"Is it done?" Aram asked, barely letting Liam enter the house.

"He won't bother you again," Liam answered, not looking at him. "I think it's time for me to leave. I heard a few other villagers talking about seeing more Salatians. It won't be long now before King Sorren sends soldiers here on patrol to keep the border area secured."

Elizabeth sighed. "Do you really need to leave? You could change your name, say you're our son."

"I wish I could, but none of that will change the look of my face." Liam's shoulders slumped. "No matter how much I wish it would."

"When will you leave, then?" Aram asked.

"I'll chop a few more cords to get you through the new year, but I can't stay much longer than that."

Aram sighed heavily. "Where will you go?"

"I don't know yet, perhaps Glessic to start and make my way east."

"Will we ever see you again?" Elizabeth's voice started to shake.

"I always find myself back in Anatalia eventually," Liam told her. "We'll see each other again, I promise."

37

Margaret blew the wisps of hair from her face. This was harder than she thought it would be. Much harder, and much more emotionally draining than she'd expected. She'd cried every night the first week they were at the Silvica cottage.

She came into the kitchen to Frances feeding her father. "Will you be all right if I ride into the village proper to find a healer for Papa?"

Frances nodded, wiping food from her father's mouth. "Of course, my lady. Take your time—the fresh air will do you good."

Clearing her throat, Margaret smoothed her skirts. Apparently, Frances had heard her crying in the night. "Right, well, I'll be back before lunch." She kissed her father's forehead before going to the stables.

"Where's Duchess?" Margaret asked when she didn't see her horse—or any horses for that matter.

Hanson stood quickly. "I put her in the pasture while I was working on the stalls, my lady." He put down his mallet and wiped his hands on his apron. "I can get her if you need to go somewhere."

"If you would, please." Margaret pulled her riding gloves on and sat on a hay bale to wait.

Margaret closed her eyes, sighing. She should have gotten Duchess herself. There would come a time when Hanson had to run an errand for her, and she should know how to wrangle her own horse.

Next time.

She'd do it next time; she was already struggling enough with the changes, moving to the country. There was only so much she could take in the day.

When Hanson finished saddling Duchess, Margaret stood. "Thank you, Hanson—I'll be back soon." She mounted her horse with his help and nudged her onward.

The sky was a light gray that looked like it could snow in the coming weeks. There was a slight chill in the air, but not enough that she thought it would make them light the fires when she got home. It didn't take her long to get to the village proper; it was only a twenty minute ride on Duchess.

There weren't many people going about, just a few women grabbing their shopping for the day. Margaret scanned the row of businesses as she walked Duchess through. She found the healer's shop at the end of the row and dismounted in front of it, tying her horse to the hitching post.

"I'll be right back," she whispered, running her hand down Duchess's neck.

Margaret walked into the shop, grimacing when bells above her rang. Surely, there was a more subtle way to announce one's presence to the healers. The storefront was empty, however, and no one came forth. She furrowed her brow—should there not be at least an apprentice running the shop? "Hello?"

She started when the curtain separating the front and back whipped open, revealing a harried looking man in a brown robe. She started to blink rapidly the longer he stared at her silently. Shouldn't he be saying…something?

"Yes?" he demanded.

Margaret pursed her lips. "I'm looking for a healer for my father."

"Can you pay?"

Margaret's mouth fell slightly open, and she leaned forward as her brows furrowed deeper. "I beg your pardon?"

"Can you pay?" The healer said each word slowly and crossed his arms in front of his chest.

"Sir, I'm Lady Margaret Doremis, daughter to the Count of Dorcia, and I'll thank you to change your attitude," she snapped.

Another healer appeared from behind the curtain and quickly bowed to her. "My lady, please forgive him; he does not typically talk to any customers."

"As he shouldn't." She glared at him, clasping her hands tightly in front of her. She resisted the urge to shoo him away. "Are you willing to help, Healer…?"

"Frederickson, my lady. Healer Frederickson." He shoved the other healer into the back. "And that was Healer Merrick, so you know who to avoid in the future."

"As I said, Healer Frederickson, I'm looking for someone to care for my father."

"We'd be happy to help, madam." He dug under the counter and pulled out a piece of parchment. "What ails him?"

"He's had a series of strokes and can no longer walk or speak, and he suffers from a palsy brought on by the strokes." Margaret rolled her bottom lip under her teeth. "Is this something you'd be equipped to help with?"

Healer Frederickson looked alarmed. "When did he last have an episode?"

"A while now," she said slowly while she thought, "a little over a month, I'd say." Not since her mother left, but she wasn't going to tell the healer that sort of personal information. She didn't want gossip flying around about them of her mother abandoning her sick husband because it became too much.

"I'd like to examine him if I could, my lady." The healer grabbed a satchel and loaded a few items before stepping from behind the counter. "Will you lead the way?"

Margaret let out a frustrated huff, throwing down a burned bannock. "I can't do it," she complained. She'd taken to cleaning much easier than cooking. For whatever reason, she could not wrap her head around it.

"You've put the bannocks too close to the fire, my lady. They're going to burn every time."

Margaret sighed heavily. "This is hopeless. I'll never learn how to cook in enough time."

Giving her a sympathetic look, Frances said, "You have to learn, my lady. We might not always be here when you need something."

Margaret fell silent as she measured out the flour for another batch of bannocks. If she couldn't master something as simple as this, she should give up on her ambition of taking care of her father and having a simple life. She knew there were times he wished he could go back to the days where it was just his family and no servants, and she wanted to give that to him again. It would make him happy, she knew. Court life had worn on him. It was likely why he got sick in the first place; the stress of the political games they had to play constantly nagged at him. Even having people wait on him stressed him more than it should.

She formed the dough and kneaded it until it sprang back at her. Next she greased her pan and put it next to the fire.

Frances sighed before saying, "Remember to put your hand over the pan to check the heat, my lady."

"Thank you, Frances," Margaret said as she divided the dough.

Margaret shaped the bannocks and put two in the pan, watching them closely. She saw them swell slightly with the heat and turned them. She grinned when she saw the other side was golden and not burned. "I did it!"

"Not until you've got both sides, my lady," Frances reminded Margaret.

Margaret glared at her.

"You're doing very well," Frances added quickly.

Margaret pulled the bannocks out of the pan and let out a small squeal when she saw they were perfect. She continued until she'd finished the batch, more of them turning out right than not. "What's next?"

"We'll make some eggs, and bacon, depending on how you feel after the eggs," Frances said. "I want you to do the eggs on your own, though."

"You're not going to tell me anything at all?"

Frances shook her head.

"Not even where everything is?" Margaret asked.

"How long have you been living here, and you don't know where basic supplies are?" Frances raised her brows, crossing her arms over her chest. "None of us will leave you if you can't care for yourself, my lady."

Margaret's cheeks burned hot. They had arrived before the winter started, and spring was starting to creep in; she'd been there long enough to know where everything was. Feeling dressed down, she searched the kitchen for all the supplies. Twenty minutes later, she had everything she needed and avoided looking at the annoyed Frances. Maybe she was right, and Margaret should call for more servants. At this rate, she was likely to starve her and father to death if Frances had to leave for more than a week. She whisked the eggs until they looked mixed, if a little foamy, and tossed a spoonful of butter in the hot pan.

She looked to Frances, but Frances only looked impassive.

Shrugging, Margaret added the eggs to the flood of butter melted in the pan and delighted in the searing sound. She stirred quickly, but the eggs were already starting to look wrong. They were brown and runny. These didn't look like any she'd seen before, and when she thought it was finished, she pulled it off the heat.

Frances moved closer to Margaret and looked at the pan. "My lady…I don't know what those are, but they're not eggs anymore."

38

Liam looked over the horizon. He'd climbed the mountain until he reached the plateau where he knew he'd find the next village. He'd been told of this village on more than one occasion—it was the place one would go to find answers, and he was desperate for answers. Answers on how to get his life back, to move on from what had happened. Liam turned to look over the valley.

It was washed with warm light, the mist from the morning dissipating in the heat already settling in the valley. He was glad he'd chosen to climb the mountain at night—he might have fainted from the heat had he not. Liam turned back to the village and moved forward. He would hardly call it a village; more of a tent city than anything else. It could be picked up and taken anywhere if they chose to move.

As Liam drew closer, he saw little heads poking out from a tent and curious eyes watching him. He smiled to himself—children were always the same, curious of newcomers and quick to accept. Liam waved, eliciting giggles as several of the children withdrew. He grinned, walking closer to the tents. It wasn't until he had passed the third tent that an adult made an appearance.

His skin was darker than the children's, likely from working longer hours in the sun cultivating the natural resources in the fields beyond. "Come," he said in a heavily accented common tongue, motioning for Liam to follow him.

Liam didn't hesitate—there was no reason not to follow the stranger. Without replenishing his supplies here, he would never make it to the next village or tent city in his travels. The sun was too hot and water too scarce to be picky. They walked in a dizzying circle of pathways until they approached the largest tent. Liam figured he was being taken to see the elders to decide if his presence was welcome or not.

The man pulled aside the flap of the tent but made no move to enter. Liam took the hint, hunching down to walk through.

There was an older gentleman leaning against a pile of pillows, the air around him hazy with smoke. He looked at Liam lazily before sitting up straight, his eyes sharpening. "No, you are not welcome here. You will bring war to us." He motioned to two servants, who peeled themselves away from the tent walls to stand beside their master. "Bring him to the city. Take the horses and give him ten Ryal for supplies when you get there so he can leave our country."

Liam looked around, shocked. He was insulted; he'd only had seconds before a judgment was made. He had come here in search of answers, and now that hope was dashed. "Can I at least rest first?" Liam asked. He was exhausted from climbing up the mountain all night. And maybe if he stayed, he could convince them to help find answers and clear his name.

"No, you must go. You can sleep in the city." He waved his hands again, motioning toward Liam as though he were a foul smell to be wafted away.

Servants pulled Liam out of the tent and took him straight to the aforementioned horses. They had several grazing behind the tents, and they came when called. It did not take long for the Radovians to saddle the mounts—they were known for their skill with and breeding of horses. Only the richest could afford a Radovian horse in Aratia. It would be an honor for Liam just to ride one; the privilege took some of the sting away.

"Why am I being sent away?" Liam asked one of the servants.

"The great shaman is never wrong about anyone. If he thinks you are dangerous, you are dangerous."

After that, the servants did not speak to him but simply got on their horses and waited for Liam to do the same. This, apparently, was going to be a silent trip for him. Maybe he could fall asleep in the saddle.

It took them only a few hours by horseback to get to one of the few structured cities in Radovan. As the years passed, they were becoming more prevalent, but many still kept the tradition of their ancestors and remained nomadic.

"Where are we?" Liam asked.

"Raniar."

Liam recognized the name; they were in the second-largest city in the country, and closer to the Frasiscan border. He would have to buy supplies here in the city and then walk his way into Frasisca. It would only take him a week or two from where he was now, and certainly not the longest walk he'd ever taken. Liam had barely gotten off his horse when one of his guides grabbed the reins and started walking away. The other handed him a small leather purse that jingled when it moved before he left as well.

"Thank you," Liam called after them, though he doubted they cared if he said anything at all.

He looked around, trying to figure out where to go. They'd dropped him in front of a coffee house. It was a good enough place to start. He could at least get sustenance and a recommendation on where he could sleep for the night. When he entered, he saw several men on pillows, smoking from long hoses connected to a water pipe.

Liam sat on an empty pillow near the back so he wouldn't intrude and waited for someone to come to him. It didn't take long, and he ordered a coffee and whatever kind of food they had available in broken Radovian.

"We can speak the common tongue here," the waiter told him after bringing back his meal. It was a thick coffee and meat roasted on a stick, along with a cup of soup and flatbread on the side.

"Thank you." Liam resisted the urge to shove the meat in his mouth before the waiter left.

It wasn't long after Liam finished his meal when someone came up to him. "Excuse me, sir," the man said. "There is a gentleman who would like you to join him, if you please."

Liam looked around to see if there were any of his countrymen in the coffee house. There weren't, but it was rude to turn down such an invitation in Radovan. He would have to go anyway. "Yes, I'd be honored."

He was taken to an older man, who had a beard that reached his waist. It was blindingly white against his dark olive skin. He was surrounded by several other men, who looked much younger by far.

Liam gave a small bow when he reached the man. "It's an honor to meet you."

"This is the wise Siam Salik."

"Liam, sir."

"Sit, Liam." Siam motioned to the cushion in front of him.

He did as he was bid, noting that the pillow was of a higher quality than the ones in the main part of the coffee house. "May I ask why you wanted me to join you?"

"I wanted to speak with you, Liam. Will you take doogh and poppy tears with me first?"

Liam hesitated. He wasn't comfortable with the drugs, but it could turn lethal if he refused. He'd seen duels fought over refusing an invitation in Radovan. It was an insult to the asker's honor if someone declined an invitation. "Yes, it would be my pleasure."

One of the men behind them rose and poured them both the milky drink while another handed them pipes.

Siam Salik waited until their pipes were lit before speaking again. "I can see that you are *alnnabil aleazim*, a great nobleman. I would like to tell you of our history so that later it might help you."

Siam told him of their great king and princes who fought for peace. Their neighbors to the south, before they became Salatia and Mekhor, waged constant war against the peaceful Radovians. They would kill any delegate Radovan sent, even though they came bearing the flag of truce to start peace negotiations. After the fourth delegate was murdered, Radovan declared war on Salatia. Radovan slaughtered nearly half the fighting men of Salatia, one of the driving forces that helped Anatalia divide Salatia into three countries twenty years later.

Liam had heard of these events before, but he was unsure of how it would be useful for him in the future. He watched as the wise man took a long pull of his pipe. Liam respectfully pulled from his own, though not nearly as deep as Siam. The smoke wafting from them was already making his head light; he did not want to partake too much.

"I will leave you with one last thing, Liam, and you'll know what to do with this advice when it comes time to use it," Siam said. "Time changes all circumstances: one day the birds are eating the ants; the next, the ants are eating the birds. Remember always: time is more powerful than you can ever be, so do good in this world while you can."

Liam looked around the room. The other men were nodding in agreement, and he followed along. "Thank you for sharing your history with me, and for the wise advice, sir."

He was unsure of what to think of that experience. He had no idea what that advice meant, much less how he would use it later. Liam left the coffee house in search of an inn. In the morning, he'd head to Frasisca.

39

Pulling on her cloak and grabbing a basket, Margaret went to their small stables, where Duchess resided. "There's my girl." Margaret patted her on her withers, smiling when the horse snorted at her. "Are you ready to get out of here?"

A flick of her ear and a nudge with her soft nose was answer enough, and Margaret saddled her. Duchess itched to move and see more of her surroundings, prancing in high spirits. Margaret couldn't blame her; Silvica and the surrounding area was beautiful, with its rolling hills and farmland. She'd only passed one home along the way, and even that was at a distance. She wished, at times, they lived closer to people on days such as this, but she did enjoy not having near-daily callers as her family had in the capital.

Margaret dismounted Duchess in front of the healer's shop and tied her to the railing. She patted her neck before going in, grimacing again at the jingle of the bells hanging in front of the door. There had to be a better way to get their attention than that, surely.

"May I help you?" one of the healers asked, flipping a page in the pamphlet he was reading.

"I've come for my father's medicines, and some advice."

"Ah, Lady Margaret." He pulled a small basket off a shelf. "We have them ready for you. What advice are you seeking?"

"It is quite a long way to come here for all of my father's needs, and though you do come weekly, there are daily concerns of mine…like when he is nauseous from eating, or if he has a headache. What can I do for him on my own, Healer Frederickson?" Margaret gripped her gloves tightly in her fists, her knuckles turning white.

Healer Frederickson nodded along as she spoke. "Mint will do well for both of those. You would simply need to boil water and steep the leaves for a few minutes. He'll feel better from drinking it."

"And where can I get this mint?"

"There is an elderly woman from whom we get some of our herbs, not much farther than you—about the halfway point between here and Fradure—who would be willing to give you clippings for a drica." Healer Frederickson pulled out a sheet of parchment. "If you are willing to wait, I can give you a list of herbs you can plant in your garden and their uses. Mrs. Fraser would have everything I would feel confident you could handle."

"Mrs. Fraser? I haven't heard of her."

"She mostly keeps to herself—I don't blame her after raising a brood of fifteen. She deserves the quiet!" Healer Frederickson laughed. "But she'll take good care of you."

Margaret worried at her bottom lip. "Would she…would she be willing to teach me how to garden?"

Healer Frederickson paused his writing. "I don't see why she wouldn't."

She smiled tentatively and loosened her grip on her gloves. "Thank you. I'll call on her tomorrow."

Finishing his list, Healer Frederickson handed it to her. "We shall see you at the end of the week to look in on your father then."

Margaret smiled with more heart this time. "Yes, of course. We always look forward to your visits."

"A good day to you," Healer Frederickson called after her as she left.

Margaret adjusted her hat as she rode up to the small cottage. It was almost small enough to be considered a cabin, but still made of stone. The gardens, however, surrounded the house and expanded outward several yards. Margaret could just see a small old woman digging in a raised bed at the far end of the garden.

"Mrs. Fraser?" Margaret called out.

The old woman turned, holding her hat down as a breeze picked up. "Yes? May I help you?"

Margaret dismounted and adjusted her skirts before she approached the older woman. "Healer Frederickson suggested I pay you a visit to get clippings for my garden…and to ask you to teach me how to garden." Margaret looked sheepish at the last admission.

Mrs. Fraser laughed, bright and loud. "Did he now?"

Worrying at her bottom lip, Margaret hurriedly said, "I can pay you extra for your services, Mrs. Fraser, if that is required."

"We'll see at the end of this, shall we?" Mrs. Fraser said.

Margaret smiled tentatively.

"What's on this list you have for me?" Mrs. Fraser asked finally.

Margaret handed it over. "It isn't too much, just a few things to help with my father's health."

"Is he sick?" Mrs. Fraser asked as she looked over the list.

"He's bedridden from strokes and palsy," Margaret said.

Mrs. Fraser pursed her lips and looked Margaret over carefully. "There are a few things that should be added to this list. Follow me," she said as she turned and went further into her garden.

Margaret followed behind. There didn't seem to be any rhyme or reason to the garden; there were herbs planted around vegetables instead of in their own boxes. She'd only ever seen them planted in clusters on their own.

"Does he have any pain in his legs and arms?"

"It's hard to tell," Margaret admitted. "He can't speak anymore."

Mrs. Fraser sucked on her teeth before mumbling to herself as she read the list again. "I want to give you the peppermint, lemon balm, and garlic they suggested, but not the tarragon. You don't need that, and neither does he—it's better used in difficult childbirths. I'll give you some valerian, thyme, and woodworm."

"What do all of those do?" Margaret asked. The only one she knew the use for was peppermint, and that was because Healer Frederickson had told her.

"Peppermint will settle stomach- and headaches; lemon balm will help with any headaches as well—and keep away the pests; garlic is helpful with any swelling and can go in your food; valerian will help your father—or you—sleep; thyme will help you with cramping, and the wormwood will also keep bugs from eating your herbs." Mrs. Fraser spoke so rapidly, Margaret could hardly keep up.

"Are...are they easy to use?"

"You'll have to grow them first, and you can ask the healers for the measurements you should use until you know more of what you're doing," Mrs. Fraser instructed. "I want to give you some lavender too. You can use it to keep your clothes fresh and keep out mice. And bay for your grain stores to keep out the crawlies."

Margaret was starting to feel overwhelmed. This was a lot of information to take in. "Thank you, Mrs. Fraser. I truly appreciate it."

"Where do you live, dear?"

"About ten miles from here, in Silvica, right on the border," Margaret said.

"I'll be by at week's end to bring you all of your herbs, but for now, I'll give you some dried peppermint to use for your father." Mrs. Fraser left her in the garden and returned with a small tin. "Just boil this with water to make your father a tea, and it will make him feel better."

"What do I owe you?" Margaret asked.

"We'll talk about payment at week's end" —Mrs. Fraser looked pointedly at Duchess— "I don't think funds will be an issue."

Margaret smiled slightly. "They will not," she agreed. "I look forward to seeing you then, and thank you for the peppermint."

Margaret made sure she kept her father as warm and comfortable as possible, and always in full supply of his mineral waters. She was hopeful as the relaxation of being away from the city noise and in the fresh air of the countryside improved her father's health. The glimmer of hope had only lasted for a short time as her father slowly deteriorated to his original state. It often left Margaret in tears, feeling that she had failed him.

The months droned on, and he no longer declined in health, but neither did he improve. It broke her heart, watching her father struggle. He would watch her with eyes that were alert and said he was there and everything would be all right, that they didn't need her mother around for support; but he had a mouth that would struggle to form words when he tried to tell her his sentiments.

She had found, though, that he enjoyed the outside. There weren't any homes near them, but there was farmland where he could watch the workers. It seemed to relax him, and he would often protest when she tried to bring him inside. While Margaret was waiting for Mrs. Fraser to stop by, she wanted to get rid of the dead plants in their pitiful garden.

The weeds had strangled what had previously been planted. Her garden reminded Margaret of her father—the shaking sickness strangling the life out of him as she could only watch. This made Margaret particularly determined to succeed in reviving the patch of earth to its full potential, unable to do the same with her father's health.

It took her several days of heavy labor, but eventually, she cleared away the weeds and dead plants so there was only clean earth. Margaret wiped her hands on her apron and grinned at her father. "What do you think, Papa? Ready for Mrs. Fraser to teach me how to garden?"

He wobbly nodded and smiled.

"I'll finally learn more than how to tell when tobacco is ready to harvest," Margaret said. "Imagine what Mama would say."

Her father's smile dropped, and he sighed.

"I'm sorry, I shouldn't have brought up Mama," she said quickly. "Why don't I bring you inside so you can rest?"

By the time Margaret got her father settled, a knock sounded on the front door. She went to answer it.

Mrs. Fraser stood at the door, a laden basket in hand. "I've brought a few extra things."

"Now is as a good a time as any," Margaret said. "Let's get dirt on our hands."

40

L iam let out a relieved sigh. As soon as Radovan grew green, Frasisca was not far away. He wiped his brow and pulled his shirt away from his chest repeatedly. The heat was always unbearable in Radovan. He didn't know how the denizens lived there with the constant high temperatures.

The Rephaim Mountains brought with them cooler air. Clouds hung over the peaks, and the ground grew spongier as grass grew thicker. The closer he got to the mountains, the cooler the air became. It was harder terrain to travel by, but it was worth the cooler temperature.

It took Liam a week to traverse around the mountains. The Frasisca River roared at the border between Frasisca and Radovan. Across the border, woods started sparsely and grew into a thick forest. Liam looked around—it was going to be dark soon. He'd camp in the woods for the night and keep going in the morning.

After making camp, he searched his supplies. There was enough left for a day or two if he pushed it—only a few chunks of dried meat, bread, and cheese remained. There was a city on the other side of this forest, if he remembered correctly; he'd resupply there and keep going.

To where, he didn't know. Liam was starting to give up hope that he'd ever find evidence to clear his name. It'd been two years since he'd escaped Jalmar, and he was even further behind than when he'd started. He hadn't heard anything through the grapevine of the goings on between Anatalia and Salatia—no disagreements, no poor trade agreements, nothing.

Sighing, Liam settled down to sleep. Maybe he'd feel more hopeful in the morning.

After walking through the forest for what felt like hours, Liam finally spotted the city. He held his arm over his head to shield his eyes, squinting, as the sun beat down on him. From the looks of it, it was nearly noon.

It was early enough in the day that the markets were still bustling when he arrived. The buildings varied from stone to wood, with the more prosperous businesses in stone. Liam found tables loaded with fruits and vegetables, and feathered animals hanging from the eaves, and the snuffling of pigs reached his ears before the smell of mud did.

Several people smiled at him as he passed, despite his muddied clothes. Frasisca was much more friendly with Anatalia; he occasionally found wanted leaflets for himself in a few of the cities he'd visited, but no one ever tried to turn him in, even if they recognized him—Liam wasn't sure why they didn't, but he wouldn't complain. He never stayed long; there was no point in testing fate longer than he already had. He'd found over the years he'd been running, the more people in a crowd, the less he was paid attention to. Especially if he acted as if he was supposed to be there.

Liam waved off a woman who shoved fabric into his face. The vendors were always pushy, but this was something else. He looked around; other vendors were doing the same to potential patrons. Were times getting tough?

Liam ventured further into the market, buying bits here and there that would save until he'd made his way back into Salatia. He would stay there for the night after he'd purchased more supplies. He still had money left from the Radovians, and often, border cities would either exchange the currency for him or take the foreign coins as well as their own.

He scowled as he watched a woman take fruit out of another woman's basket in the market. He opened his mouth to say something but shut it when he caught sight of a familiar face: Alton Bryant. He was there, flitting around free as a bird while Liam suffered for his crimes. Liam moved closer, only to lose sight of Alton in the crowd.

No, he couldn't get away! The previous night's malaise evaporated with a new fire to find evidence to prove his innocence. He could get that evidence from Alton.

He stood on his toes and then scolded himself. He could not look conspicuous, not while there was a price on his head, and Alton would be primed to take him back to Anatalia for an execution. Or even do it himself and save the king the trouble of hiring an executioner. No doubt, Alton would be happy to save His Majesty's coin.

Liam moved further into the crowd to find his enemy, sliding between the people as he inched closer. Alton walked without a care in the world—he even greeted people around him. His freedom made Liam sick. Sick and angry.

Alton turned to look at some wares, and Liam quickly hid behind one of the stalls.

If he wasn't careful, Alton would catch sight of him, and he'd disappear before Liam could get his hands on him. He wanted blood for what Alton had done to him. Maybe not a lot of blood, but there would definitely be blood on his hands by the time he was done with him. He couldn't let Alton get away without a scratch, not after he'd put Liam in prison for three years and was the reason he'd aimlessly wandered for two more.

Liam continued to follow Alton. The longer he stalked, the angrier he got. This was the man who'd ruined his life—he and Lord General Crompton, but the lord general wasn't accessible. He waited until they were out of the market before he made his move.

He grabbed Alton by the shoulder and turned him around, grinning satisfied when he saw the surprised fear on Alton's face. "Remember me?"

 **41**

"And you think he's going to keep improving?" Margaret asked, hope fluttering in her stomach.

"Minimally, my lady," Healer Frederickson said, his voice cautious, "and I won't promise you that he will even keep the progress he's made now."

Her shoulders sank momentarily before she straightened them again. No, she couldn't let her hope fade. "We'll just pray that it stays."

"Of course, my lady," he said quickly. "I'll leave you his lordship's usual draughts in the kitchen on my way out."

"Thank you." Margaret smoothed back her father's hair and kissed his forehead. "I've taken some herbs from the garden for the shop. Frances should have them for you."

Healer Frederickson bowed his head to her before leaving.

"Well, I think you're going to keep getting better, Papa." Margaret smiled at him, one corner of her mouth upturned. "Do you feel like eating?"

He nodded wobbly, patting her hand.

Margaret's heart swelled. Even last month he didn't have the dexterity to touch her hand. "Let's get you in your chair and into the kitchen, then."

When Margaret pushed her father into the kitchen, she found Frances reading a letter with her hand to her mouth. Frances jumped and hid the letter when Margaret said, "Frances, is everything all right?"

"It's my sister, my lady." Her voice trembled as she spoke. "She's taken ill."

Instinctively, Margaret put her hand on her father's shoulder as though speaking of sickness would bring it to him. "Oh, I'm sorry, Frances—I hope she recovers quickly."

Frances swallowed hard, shifting from foot to foot. "Lady Margaret, I would like to take care of her, if you'll allow it."

Margaret frowned. Was she afraid to ask her for a simple favor? "Of course, Frances." She pushed her father further into the kitchen and settled him at the table. "Will two weeks be long enough?"

"That should be more than enough, my lady." Frances brightened, her face looking less strained as she smiled. "I'll write down some easy meals for you to make while I'm gone before I leave, and dinner for tonight."

"I suppose this will be our test of whether I need to hire more help or I can manage with only you and Hanson if one of you needs to leave for a while."

Margaret certainly hoped that, after months of learning the basics of running a home and cooking, she could manage two weeks on her own.

Margaret left Frances to her own tasks and prepared her father's lunch of porridge topped with mashed fruit and eggs. It was mostly what her father ate, other than soups. They were the things he could eat easiest and meals she could readily make.

After she fed him, Margaret turned her attention back to Frances. "How far away is your sister?"

"About a day and a half's walk." Frances continued with her work as she spoke. "If you'll allow it, I would like to leave this afternoon."

"This afternoon?" Margaret internally scolded herself for sounding so panicked. "I'll have Hanson take you in the carriage tomorrow to save you some time. And, of course, retrieve you at the end of two weeks."

France dropped her spoon, looking up quickly. Her mouth fell open, and her eyes widened. "Really, my lady?"

"Of course." Why was this so shocking to her? It wasn't as if Margaret denied her servants any resources they asked for. "It will make me feel better, knowing you'll get there safely, and you won't have to spend any money on an inn for the night." Margaret picked up the spoon and handed it to her. "And it will make sure we aren't without you for too long. Does that sound amenable?"

"Very."

The house sounded quiet—too quiet. It was their first day alone in the two years since they'd moved to Silvica. Frances and Hanson left in the early morning hours to make sure Hanson could be back before nightfall. Margaret checked on her father and found him still asleep. Inhaling deeply, she let out a frustrated noise and went to the kitchen.

She didn't know what to do with herself. Frances usually had a plan for the day, and Margaret helped with it or did something of her own with her father. She rapped her knuckles against the counter, letting out a huff. This would be a long two weeks if she couldn't figure out what she was supposed to do with herself.

Margaret let out a pleased noise when she heard her father groan. Thank Theotes there was something she could focus on—she'd let her father's needs dictate the day. She grinned. He was rubbing the sleep from his eyes; she hadn't seen him do that since before his last stroke. Healer Frederickson would have to eat his words the next time she saw him.

"Good morning, Papa."

He grunted back, glaring at her through a single half-lidded eye. She laughed—he did not like getting up in the morning.

"It is, Papa. You're moving much better than you have in a long time."

He gave her a small smile—or, at least, the best version of a smile he could. He struggled to keep his mouth tight, the corners of his mouth twitching rapidly.

After she fed and bathed him, she wheeled him out into the garden. He seemed to be happiest when he was in the fresh air. Margaret settled him between the vegetable beds where he could see the farmers work the land. It brought him joy to see others work the land; he'd always told her it was what he missed most while they were at Cerule House.

She gathered a few vegetables for their dinner that night, along with herbs to cook them in and some to dry for the healer's visit next week. The healers needed the herbs, and it made her feel good to contribute. Her father would have done the same.

Margaret looked back to her father and found him leaned back in his chair with his eyes closed. She hummed a pleased sound, turning back to her work. She enjoyed gardening once she understood it more, but she did not enjoy the dirt. Or the bugs, but luckily, Mrs. Fraser had given her plenty of herbs to reduce the number in her vegetable beds.

She pulled out one of the carrots with a large top and let out a yell, falling back on her rear.

A large black snake slithered out of the open patch of vegetation, flicking its tongue at Margaret. She held her breath and stayed frozen in place as it rapidly undulated past her. She couldn't take her eyes off it for fear it would turn around and bite her.

When it was clear away, Margaret let out her breath and ripped several other carrots from the bed and threw them in her basket. She was done outside for the day. Maybe even the next few days. Margaret would make Hanson come up with…something—he could figure it out for himself—to scare away any other snakes before she put her hands in the dirt again.

She wiped her hands on her apron and went to her father. He looked at her alarmed, his brow knitted together.

"I'm all right, Papa." She put her basket in his lap and wheeled him inside. He wouldn't want to be outside with the snakes any more than she would.

Margaret wheeled him into the common room and settled him near enough to the window he could see out but not so that he'd have the sun directly in his eyes. Once he was comfortable, she went to the kitchen with her basket. She itched to get the dirt from under her nails. She picked up the pitcher and groaned.

Empty.

At least she could fill it in the bathing house and didn't need to use the outside well. Her hands still shook slightly from her encounter, and she held on tighter to the ceramic pitcher so she wouldn't drop it. Margaret gave her father a shaky smile as she passed.

She pumped the handle on the pump until the pitcher was full. A crash sounded from the common room behind her. Margaret turned sharply, gasping when the pitcher collided with the door. She didn't have time for this. She dropped the handle and ran to the common room.

"Papa!" Margaret gasped.

He was on the floor, his chair tipped over. How could that have happened? Had he tried to move and fallen over?

Margaret pulled up his chair first. "Papa, how did you manage this?" She looked around the room for anything she could use to help her pull him up.

She let out a frustrated growl. Nothing.

There was nothing.

How was she going to pick him up without Hanson? She couldn't leave him on the floor until he got back—he'd only been gone a few hours; he wouldn't be home for a dozen more.

She ran her hands over her face. "Pull yourself together, Margaret," she scolded herself. "Just do it."

Margaret squatted and hooked her elbows under her father's shoulders. She closed her eyes tightly and took a deep breath. She could do it. No—she *would* do it. She had no other choice but to do it. Margaret braced herself and pulled him back. She just had to get him in his chair.

She strained under his weight and nearly dropped him as she shifted her weight. Margaret unceremoniously shoved him into his chair before she lost her grip again.

Margaret let out a small laugh. "We did it, Papa." She cupped his cheeks and smiled at him. "We did it."

When she was sure he was all right, she returned to the bathing room to clean up the broken pitcher. Surely, if she could survive these first few hours of everything going wrong, she could last the two weeks Frances was away.

Margaret smiled when she heard the carriage pull in. It would be nice to have Frances back. The time she was gone had been harder than she expected, but she had done it. She went outside to greet them, her smile falling when she saw Frances. Her eyes were rimmed red and her face stained with tears.

Margaret grabbed her shoulders and held her at arms length, looking her over to see if she was injured. "Frances, what's wrong?"

"Things are worse than we expected, my lady." Frances's voice was thick. She hastily wiped new tears from her face. "She'll not last the year, the healers said."

"Oh, Frances." Margaret pulled her in for a tight hug. "I'm so sorry to hear that. Why don't you take tomorrow to rest?"

"Won't you need me, my lady?" France looked up at her, surprised.

"I've been without you for two weeks," Margaret reminded her, "I should be fine for one more day."

Weeks passed as Margaret fell into a schedule with Frances again. Margaret was growing concerned as she noticed Frances drifting around the cottage in a fog the longer she was back.

Margaret jumped when she heard something shatter in the kitchen. She set aside her needlework and went to find what broke. "Is everything all right, Frances?"

"I'm sorry, my lady," Frances said between small sobs. "I don't know what came over me."

Margaret reached out to offer some form of comfort but pulled her hand back quickly. She was no good in situations with people who were crying. "Frances…are *you* all right?"

Frances shook her head silently, her mouth twisted in a hard line as held back another sob.

Margaret guided her to a seat. "Stay here," she commanded before going out to the garden. She looked around and found the chamomile in the back bed, grabbing a few stems. That should make Frances feel better. On a whim, Margaret snagged a few pieces of mint. Margaret cleaned the mint and flowers and set a kettle to boil. She turned to Frances and braced herself. Even if she wasn't good at giving comfort, she should at least try. "Why don't you tell me what's wrong?"

"I've had another letter from my sister." Frances hands shook on top of the table. She quickly moved them into her lap. "She's getting worse. It won't be long now."

"I'm sorry to hear that, Frances." Margaret rose with the kettle's whistle and poured them both a cup. "Would you like to go back for another visit?"

Frances wiped fresh tears from her cheeks. "My lady…"

Margaret's stomach sank at her tone. "You can speak frankly, Frances."

"My lady, I wish to leave your service to care for her." She choked back a sob. "Her children will need me, and I can't bring them here."

"You didn't mention the children before." Margaret furrowed her brow. Had she been planning on leaving this whole time?

Frances blew on her tea before she took a sip. "I thought she would have more time, my lady—" she took another sip as her eyes watered "—that maybe their father could handle them on his own, but her letter has said he's fallen apart with grief."

Margaret took a long drink from her cup to calm her nerves. She had survived without her maidservant; she could do it again. "You may leave my service, Frances, and I hope that you will be well."

42

Liam pulled Alton into the alleyway, slamming him into the wall. He put an arm against Alton's throat. "What the hell are you doing here?" He leaned heavily on Alton, pushing him back into the craggy stone behind him.

Alton glared at him. "I should be asking you the same thing. Don't you know you're easy to extradite here?"

Liam shoved him again. "Answer my question."

"It's no concern of yours," Alton said after he caught his breath.

"Anything you do is a concern of mine since you took my life from me."

Alton laughed. "You shouldn't have been stupid enough to follow the lord general. You were an underling and had no business following anyone, but you certainly did us a favor by taking the fall."

"Don't you even feel bad that you've ruined my life?" Liam asked, incredulous.

"Why would I?"

Liam's anger grew molten in his chest. How could he be so blasé about ruining someone's life? Liam shoved Alton into the wall again before punching him.

Alton threw a fist back at him, his ring tearing the soft flesh of Liam's cheek.

Liam stumbled back into the street, blood oozing from the cut. That ring was sharper than he expected, but that wouldn't stop him. He ran at Alton, fist raised above his shoulder. He wouldn't lose his opportunity for retaliation. Not when he'd been waiting for years. Not when he'd been dreaming of what he'd do to Alton and Crompton if he ever saw them again.

Knocking him on his back, Liam straddled Alton's chest and brought his fists repeatedly down on his enemy's face. He distantly heard a woman calling for soldiers over the blood pounding in his ears, but he didn't care. In front of him he had one of the people who'd ruined his life, and he was not leaving now. Not until he'd gotten some modicum of justice by his own hands.

Liam yelled when he was pulled up from behind, hands under each arm. "No!" He struggled against the grip.

Other soldiers picked up Alton. He spat on the ground, red dripping from his lips.

"You are both under arrest for disturbing the queen's peace."

Liam's shoulders slumped. He'd let his anger get away from him, and now he was going to jail. No doubt, Alton would tell them exactly who he was, and he'd be brought back to Anatalia to finally face his execution.

"You can't take me to jail!" Alton struggled against his soldiers, his eyes wild. "I've done nothing wrong—he attacked me!"

Liam furrowed his brow. Why did he look so panicked? Did he have something to hide? Hope bloomed in his chest. Did Alton have something incriminating on him that could clear Liam's name?

The soldiers dragged them to their jail. In the front room, the soldiers stripped them of their possessions. "You'll get these back when you leave—if you leave."

Liam sighed. He knew well enough the guards would eat everything he'd just bought and take whatever they pleased, no matter how long he was in this jail. He looked at Alton and nearly laughed. The other man looked angry enough to burn the entire city to the ground. Liam couldn't say he wasn't enjoying Alton's misery and anger after what he'd done to Liam.

The guards took them down a hallway with several branches. It was a lot bigger than Liam had expected, seeing it from the outside. Several closed doors lined the hallways and the branched corridors as well. At the end of the hall, they entered a block of cells. None were occupied—how lucky for him, they would have privacy for what Liam wanted to discuss.

The soldiers shoved them both into the same cell and closed the bars behind them. "Enjoy your stay, gentlemen."

"Piss off!" Alton grabbed the bars and shook them.

One of the soldiers laughed as they walked away, leaving the pair alone.

Alton whirled on Liam. "Do you have any idea what you've done?"

43

"Happy Yuletide, my lady," Hanson said as he came into the kitchen. He held up a sealed parchment. "We've had a letter from Frances."

Margaret smiled. "It's been months since we last heard from her." She took the letter and read it quickly. "Her sister passed, and she's married her brother-in-law."

Hanson's mouth twisted in a smirk. "Frances looked remarkably like her sister."

"Did she?" Margaret looked away from the letter and raised a brow. "I suppose it's none of our business why he married his wife's sister." She picked back up the letter and continued reading. "She also says she's with child and will give birth in the spring."

"Well, now we know why they married." Hanson laughed, grabbing a cup and pitcher. He poured himself a drink and attempted a sip several times but could not stop chuckling long enough to take one.

Margaret groaned. "What do you mean?"

"The spring is only just three months away, and her sister recently died?" Hanson set down his cup and looked at her, surprised. "Surely, you cannot be so naïve, my lady."

Apparently she was that naïve. Blushing, Margaret said, "Oh."

Clearing his throat, Hanson looked away. "My lady, I was wondering if I might ask you a question?"

"Of course, Hanson." Margaret put aside the letter and looked at him. "You don't need to ask my permission for questions."

"I spoke to the smith in town, and he's looking for help." Hanson ran his finger over the edge of the cup and fell silent. After a moment, he continued, "He asked if I would be able to help him."

Margaret was wary after Frances left. She didn't know if she could lose Hanson too. "How often would you be gone?"

"Only a few days a week," he said quickly. "And I would still have plenty of time for my chores here."

"If you think you can handle your responsibilities here as well as there, I have no objection." He didn't have much to do here, and if he could help someone else close by, who was she to deny them? She did all she could to help the people of Silvica; it would be hypocritical for her to tell Hanson he could not do the same.

Hanson smiled. "Thank you, my lady. The smith will be pleased to hear it."

Margaret watched Hanson ride away through the window. Spring was starting to bloom, and with the warming weather, more work came from the smith and the people of Silvica. Hanson seemed happier than she had seen him since they had moved to the cottage three years ago.

It would only be a matter of time before Hanson asked to leave like Frances did; she could feel it. He was gone far more than he was with them. She didn't want to dwell on that now. She went into the kitchen to start her father's breakfast.

"Papa, once I'm done in here, I'll come get you," she called.

She went through her normal routine for the morning, cleaning from last night before starting the new tasks. She lit the fire in the hearth and set the pan next to it to heat. Margaret put the oats and milk in and waited for it to boil. When it was finished cooking, she mashed the fruit that would go on top.

"Papa, breakfast is ready." Margaret picked up the bowl and turned to take it to the table. She gasped and nearly dropped the bowl. "Papa!"

Her father sat in the doorway, breathing heavily.

"Did you roll yourself in here?" Margaret hurriedly put down the bowl and went to his side. "Papa are you all right?"

He nodded wobbly. His face remained determined as he pushed himself further into the kitchen.

Margaret let out a single noise, a mix between a laugh and a sob, as her eyes started to water. Healer Frederickson would certainly have to eat his words now.

"I've brought you a gift, my lady," Hanson announced as he entered the kitchen. "From myself and the smith."

"A gift?" Margaret grew wary. It would be inappropriate to take a gift from a man she was not involved with. "I don't know if—"

"It's a parting gift," Hanson said quickly, holding out a small package wrapped with cloth and ribbon, "and one of appreciation." It wasn't a question; it was a statement of fact. He was leaving.

Margaret's shoulders slumped. She knew it was coming. Hanson had been watching her carefully while dropping small hints of how busy the forge was. "So you're leaving."

"Yes, my lady." He set the package in front of her. "But I would still like your blessing, and I'm happy to return whenever you need something repaired." Hanson motioned at the package in front of her. "Please, open it."

She hesitated a moment before she pulled the ribbon free of the cloth. She gasped when she saw the contents—a broach of her family crest. Three tobacco leaves overlapped each other in a trident shape, their stems twisted together, topped with a garland of the five-pointed flower that bloomed as tobacco grew. At the center of the flowers were small round-cut emeralds. "Hanson—"

"I made it myself." He gave her a lopsided grin. "I have learned much from the smith."

"I can see that." Margaret pulled the broach to her chest. "I'll treasure it forever."

Hanson looked at her, hopeful. "Do I have your blessing to leave, then, my lady?"

"Yes." Margaret nodded, though her heart was heavy. "You have my blessing, and I will be coming to you soon for another one of these for Papa."

"It would be my honor to make it, my lady."

Margaret stood and took him to the door. "You may have the other horse—I will not need him, and Duchess will be as much as I can handle on my own."

"Thank you, my lady." Hanson picked up her hand and kissed it. "Be well," he said before he left.

Margaret closed the door, leaning her forehead against it while her chest tightened. She was alone with her father now. She didn't know what to do… That wasn't true. She did know what to do, but she didn't know if she could do it entirely by herself. But she would prove to herself that she could take care of the two of them. And that she wouldn't abandon him as her mother had or rely solely on their staff to go about her day, only seeing him on rare occasions.

She let out a sigh when she heard her father snore. She would have a few hours to herself. Margaret needed to go into Silvica to visit the healers for more draughts and replenish her fresh food. It had been some time since she'd seen them, and it would be a welcome reprieve to speak to another person.

44

iam glared at Alton from across their cell. After Alton's accusation, they sat in silence. At the very least, the guards could have separated them. The last thing he wanted was to spend one more minute with that traitor. Liam crossed his arms and looked away from him.

"Liam—"

"Don't talk to me."

"Liam—"

"What did I just say?"

"We have to get out of here," Alton said before Liam could cut him off again. "I have some documents in my satchel they took from me that will get me killed." Alton stood and paced his side of the cell. "And when they figure out who you are, you'll get sent back to Anatalia for your very delayed execution—or Frasisca will volunteer to do it for the king."

Liam crossed his arms over his chest. It gave him a small bit of satisfaction, knowing that Alton could be killed as well. "Why would I want to help you? If you ask me, you deserve what's coming to you."

He looked at Liam, exasperated. "If you don't want to help me, at least help yourself, and we can part ways once we're out."

Liam rolled his eyes. He halfway wanted to stay in the prison just to spite Alton and Crompton. But Alton was right; at the very least, Liam should save his own hide. "Fine. We get out of here, and then we part ways."

"If you help me get out of here, I'll make sure you get exonerated when our plans come to fruition," Alton promised.

"I'm sure you will," Liam said, his voice deadpan. He would trust nothing that came out of Alton's mouth.

"Are you ready?" Alton asked in hushed tones.

Liam sighed. "As ready as I'll ever be."

Alton nodded. "The guards are coming. Get on the floor."

"This better work." Liam lay on the floor, his back to the bars.

"It will. Now be quiet."

Liam sighed again, closing his eyes.

"Help!" Alton yelled. "Help, my cellmate has fainted!"

Liam heard hurried footsteps and their cell door opening. "What happened to him?"

"I don't know," Alton said hurriedly, "he just collapsed, and I can't wake him up."

One of the guards rolled Liam onto his back and patted his cheek. "Wake up," he commanded.

"Should we get the healer?" the other guard asked.

The first guard smacked Liam's cheek harder. It took everything Liam had not to react to the hits. "Go get the healer," the guard finally said.

Liam waited until he could no longer hear footsteps before he grabbed the guard by the collar and brought him down to a headbutt. The guard yelled out, and Alton grabbed him from behind, wrapping his arm around the guard's neck. He held him tightly until the guard stopped moving and dropped him to the side.

Liam grimaced, rubbing his forehead. "Grab his keys."

Alton grabbed the keys and poked his head out of the cell door. "It's clear."

"Let's go." Liam slipped past him, his eyes roving the halls to catch anyone coming.

They traded off who was in front, one reaching a branch in the hallway and waving the other on when the coast was clear, being careful to avoid anyone seeing them.

"There's the exit," Liam said.

"I have to get my satchel," Alton reminded him.

Liam hesitated. He didn't want Alton out of his sight. And if he left now, he'd never know if he could use the information in the satchel against Alton and clear his name for himself. That was all he'd wanted for the last two years he'd been wandering the continent.

Liam sighed. He had no other choice but to help. "Where would they keep it?"

"In the head office, likely." Alton looked around a corner.

"And do you know where that is?" Liam raised his brows.

"No."

"This has been a great plan, Alton," he said acerbically. "How did you manage to get where you are in life?"

Alton glared at him. Instead of saying anything, he rounded the corner and began opening doors at random. After the fourth door, Alton let out a small whoop and snatched something out. Liam looked around. This felt too easy: they'd overcome the guard too easily, they hadn't seen anyone in the halls, and Alton was able to get his satchel with relative ease.

"What are you playing at?" Liam demanded, blocking Alton's way out of the room.

"I'm not playing at anything," he said. "We're escaping, but if you hold us up, we might not be able to get out without being seen."

Liam heard footsteps coming their way and ran with Alton. They retraced their steps to the main passageway and found guards coming down the hall. Alton growled an expletive and grabbed Liam by the arm, pulling him in the opposite direction. There was an exit on the opposite side, but it was to the entrance where they'd come in and other guards gathered.

Liam pushed through the door first, startling several guards in the room. Alton pushed in after him and shoved him through the entrance. They wouldn't have much of a lead with their escape now. After they cleared the prison, they knocked no fewer than six people out of their way and headed for the wooded area at the edge of the city.

"Get to the river!" Alton yelled.

If they could get over the river and into Radovan again, no Frasiscan would follow them; it was outside of their authority to arrest them there. Liam pumped his arms to catch up with Alton. He would not let him out of his sight, especially not now. He wouldn't lose his chance to exonerate himself now.

Liam looked over his shoulder when he heard shouting and saw three soldiers chasing them. "Hurry!" he yelled as their feet pounded on the wooden bridge.

They made it over the bridge but did not stop. He and Alton ran for nearly two miles along the river where the soldiers would not see them. Liam leaned down, hands resting on his knees. It had been a long time since he'd run that fast and that long. He gasped for breath and sat on the ground.

Alton looked to be in only slightly better shape but remained standing.

"Now what?" Liam asked between breaths.

"Now we go our separate ways," Alton said between breaths, adjusting the satchel over his chest. "And we never see each other again."

Liam eyed the satchel. "That's not good enough," he said while he rose. "What's in the satchel?"

Alton backed away from him. "None of your business."

"Not good enough," Liam repeated, advancing on Alton. "I want to know what's in there and if it will exonerate me."

Alton didn't reply and, instead, started running again.

"No," Liam growled more to himself than Alton. He would not let him get away. Liam ran after him, grabbing at the satchel. "Give it to me!"

Alton whirled and punched Liam in the face.

Liam yelled a curse and tackled Alton to the ground. "Give it to me!"

Alton shoved him off and ran toward the river.

Liam couldn't let him cross again; he couldn't risk being arrested again—he wouldn't be able to escape fate a third time. He caught up to Alton, tackling him again. Liam struggled to grab the satchel and yelled triumphantly when he got it past Alton's shoulders.

Alton ripped it from Liam's hands and scrambled to stand.

Liam grabbed it back and started running north along the river. If he could make it far enough, he could escape in the Rephaim mountains. There were several caves around the base that were easy to hide in, and Liam had spent a few nights in some of them.

Liam yelled as he fell forward, Alton slamming against his back. Liam watched in horror as the satchel bounced into the river and was carried away by the fast pace of the water.

"No!" Alton yelled. He turned Liam over and punched him several times in the face before he wrapped his hands around his throat. "You bastard!"

Liam swallowed hard, trying to take in air. Alton's hands tightened, and black came in around the edges of his vision. If he didn't get him off soon, he didn't know what would happen. Liam clawed at Alton's hands, but Alton did not relent.

"What have you done?" Alton tightened his grip.

Liam's lungs burned.

"I needed those papers!"

His head swam.

"The king isn't going to need to execute you when I'm done with you!" Alton yelled in Liam's face.

His vision went dark.

45

Margaret tied Duchess up outside the healer's, patting her thigh before grabbing her packages of herbs out of the saddlebags. The familiar bell chimed as she walked in the door. "Good morning, Healer Frederickson," she said pleasantly.

"Lady Margaret." He smiled. "What have you brought for us today?"

"About the same as before, but in higher quantities," Margaret said. "My harvest has been bountiful this time around."

"Mrs. Fraser has taught you well," Healer Frederickson said. "We can use all the extra we can get this time of year when all come down with sickness."

"I have more at home for you; you can get it upon your next visit to my father."

Healer Frederickson shifted uncomfortably. "Lady Margaret…"

Margaret frowned. She did not like the tone with which he said her name, a pit growing her stomach. "What is it?"

"My lady…in the four years you've been here, your father hasn't gotten any worse," he said slowly. "He's even improved enough that he can wheel himself around in his chair. I don't see a reason to continue our visits; there's nothing more we can do for him, and you've begun making all the draughts at home from your garden."

"Oh," Margaret said simply. "Oh."

"It would be wrong of us to continue taking your money for no work." Healer Frederickson grimaced. "If need does arise for us, we are happy to come, but it won't be on a regular basis."

"I see." Margaret clutched her hands tightly in front of her. She would not allow herself to tremble in front of him.

"While you're here, is there anything else we can do for you?"

"No," she said quickly, her voice wobbling, "no, there's nothing else I require at the moment." Margaret stared awkwardly at the healer before finally saying, "A good day to you."

"And you, my lady," he returned, nodding.

Margaret left the shop in a hurry. She had looked forward to the healer's weekly visits to break up the monotony of caring for her father, to talk to someone who could talk back without having to leave her father's side to do so. Now that was being taken away from her in the name of kindness and saving funds.

She supposed she at least still had her monthly visits to the village to share the spoils of her garden. It was more than she and her father could eat, and the food would only rot if she didn't share it. He couldn't say it, but Margaret knew it pleased her father that she did so as well. She delighted in the brightness of his eyes when she told him of her plans, and would not stop as long as they lived in Silvica.

Margaret patted Duchess before she untied her reins and walked her through the village, stopping at a few vendors to parcel out vegetables and herbs from her garden. She took her time to visit with each villager she came across. They told her of their days, children, pets until they had talked themselves out.

Down to her last bit of food, Margaret squatted down to be level with the Widow Dover. She smiled, taking her hands. "How are you today?"

"Well, child," she said, her voice frail. "I've strength yet in these old bones."

Margaret squeezed her hands. "You do; I can see that. I've got some vegetables for your pot."

"What do you have this time?" Widow Dover asked.

"Some cabbage, carrots, and a few herbs to go with your stew."

"Theotes bless you, my dear." She kissed her hands.

"I'll see you next month, all right?" Margaret said as she stood.

Widow Dover nodded wobbly. "Safe ride."

Margaret took her time coming back to the cottage. It would be some time before she ventured out again, and she wanted to enjoy it. She closed her eyes as the sun beamed down on her. It was a nice enough day; when she arrived home, she would bring her father out to sun. He would enjoy it as much as she did.

The familiar pinks and purples of the wild lupine in the field leading up to their home came into view, and sadness crept down her spine. Margaret slowed Duchess when she saw the cottage and dismounted. She would walk the rest of the way to cool her mount. When she reached the stable behind the house, she unsaddled her horse and wiped her down. Margaret let Duchess out into the back to graze and filled her trough with water. That should do her for now, and she'd bring her back in before the sun set.

"Papa?" Margaret called when she entered the cottage. She didn't need to; he never left the cottage when she was gone in case he fell from his chair.

He was in front of the back windows so he could look out and watch what would come out of the forest. Margaret came to his side and kissed his cheek. "Shall we go outside, Papa? The sun is bright, and the breeze is cool."

He wobbly nodded, and Margaret opened the door before she pushed him out on the back path. Her father let out a sigh and leaned his head back.

Margaret sat on the grass next to him when she found the perfect spot. "Papa, Healer Frederickson has told me that they will no longer be coming on a regular basis. He says you're doing too well for them to come, and they don't feel comfortable taking our money for no work."

Margaret looked down at her hands, letting the silence settle between them. She wiped away the tears that sprang, sniffling. Her father placed a shaky hand on her head and tried to stroke her hair, but his ailment prevented any gentle movement. Despite the comfort he tried to give, it made her feel worse. Margaret covered her face with her hands and took several deep breaths.

Finally, when she calmed herself, she said, "We should prepare to be alone for a long while."

46

iam returned to Anatalia through the Glessican border. He never went the same way twice. In the seven years he'd been wandering, he'd become so familiar with Glessic, Salatia, and Anatalia that he could navigate them in his sleep. He put his hand to his growling stomach as he walked; he would have to stop soon to find food. Game had been uncommonly sparse the last few days as it grew colder, and his supplies were running low.

Liam approached a small town he had been to a few times before. Silvica was nice enough, but it was starting to look old and worn. It had severely changed in the years since he had last been here. Many of the buildings that he saw had warped planks of wood, and the paint was starting to shatter and flake off.

Liam went around the town. There were cottages and shacks where he could stop and no one would take notice of his presence. He did not want to draw attention to himself by knocking on every door in the small town. There had been more than one occasion where someone had recognized him and Liam had had to flee from whatever place he had stopped. He did not want to bring the soldiers' wrath down on him or the town he was begging in. Liam had seen some of the king's soldiers outside of Silvica a few hours ago, stopping for lunch.

He walked through a field of purple and pink flowers he couldn't identify. They were pretty enough and added to the charm of the cottage he could see in the distance. Liam waited as long as his growling stomach would allow him to ensure there were no soldiers near the cottage he approached.

The large cottage had a well-kept garden, holding herbs and crops that would be useful to the inhabitants. It would be a shame in a matter of weeks that would all be lost to the cold. Liam went to the front door, running his fingers through his hair in an attempt to make it look neat, and he straightened his tunic. He had not bathed for quite some time, but he could at least try not to look slovenly. Liam looked around to make sure there were no soldiers in the area and inhaled deeply before knocking on the door.

CONTINUE THE STORY!

THE ANATALIAN COUNTESS

BOOKS2READ.COM/ANATALIANCOUNTESS

ACKNOWLEDGMENTS

Gosh.

The time has come for me to write my acknowledgments, and after writing a whole novel, I feel like I should be prepared. Or at the very least, better at it. If I were to thank everyone who helped me with this novel, and subsequent books in the series, I would run out of pages, so I want to thank a specific few instead.

First, I want to thank my husband, whom I affectionately call Mr. M on social media—at first to give him privacy, and now to keep the air of mystery about him. Without you, I never would have found the courage to finish my novel and join a critique group. And I never would have met the wonderful Brandi Spencer and Renee Frey, and started Authors 4 Authors Publishing. Really without him, none of this would have ever happened—had he not dragged me off to live in South Korea, I never would have started writing this book in the first place. For that, I am ever grateful. I love you as far as the East is from the West, Mr. M.

To my best friend Paige: your face, it's face pale face. Thank you for letting me read you my novel in person and on the phone to try to catch all of the mistakes, especially our favorite one.

To my parents, thank you for always encouraging me every step of the way—and sorry for waiting for years to tell you I was even writing a book in the first place.

And finally, to Brandi and Renee: thank you for going on this adventure with me and throwing money into a pot with someone you've never met in person to start a publishing company. I didn't even know being a publisher was a dream of mine until you both helped make it a reality. I wouldn't want to be in this business with anyone but my found sisters. I love you both.

ABOUT THE AUTHOR

Rebecca Mikkelson has been writing fantasy stories since her early teens for fun and was thrilled to turn her dream into a reality when she was published for the first time in an anthology. She currently lives in Maryland with her husband and three cats.

In her free time, Rebecca likes to cross stitch to relax when her cats aren't hogging the embroidery floss. She also enjoys reading a wide variety of books, ranging from non-fiction biographies of historical figures and families to high fantasy.

As well as being an author, Rebecca works as the editor-in-chief at Authors 4 Authors Publishing, which she helped start in 2018.

Follow her online:

RebeccaMikkelson.com
TikTok: **@zebookverm**
Twitter: **@zebookverm**
Instagram/Threads: **@authorRebeccaMikkelson**
Facebook: **@RebeccaMikkelsonAuthor**

Authors 4 Authors
Publishing

A publishing company for authors, run by authors, blending the best of traditional and independent publishing

We specialize in speculative fiction: science fiction, fantasy, paranormal, and romance. Get lost in another world!

Check out our collection at https://books2read.com/rl/a4a or visit Authors4AuthorsPublishing.com/books

For updates, scan the QR code or visit our website to join our semi-monthly newsletter!

Want more historical fantasy? We recommend:

One Thousand and One Days
by Renee Frey

Sutaita, daughter of the Sultan's vizier, planned on a life of quiet study. But when she learns she and her sister must be the next two brides for the bloodthirsty Sultan Shahryar al'Mamun, Sutaita decides to change their fortune. Staying alive by telling stories every night, she must buy enough time to solve the mysteries surrounding the Sultan's edict. In this retelling of the Arabian Nights frame story, can Sutaita slip past the walls around the Sultan's heart and soul? Or will she end up like so many brides before—with her head on a chopping block?

books2read.com/1001Days